THE OUTFIT: BLOOD AND ASHES

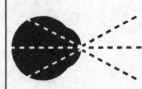

This Large Print Book carries the
Seal of Approval of N.A.V.H.

THE OUTFIT: BLOOD AND ASHES

MATTHEW P. MAYO

THORNDIKE PRESS
A part of Gale, a Cengage Company

Farmington Hills, Mich • San Francisco • New York • Waterville, Maine
Meriden, Conn • Mason, Ohio • Chicago

Copyright © 2017 by Matthew P. Mayo.
Thorndike Press, a part of Gale, a Cengage Company.

Thorndike Press® Large Print Western.
The text of this Large Print edition is unabridged.
Other aspects of the book may vary from the original edition.
Set in 16 pt. Plantin.

LIBRARY OF CONGRESS CIP DATA ON FILE.
CATALOGUING IN PUBLICATION FOR THIS BOOK
IS AVAILABLE FROM THE LIBRARY OF CONGRESS

ISBN-13: 978-1-4104-8358-4 (hardcover)

Published in 2018 by arrangement with Cherry Weiner Literary Agency

Printed in Mexico
1 2 3 4 5 6 7 22 21 20 19 18

Para Mi Hermano, Jeff . . . Och!

"Hateful to me as the gates of Hades is that man who hides one thing in his heart and speaks another."

—Homer, *The Iliad*

OUT·FIT (noun): A group of people engaged in the same occupation or belonging to the same organization, occasionally with the implication of being unconventional or slightly disreputable; a collective of cowboys employed by a cattle ranch.

CHAPTER ONE:
MEANWHILE, BACK AT
THE RANCH

"Cookie McGee! If you dip your grimy finger in my biscuit batter one more time I'll lop it off and wear it around my neck!" Arlene Tewksbury poised the gleaming cleaver high above her head as if she could not wait to drive it downward, batter or no, and make good on her frightening promise.

That stayed the old trail hound's knobby hand, a curled finger dripping golden biscuit batter from the generous dollop he'd scooped for himself.

"Oh," he said, his Adam's apple bobbing in his reedy neck. "Miss Tewksbury, didn't see you there . . ."

"I'm here, all right, Cookie. I'm always in the kitchen, fixing up a meal for you and the rest. Don't think I don't see everything that happens in here. Besides," she said, turning back to her work, "you eat raw dough, it'll give you pinworms."

"Pinworms!"

11

"Oh, yes." Arlene tried to hide a smirk. "I'd be surprised if you aren't already afflicted."

"Pinworms!" Cookie's knuckled hands trembled and he shook his head in denial. "Can't be such a thing as that." His voice dwindled to a whisper as he made for the door. "Can't be." He rubbed his belly as he walked, and with each step grew convinced she was right. He had been feeling a mite queasy since he woke.

Course, it could have been the whiskey of the night before. But then again, a splash or six of tanglefoot had never bothered him all that much. But worms, now they were a different matter. He leaned against the corral, a hand lightly massaging his gut.

"Cookie." Sue Pendleton, lugging an armload of firewood, nodded at the bedraggled old man. "Are you okay? You look a little rough this morning."

"I do?" Cookie raised a trembling hand to his throat, gently pressing one cheek with his fingertips. "Oh . . ." He kept walking toward the pole barn they'd hastily constructed on settling in at the Barr-McGee ranch months before.

Sue shrugged and walked on toward the kitchen. "What's wrong with Cookie, Arlene? He looks like he bumped into a phantom."

Arlene turned to her, tears slipping down her cheeks. She caught her breath. "He thinks he has . . . worms!" She barely uttered the word before a fresh round of giggles burst from her.

Sue had no idea what Arlene was talking about, but the jolly older woman's cheer was catching. She found herself laughing along. Minutes later, when Arlene had control of herself once more and stood stirring spices into the beef stew, Arlene told Sue what she'd said to Cookie.

"Oh, that's terrible. Poor Cookie."

"Poor Cookie, my foot! I have had enough of that rascal sticking his grimy paws into whatever it is I'm trying to cook in this kitchen. It's a wonder we aren't all afflicted with something he brought in."

"Well, you'll be shed of him for a while. Rafe says they have to round up strays and it might take two days."

Arlene's expression grew stern. "And that one," she said, driving the big blade through a particularly large potato. "Here," she handed Sue a paring knife and nodded toward a bowl of apples. "You can peel those while we gab."

"What's wrong with Rafe?" said Sue, setting to work on an apple. She preferred outside work, checking the herd with Jack Smith or fetching lumber for Rafe. Or even listening to Cookie rant and ramble.

"You can't be that blinded by love, girl." Arlene rapped the wooden spoon hard twice on the rim of the Dutch oven.

Sue turned, unable to quell a blush. "I . . . I don't know what you mean."

"Oh, come now." Arlene chuckled. "We all know you're sweet on Rafe. No call to hide your light for him. But he's . . . well, don't you think he's changed? And not for the better, either. I have never seen a man angrier all the time, though about what I can only guess."

"Arlene, do you think it's me?" Sue paused, a peel dangling from her knife. "I mean, do you think he's angry all the time because of me?"

"You? No, it's not you, girl. I think he's angry with himself, with the people who wronged him here at this ranch all those years ago. The ones who killed his wife and son. That's who he's angry with. Not any of us, that's for certain."

They worked quietly for a time, then Sue said, "Arlene? Do you think he regrets rescuing me from Al Swearengen up in Deadwood? I know I wasn't the most pleasant person to be around. Maybe I'm still not, but I'm trying. Really trying to be what he wants me to be, Arlene. He can be so difficult."

Arlene wiped her red, work-hard hands on her apron and hugged the young girl tight about the shoulders. "I don't think he regrets a single thing he's done for you, Sue. Rafe is a good man, but he's a man. And like most of them, he's both complicated and simple. Though in his case, I'd say he has more of the former and less of the latter. He has packed a pile of living into his years, more than most people get up to. It's the way he's made." She scooped up a pile of rough-chopped potato chunks and dropped them into a stewpot. "Cookie has told me some things about Rafe, the things he did on behalf of his country. Why, it makes me ashamed to think of how little I have done in comparison."

"You think he'll ever . . ." But Sue could not finish the thought.

"Come around to appreciating you? He might, Sue. But a man like Rafe, if I have any right to judge him at all, he's different than most folks. One thing I know for certain: He will make the decision he thinks is best for everyone around him, then he might, mind you, think about himself. You can take that to the bank."

"Why, Arlene, you are beginning to sound not a little like Cookie McGee."

The older woman nudged a flyaway strand of chestnut-streaked white hair from her forehead and turned back to the stove. "I have no idea what that means, Sue. You best get back to whatever it is you were doing before you came in here to pester me. Shoo!" She waved the wooden spoon in the air, but didn't turn.

Sue was fairly certain it wasn't the stove's heat that had reddened the woman's face. As she headed out the door, smiling, she heard Arlene say, "Cookie McGee? Honestly. That man . . ."

CHAPTER TWO:
WHEN OLD FRIENDS MEET

Turk Mincher suppressed a belch and rapped knuckles to his chest. "Seems to me a fellow ought to have more of a reason to drink beer beyond getting stupid in the head."

The man leaning on the sticky bartop next to him paused, swallowed the last of his own beer. "Well, I like the way it tastes."

Mincher's eyes narrowed and a grin tugged up a corner of his mouth. "I bet you do." He pushed away from the bar, stretched his back, and yawned. "Me, I like the way my thumb stops throbbing after I'm done hitting it with a hammer."

The man canted his head and eyed Mincher. "You wouldn't be funning me, would you, mister?"

"Me?" Mincher recoiled as if slapped. "Why, no, sir. I intended only to prove a point. And that point is . . . I have decided if I am going to spend time in my life imbibing, and I most assuredly am, then I will drink something with more kicking power and less time spent out back leaking out all that tonic I took in but moments before."

"Mister, I don't understand half of what you said." The man shook his head. "You are an odd duck and no mistake," he said as he walked toward the batwings.

Mincher smiled at himself in the bar-back mirror. "And that, Turk, is how to either get your head stoved in or get rid of a person." He glanced at the fine mantel clock nested among all manner of fancy-shaped bottles and sighed. "I reckon it's time." He made his way to the door. As he walked past the other patrons, they hushed their chatter and watched the rail-thin man pass by.

He was no taller than the average fellow, but seemed big, somehow. No one in the crowd would have denied it. He carried himself straight and assured, as if he wasn't about to take anyone's word for anything, nor take no for an answer. He also looked familiar. Was he a lawman? Or worse, was he on a "Wanted" dodger? No, that didn't seem right, either. He was far too well-dressed for that.

Turk Mincher wore a black leather vest, tassels swung from silver conchos. Beneath, a crisp shirt the rich, deep color of red grape wine. His trousers were of serge, black with faint gray lines running the length. Blunt-toe boots, also black, shone from the polishing he gave them each morning before tugging them on.

About his middle, Mincher wore a single, nickel-plate LeMat revolver snugged in a shining black leather holster, buscadero style, with its concho and hide-tassel swinging with his sure-footed walk.

Atop his head sat a low-crown, wide-brim black beaver hat with a faint curling at the edge. Small silver conchos akin to those on the vest ringed the crown. But it was the face beneath the brim that drew the most attention of all.

Turk Mincher was a handsome man, or rather would have been did he not bear two nearly identical welted red scars cut in a diagonal fashion down each cheek. They ran from his earlobes down below his mouth, doglegging twice before meeting at the point of his sharp jaw.

If the scars, odd enough to draw stares unbidden from strangers, were in part what caused folks to look his way, it was his eyes, mouth, and sharp-ended nose that prevented them from uttering a greeting. The man's nearly black eyes shone with a spark that defied welcome. The mouth sealed the deal, always, it seemed, set in a near-grin, as if his mouth had decided halfway there to call a halt to the proceedings.

When asked by the occasional daring soul, usually a young man mistaking impertinence for boldness, how he came about his unusual facial adornments, Turk would smile. Then he would fix him with his dark, shining eyes, lean close, and in a low, even voice that sounded of leather dragged over rusted steel, would say, "In life, son, sometimes you give, and sometimes you get." He would let that hang in the small, tight space between them for several quiet moments, then say, "Any other questions I can answer for you?"

Never once had anyone taken him up on the offer. He rarely received more than a quick, tight headshake and a gulp from his questioner.

All tallied, the details of Turk Mincher's appearance were mighty in their ability to convey superiority among his fellows. And that was precisely how he liked it. He'd been that way since childhood and it suited him fine.

Mincher strode from the Hot Dollar Saloon and Gaming Emporium, one of dozens of such establishments along the main street of Bitterwater, South Dakota. A spring sun angled down at him, warming his shoulders, his face in brim shadow. He almost felt like whistling. Almost. But since he saved such bursts of enthusiasms for his work, he refrained. Women, children, men, didn't matter who, all parted before him on the boardwalk. He suspected he would make it to Hawley's Stables with time to spare. He checked his pocket watch, a silver affair that glinted in the sun. Yes, mere minutes early, as he intended.

Mincher nudged open the side door of the place, peered into the dark interior of the barn, and heard a rustling to his left. It came from one of the stalls lining the wall before the big double-door, half of which had been left swung open to let the fresh March air numb the nostrils.

He leaned in further and saw a big pink knob of a head rise into view in one of the stalls far down the left side of the stable. The man he'd seen bent to his task once more, then stood again. This time the top of a brown leather saddle rose into view, higher, and the pink-headed man grunted as he worked to drape it over an unseen rack. Behind him, out of Mincher's sight, a horse whickered. The bald man looked at the horse, gestured with his head, and pawed the horse's long snout once, a clumsy show of affection.

Mincher smiled, nodded. This was going to be so very much fun. He stepped into the stable, closed the door gently behind him, and walked down the central alley with casual, sure steps. The bald man, busy fiddling with saddlebags, did not hear him until Turk cleared his throat.

The thick plug of a man spun, his wide hands held stiffly out to his sides as if ready to draw guns. His eyes took in the face, half-lit from the sun angling in the doorway, half-shadowed from the dark of the stable's depths. The bald man's eyes widened, his nostrils flared, his mouth followed suit, opening wide in a growl of hate-tinged rage. It revealed two rows of short, white teeth, and behind them . . . the wet, ragged stump where a tongue had once rooted.

"Feeney," said Mincher. "So glad you made it. Ah, I see you still don't have a tongue. Now how do you suppose a man might lose such a thing? Bad poker game? A foolish dare? Oh, I bet I know. You let yourself get sneaked up on by someone with a straight razor. Someone who happens to be me. Am I right?"

The bald man forgot everything told him by his boss, Warden Talbot Timmons, who he knew was at that very moment seated at his oak desk a thousand or more miles away, blowing rings of blue cigar smoke at the ceiling in his office at Yuma Territorial Prison.

Feeney forgot that the warden had told him, weeks before, on no condition at all would he allow Feeney to incapacitate Mincher in any way. "I am counting on you, Feeney. I know there is bad blood between the two of you. Hell, I can sympathize to a point. But there is nothing you can do to him that will bring your tongue back. I know it's a hard truth," said the warden, his hand held up as if to stop a torrent of impossible words — or grunts — from the bald man.

"But the truth has teeth, and it frequently will bite us when we're not looking. So I want you to make nice with Mincher. We need him, have need of his skills. I see that now, should have seen it before I hired that buffoon, El Jefe, and his band of idiots, the Hell Hounds.

"Bring him back here in one piece, alive and kicking, and you will be richly rewarded, I promise you that, Feeney. You will never want for anything ever again. Well, except for that." The warden grinned at his feeble joke about Feeney's vanished tongue. The smile slid from his face as he took in his strong-arm's dead-eyed stare, heard the low rumble in the man's bull chest like a far-off train pounding steel tracks into submission.

That joke had been too much, even for Timmons. He'd offered a weak smile, turned away, and fumbled with his cigar. "Remember, Feeney. Don't kill Mincher. Yet. Your chance will come in good time. I promise. I suggest you begin your quest in Denver. It is one of the few locations I know him to frequent. If he is not to be found in that nexus of chicanery, try these other towns." Timmons handed Feeney a folded slip of paper.

In the stable in Bitterwater, South Dakota, Feeney faced the man, no, the thing he loathed most in all the long days of his life. Even more than he despised his employer, Warden Talbot Timmons. He faced Turk Mincher, killer for hire, his quarry for weeks now — Bitterwater had been the third locale on the warden's list — the man who'd hacked out his tongue years before, the man he'd once trusted with his life — had he ever been that foolish? Yes, in hindsight he had expected too much and received too little from Mincher, once his partner in the bounty trade.

How in the hell had Mincher known he

was in town? Feeney stared at those cold, dark eyes that smiled but didn't. There was that same smug face, the scarred cheeks Mincher had earned at the hands of a savage Apache long before Feeney had met him.

Turk Mincher stared back, but not for long. "You know what's about to happen, don't you?" said Turk. Even as he said it he leaned back, his left boot rising up fast, snapping hard into the nexus of the big man's legs. He kicked Feeney so hard in the crotch that despite the man's girth, the blow lifted him up onto his toes. Mincher's gritted teeth broadened into a quick smile as he felt something like eggs popping across the top of his booted foot.

Feeney's broad red face drained of color and his leer drooped into a long "O." His bottom jaw sagged as if weighted by rocks. His eyes twitched and filled with tears. A wheezing moan leaked out of his mouth and his thick hands grasped at his crotch, hugging the source of this unexpected bloom of agony.

Mincher pulled his leg back, held it up in the air a moment, then pressed the sole against Feeney's broad chest and gently pushed. With a groan the thick man toppled backward like a felled tree into the straw beneath his horse's churning feet. A thin whimper escaped his mouth.

Mincher untied the stamping horse and led it gingerly to the neighboring, unoccupied stall. He returned to the first stall and looked down at the quivering mass of man.

"A shame I can't bring back your tongue. You know, to prove to that garble-mouth Timmons that you weren't the right choice for tracking down ol' Turk Mincher. I'm sure we can find something else to prove our point, though, eh, Feeney?" Mincher leaned forward, out of range of the chunky man's foot. "If we put our heads together, that is." Only Mincher's mouth smiled.

"Oh! That gave me an idea. I'll be darned if good ideas don't drop out of the sky onto your head sometimes. Oh, there it is again. Why, if ever there was a sign from the universe . . ."

As quick as he was in kicking Feeney, Mincher's next movement stunned the whimpering man. In the shaded depths of the stall, Feeney didn't see what it was Mincher had retrieved from a pocket inside his vest. Not until it was too late.

A sliver of afternoon light shafting through warped planking glinted off the polished steel of a straight razor. All in one smooth-as-pie motion, Mincher worked his fingers and palm until the razor sat comfortably. He leaned in and swung his arm low like a clock pendulum. Down it went shining and silver and bright. Up it came, the keen edge rimed wet with the surprising redness of fresh-drawn blood.

For a long moment, Feeney stared upward, mouth wide, the pain in his groin hammering his body in dull waves. Then came a new feeling, not yet pain, far from pleasurable. Within seconds he realized what Mincher had done. Feeney snatched with one hand at his waist, where his revolver rode. But then he recalled he'd taken it off and draped it on his saddle horn while he tended the horse. His other hand grabbed at his throat, his clawing fingertips wedging briefly in the welling gash. He raised the hand before his bulging eyes.

The tongueless man's mouth opened even wider and he screamed — but the only sound to rise out of him now was a wet gurgle. Droplets of blood sprayed upward, forced by his throat's jerking efforts. The wetness ran back and inside, flooding his throat and his mouth, spuming out his nose with his efforts to rise.

Weakening by the second, Feeney tried to rise, scrabbled, and clawed at the glistening

27

straw, the dust, the soft knobs of fresh horse dung. His head flopped backward as blood welled in his blinking eyes. Awkward, grunting animal noises bubbled through, matched with Feeney's pulsing nostrils sucking in air that went only so far before pushing blood out and in through his new wound.

Turk matched Feeney's gurglings note for note with low, wry chuckles, as if he'd been told a joke so fine he wanted to savor it. He stared down at the man, head leaned to one side, and regarded the ineffectual display as an amusement. "You know, you really ought to do something about yourself. This is no way to behave in public. Especially not when you first greet a former pard from the trail. This is one hell of a note, I must say."

Without warning he swung down once more, right to left, then twisting his wrist, swung back, left to right. Feeney's head flopped, a wide red wound pulsed blood, the head now all but separated from the thick, stocky stalk it had rested on for all its days. Feeney's nostrils flexed once, his eyes snapped open. His blood-filled mouth stretched wide, the gore-covered tongue-stump the last thing to quit twitching.

Turk Mincher let out a slow breath, one corner of his mouth angled high in a grin as he stared at his work. "What's that,

Feeney?" He bent down, leaning an ear toward the corpse at his feet. "What? Oh, I see, you want to know how it is I knew where you'd be?"

Mincher drummed fingertips on his chin, then shrugged. "Normally, I don't share my secret ways with anyone. But us being old friends and all. Oh, and you being dead, I guess it can't hurt to tell. You see," he leaned closer. "I had no idea where you thought I'd be. But I knew where you were. Oh, yes, oh, yes, don't look so blamed shocked, Feeney. I've fogged your backtrail nearly all the way from Yuma. I wanted to know what sort of game Timmons was playing. I'd about given up when you jiggled on into this town. You see, it occurred to me some time ago this South Dakota sinkpit is one of the places I told Timmons a year or so back he'd be liable to find me if he needed to. At the time, it seemed as good a place as any. In truth, if I had known it was going to take you so long to get here, I might have been tempted to lay you low a lot closer to Yuma." He sighed, shrugged again. "Reckon I'll have to make my way back there, talk with the warden about our little encounter here."

Mincher looked down, leaned in, and nudged Feeney with a boot toe. The thick man's head jostled. The eyes had glassed and his wide face sagged.

"Aw now, see? That is why I don't like to chat about my private doings. People are forever dozing off. So rude." He shook his head, then angled in beside the man and hunkered down, hands dangling from his knees, the straight razor held lightly in one hand. He made one more quick reach, the blade disappeared into the wet, shadowed stump of Feeney's neck, and sawed at it. The head flopped to one side, severed at last.

Mincher held up the blade and eyed it. "Going to need a good stropping, I fear." He dragged the blade back and forth along the black wool of Feeney's trouser leg, then folded the tool and stuffed it neatly into its inside vest pocket.

Turk grabbed Feeney's cannonball of a head by the right ear. He held the face up before his own, tilting his head to mimic the angle of Feeney's. "I think we should be heading out now, don't you, Feeney?" He winked. "Oh, I'm only funning you. But it will be nice to have someone to talk to on the trail. One thing I don't like is someone who talks too much. Not that you ever did. Come to think on it, might be I didn't have to lop off your head after all. Not like you were going to yammer overly much on the trail." He shrugged. "Oh well. Live and learn — one of us, anyway."

Giggling, Turk Mincher carried Feeney's head down the length of the barn, stopping at a stall in which stood a saddled black horse, tall and gleaming. He wore tack of black leather with silver accents. Turk dropped Feeney's head into a thick canvas sack awaiting its task. He dumped two tin cups of lime into the sack, cinched it tight, and shook it. Then he dropped that sack inside another sack, this one of oiled canvas. He snugged its drawstring tight, wrapped it well, and secured the parcel behind the cantle, tying it tight to minimize bouncing on the trail.

Then he led his horse out of the stall and toward the far double doors, the one on the left still half-open. As he walked, taking his time, smile in place, he paused beside a door to a shed on the side of the barn. He leaned in, pinched free a silver coin from his vest pocket, and flicked it into the dim space with a thumb. "Much obliged, hostler. I'll recommend your fine establishment to all my friends." He chuckled and resumed walking to the barn door.

Behind him, in the hostler's room, the stiff body of a thin, old Mexican man lay curled on its side, eyes wide and unblinking. His clawed hands cradled a flyblown clot of entrails covered in straw and filth.

Not twenty feet away, in a darkened stall, Feeney's headless body lay sprawled on its back, as if he'd decided to stretch out and catch forty winks.

Already disappearing behind the clutter and jumble of buildings that made up Bitterwater proper, Turk Mincher heeled his horse into a lope, the wrapped sack beginning to stain as it thumped in counterpoint to the big horse's mile-eating gait. The rider chuckled low and long.

CHAPTER THREE:
THE PAST IS PRESENT

"Hey, Rafe." Jack Smith jerked a chin toward the broad back of the big man before him. The man didn't move.

"Rafe? You okay?" Jack rapped the big man on the arm.

Rafe Barr flinched and spun, both hands clenched into ham-size fists, eyes narrowed to slits, and nostrils flexed. Long moments passed as both men stared each other down.

"Easy, now, Rafe. Only me." Jack spoke low, calm, above a whisper.

Rafe's eyes focused on the man, where seconds earlier they had fixated on a memory, a torment come to life before him. The eyes relaxed, widened.

Jack lowered his hands from their defensive pose, leaning once more on the hardwood cane that had become an unwanted but vital part of his life since his run-in with El Jefe and his Hell Hounds. "Sorry to startle you, Rafe. I'm only the messenger.

Come to tell you dinner's about ready."

Rafe shook his head and ran a big hand down his face. He nodded. "Okay, thanks. That loafing shed done yet? I could use another pair of hands on this chimney. It needs to be finished soon."

"Yeah, Rafe. She's about done. Another hour or two, I should have it."

Barr turned back to stacking rocks for the chimney off the stone boat. "Good. And don't get jawing with Cookie. That man can wear out a shovel by leaning on it and talking . . ." He stood, straightening his back, rubbing it. Jack was heading away when he heard Rafe speak his name. "Jack. I . . ."

He turned back but the big man's words had already trailed off as he looked at the rise of land beyond the newly built ranch house toward the grave of his wife and son.

He backed away and left the big man to his silence. As Jack walked to the house, the air around him felt thick with something that didn't have a word to describe it. Grief? Anger? Confusion? All those and more. And he guessed why Rafe Barr, the big man, part owner of the ranch, along with his sidekick, Cookie McGee, was so lost in that direction.

From what Cookie had told Jack, well out of earshot of Rafe, the man's family had

34

been murdered, and the entire sad mess was pinned on Rafe. He'd been sent to the hellhole, Yuma Prison, in Arizona, but released by a warden who seemed to have something more in mind than the odd mission he'd sent Rafe on.

The situation was mud-clear to Jack. In truth, Cookie was in his cups when he'd told Jack all this. The old coot had a way of talking around and around a thing until as the listener, Jack had no idea what Cookie was yammering on about.

Still, he'd gleaned enough of the conversation to know Rafe was not a free man, not cleared of the false charges of murdering his family. Normally, Jack Smith would hear such a story, say, in one of his more usual haunts, a gambling hall back in Kansas City, and he would assume the man was guilty. Why not? People did bad things to other people all the time — killed their families, killed strangers for pennies, enslaved other people — Jack had the whip marks to prove that. The welted scars laced his back like a jumble of tossed train rails or snarls of barbed wire.

But he'd gotten to know Rafe Barr and Cookie McGee — owed them his life, and for more than one slip-up, too. He'd have to say he'd never met a more honest or a more troubled man in his life than Rafe Barr. And that was saying something.

Jack himself was no wilting daisy — born a slave, clawed his way to freedom, then he became a professional gambler. And now here he was, head of cattle operations at Barr and McGee's ranch. Course, they would have found someone else to do the job, but Jack was here, and mighty grateful they had saved his skin some months back — twice. It also helped he could sit a horse, always had been able to. In a surprise even to himself, Jack found the work with the cattle suited him.

The title was a nicety that Cookie and Rafe tossed his way. They didn't have to take him on, but they had, and paid him a wage, too. And Jack had been quietly saving every cent to spend on his one true love, his passion, what he'd long ago considered his calling in life — poker. He loved everything about reading faces, raising hands, and setting bets around the green baize mistress, the tables of a gambling hall.

Any hall would do, though he had developed a taste over the years for the finer spots, among them the Top Hat Room in Kansas City, Chauncey Miller's Emporium in Denver, and Sacramento's Lavender

Palace. Hoo-boy, but he'd had a time of it so far.

Despite the solid company, fine food, and good, though hard-earned, pay at the ranch — Rafe Barr could work a man — Jack had a growing urge to dust off his city clothes, take a long trip, and flex his gambling muscles again.

This past week he'd settled in for a game at the local watering hole in Dibley, the town nearest to the ranch, mostly to keep an eye on his fellow ranch compadre, Doc "Deathbed" Jones. Rafe had asked him to make sure the old soak didn't wedge himself too far down into a bottle of hooch. That's when Jack saw a notice tacked to the wall of Mean Pete's Place, for a big — and it looked big, with a big "B" — poker tournament down Santa Fe way. It had been three years since Jack had been to that fine city, he recalled, scratching his chin and staring at the poster. He'd give it some serious cogitatin', as Cookie would say.

Jack smiled at the thought of the roosterish old man. He was a peculiar character, but a finer gent he'd not come across. All of them at the ranch were solid individuals, in fact: Rafe, Cookie, Doc Jones, Arlene Tewksbury — mother hen and one hell of a cook. And then there was pretty young Susie

Pendleton, daughter of none other than California Governor Pendleton. She was a fine young woman. It had appeared for the longest time as if she and Rafe had taken a shine to each other, though Jack wasn't so certain anymore.

Seemed like Barr was only interested in one thing: work. Sue might still have her cap set for the big man, but with the way he'd been lately, who knew? Might be Jack himself stood a chance . . . nah, Jack. Give up that thinking. You might well be a dandy gambler turned ranch hand, but you forget one crucial fact, mister. You are a black man, a Negro, a former slave. She is a white woman, the daughter of a prominent white politician, and that, Jack, is a recipe for a lot of headache.

Jack shook his head and smacked the dust off his rough-cloth work trousers. He wished, not for the first or last time that day, that he was in a city, any city, wearing a suit of fine clothes, puffing a cigar, and reading the faces of the other men gathered around the card table.

Was the pursuit of professional poker dangerous to his health? You bet it was; the beatings he'd taken in the past year, all gambling related, were proof of that. But what was a man's health if he found distasteful what he did with the hours in his days?

Yes, sir, he told himself. Maybe it was time he paid a visit to a place with more people than cattle, get himself reacquainted with his old mistress, Lady Luck, the one who didn't much care what color a man's skin was. She only judged a man by how much daring he had in his heart, how much spark he had in his eyes, and how much cash filled his coin purse.

Jack went on into the little ranch house, smiling and ready for stew, dumplings, and what was that he smelled? Apple pie?

Chapter Four:
A-Questing He Shall Go

"Now, see, that's what I'm talking about." Cookie rapped his dusty topper against his thigh, raising another cloud. He mopped the top of his gleaming pate with a grimy bandanna, once red but now pinked and pocked with holes. He'd had the same funky rag in his pocket since Rafe had first made the old rooster's acquaintance back in the war.

Rafe sighed, didn't look at Cookie lest his old pard see his smile. He knew Cookie was waiting for him to ask him what he was talking about. Rafe pulled a nub of cigar from his breast pocket and made a show of lighting it.

"Confound it, boy, you got mattress ticking stoppering up your head? I'm talking to you!"

Rafe rounded the flame nicely on the cigar until the end glowed a satisfying orange, crusted with blue ash. He puffed, blew out the match, shook it a couple of times, then jammed it into his shirt pocket. "I heard you, Cook. What's the trouble . . . this time?"

"This time? This time, is it?! You ungrateful cur, I've a good mind to . . ."

Rafe's eyebrows rose. "Oh? What's that, you say? You're going to do something, eh?"

Cookie surprised Rafe then and narrowed his eyes and nodded. "I see the game now. Don't think I don't. You have to work pretty hard to pull the wool over ol' Cookie's eyeballs, no mistake, mister."

"Okay, Cook," Rafe blew out a cloud of thick smoke. "I expect you want to get down to it."

"Yep. Known each other too long to keep on playing these games. You're fixing to leave, ain't you?"

The big man nodded, pooching his lips as he studied the setting sun. "I have to, Cook."

"But why?" Cookie angled around to face Rafe. "Everything's been going right good around here, ain't it? We get three square feeds a day, cattle side's building up faster than we both expected, and everybody's gettin' along." He winked and nudged Rafe with a bony finger. "I dare say some of us get along better than others, eh?"

Rafe knew Cookie was referring to Sue

Pendleton, the girl they'd rescued from that whoremonger, Al Swearengen. The big man shook his head, looked at Cookie, and plucked the cigar from his mouth. "Cookie, I told you months ago if we were still alive after that mess with El Jefe and his Hell Hounds then I would be on Warden Timmons's most-wanted list. Likely right at the top. The man hates me and the feeling is mutual."

"What's that got to do with this place? They let you go from Yuma fair and square."

Rafe stuffed the cigar back in his mouth and turned away. "Not exactly."

"What do you mean?" Cookie backed up as if he'd gotten a whiff of a week-old gut pile. "You didn't break out, did you? You lie to me, boy?"

"No, nothing like that. But Timmons expected something in return for releasing me."

Cookie nodded. "Yeah, he wanted us to bring Sue back there to him, nice and trussed up with a bow on her head so he could use her to blackmail her father. Well, Governor Pendleton would have enough power to deal with a worm like the warden."

"Keep your voice down, will you, Cook?" Rafe growled, looking around them. "Sue's liable to hear. I don't want her to think any of this is her fault."

"Well, it is, in a way."

Rafe sighed. "I know that, but I don't want her feeling guilty. Besides, if it weren't for her, I'd still be locked up." Rafe smiled. "It's a complicated situation, Cook."

"I still don't see why you need to up and leave, not when everything's going so well."

"Don't you, Cook? I'll never be a free man if I still owe Timmons. But it's deeper than that. I can't live like that. I won't live like that, like a fugitive for the rest of my days. As far as the law is concerned, I'm a killer. On the books and in my records at Yuma, I'm still a lousy murderer." Rafe's big hands opened and closed; his voice lowered and came out in a raspy growl. "Even if that bastard is the one who sent El Jefe and his goons after me."

"Course he did. Wanted you to do the hard work and find the girl, get her out of there. I expect he knew such operations were your specialty in the war. I know that warden wanted you dead. Still does. All the more reason to stay put. If they come here a-knocking for you, we can settle his hash once and for all."

"No," Rafe shook his head. "I'll not bring more trouble down on the heads of my friends. I've done enough of that."

43

They were silent for a time. Rafe smoked and Cookie chewed a wad of tobacco big enough to choke a mule. "What I can't figure out, no matter how much cogitating I do, is why that Timmons wants you dead so bad. In his eyes, you should be a prisoner like all the rest. Keeping convicts locked up is what he does, right?"

Rafe sighed. "You'd think so, but that's the same piece of this puzzle I snag up on every time I think about it. No," Rafe straightened, flexing his back muscles. "There's more to Warden Timmons than that. Any man who would blackmail another, using the man's daughter as his pawn, all for his personal gain . . ."

"Can't be trusted."

"Exactly, Cookie. And what's more, he'll stop at nothing to get what he wants. I have to confront him, stop him. Somehow. The only way I can think to do that is to prove myself innocent of . . . what it is they're convinced I did." Rafe's eyes stared off toward the cluster of aspen on the little rise where his wife and son were buried. "I can't forget Swearengen, either."

"Not likely many folks who've done him wrong and lived to tell about it could forget him." Cookie let loose a sloppy stream of spittle, and dragged his cuff across his mouth.

"All the more reason for me to fix all this. It's a matter of time before the government shows up and hauls me off in leg irons and shackles. But if I go now they won't expect it. They'll think I'm on the run, holed up somewhere, cowering." He spat out the distasteful words.

Again, a silence fell between the men, the sort that happens when two people have known each other a long time.

When Cookie spoke, his voice was raw, husky, as if he'd been shouting all day into the wind. "You do what you feel you need to, boy. I'll not stand in your way. Don't mean I'm happy about it, nor that I agree with the path you've chosen. But Cookie knows the harm can come when a man gets gnawed on from the inside out." He sent a last stream of brown spittle caroming off a flat rock, then stalked toward the barn.

Rafe half-watched him leave, growled, "Dammit," and ground the last of his cigar into the dirt. It had gone out anyway.

"Why, Rafe Barr, what is all this brooding I see going on?"

The big man turned to see Susie Pendleton walking up with a battered pewter pitcher, the sides frosted with condensation. She held two tin cups by the loops in her other hand. "You ready for a cool drink of water?"

She smiled as she filled the cups.

"Thank you, Sue. As long as it's wet."

"Sounds like something Cookie would say."

Rafe smiled around the rim of the cup. "Where do you think I learned it?"

She stepped closer to him, her sleeve touching his, as she fiddled with her cup.

"No," said Rafe, his voice thin, strained. "I . . . I am sorry, Sue. This won't work."

"The water?" she said, trying to keep it playful, a joke.

"Sue." He turned to face her. "I have to go. I have things I need to do if I'm ever going to be free."

Sue gritted her teeth tight. Dammit, she hated that she was a girl sometimes, hated that she cried so easily. She could feel the tears creeping up on her, well, she would not give the satisfaction. "No."

"Sue, if I've ever given you cause to think there might be . . . that we might be . . . well, I'm sorry, that's all."

She cleared her throat. "Rafe . . ."

But he stared hard at her. "You have to follow what your mind and your heart tell you. You have to do what's right in life, do you understand? Look, I've always tried to play fair, treat others decently in life. With you, with Cookie, with everyone."

He waved an arm weakly around them, taking in the new ranch house, the pole barn, the corral, the little bunkhouse, smoke rising from the chimney. That meant Arlene was working on yet another meal. And beyond, the green meadows losing themselves in the distance to ragged lines of trees stippling the lower slopes of the foothills that grew up to be mountains, far, far away.

"Rafe, I don't need advice." Sue's voice sounded tight, her words angrier than she intended. She dragged the back of a hand across her eyes. "I mean, maybe I do, but . . . look, I've changed, I'm getting better all the time."

"I know that, Sue. I only meant —"

"No," she held up a hand. "Hear me out. You honestly think that keeping me, and everyone else here, at arm's length is the right thing? That's what your own mind, your own heart is telling you?" She had turned his own words on him, not sure if it would offend him. She didn't care if she hurt his feelings. He'd been a bear for far too long. Each day he'd grown angrier and more sullen, withdrawing, becoming a man who did little else but work and eat and sleep. And even where sleep was concerned, she wasn't certain how much of that he actually got.

"If that's the case, Rafe, then fine. I'll go and you won't have me to worry about anymore."

"I didn't mean you need to leave. This is your home for as long as you want to stay here, Sue. I'm the one who has to go. I told you, there are things I need to do."

"No, you're wrong, Rafe. It's both of us who have to go. Different directions, I guess, but it's time I made my own way in the world once again. I have you and Cookie to thank for saving my life. I will never forget that, Rafe. I don't know how, but I will try to repay you, somehow, someday."

"That's not necessary, Sue. You've already done more than you know." Rafe stared off toward Grizzly Peak and the lesser peaks in the distance. After long moments of quiet, he said, "Where will you go?"

"California. I have to get to know my father again. To most people he may be the governor of California, but to me he's Daddy. I am certain that telegram I sent after the mess with El Jefe was precious little for him to hang onto."

Rafe looked at her, concern raising his

eyebrows. "You shouldn't travel alone, Sue."

She shrugged as if to say that it's not really up to him, is it?

As Sue turned away from him, Rafe saw a sly smile on her face where moments before there had been fear, perhaps sorrow. At least he had said what he felt he needed to say to her. Didn't make any of it easier, though.

"That's the way it's gonna be then, eh, boy?"

Rafe paused in the midst of cinching the saddle on his horse, the same buckskin he'd been given when he rode on out of Yuma. The big horse was solid, and held up to long hours on the trail. Couldn't ask much more of a horse. He hoped it would continue to serve him well.

Rafe let the stirrup down, resting a hand on the smooth-worn saddle. "Look, Cookie. We already talked about this. I have to go."

"Run out without so much as a final cup of coffee? After all we been through together?" Cookie shook his head and turned away, crossing his arms.

"You know I'm not much for making a big show of these things. Thought I'd hit the trail early, get a good start on the day. I'll be back, Cook."

"Yeah, if you don't get yourself killed off first."

Before Rafe could answer, Cookie spun on him, a bony finger pointed up at him. "If you do meet your end, wherever it is you're going, you'd best look over your shoulder, 'cause I will track you down and kick the stuffing out of your sorry dead backside, you hear that?"

"Cook, look, I . . ."

"No, don't do me any favors. You get on the trail and tend to your business. I'll be here doing the same." He stomped off toward the bunkhouse, smoke already rising from the chimney.

CHAPTER FIVE:
TWO FOR THE TRAIL

"I do believe you are the quietest person I've ever ridden the trail with, you know that?" Mincher looked over his right shoulder at the sticky, begrimed canvas sack, cinched tight and secured to the saddle with a second hemp rope around the middle. "I would be offended, naturally, but I recall you are a man of few words."

Mincher waved a hand at the sack. A swarm of bluebottles swirled, then settled once more on the bloody thing. He chuckled. "Oh, I plumb forgot you are little more at present than a tongueless head. You are also fast becoming ripe — stinking to high heaven, in fact. You really ought to wash. Why, even Buck, my trusted steed, is beside himself with concern for your current state. I reckon we'll have to find more lime the next settlement we come to."

Turk Mincher chattered with the head of Feeney as they slowly made their way southwestward toward Yuma Territorial Prison. They stopped in Pillory, Colorado, and managed to procure another, larger sack in which he swaddled the swollen head, then dumped a heaping dose of lime on top of the grisly clot before cinching it tight once more.

Late on the third day, Mincher holed up under a mesquite tree in a small copse, waiting out the last of the long afternoon's sun. It wasn't near as bad as summer sun, but any sun, in his book, was sun that should be spending its time tormenting someone else.

He hated to sweat, hated to have to loosen his kerchief, hated to be in a place without a breeze. But his job, such as it was, required that he spend time in hot places trailing desperate men or stupid men or men seeking him who wanted to best him. Such had been the case with Feeney.

And now here he was. Though later in the day he was still holed up under a clump of rabbitbrush, lazily puffing quirleys and shifting every so often to take advantage of the increasing cooling shade. His horse, tethered twenty yards away and cropping spike grass at the bottom of a gully, perked its ears and whickered. Turk sat up, still crouching beneath the bush, and tipped his black hat lower over his eyes. He squinted southward. "What's that, boy?" he whispered. "Got ourselves a new neighbor?"

Whoever it might be was far enough off that Turk figured he could risk a slide down the bank to the horse. He rummaged in his saddlebag, tugged out a brass spyglass, and racked it open. "You hang on to your hat there, Feeney, I need to see who's coming to dinner."

Turk knee-walked back up the slope, selected a spot free of prickly pear, and set his hat down next to him. Prone, he balanced the spy scope on the outstretched fingers of one hand, holding the focusing ring close to his eye with the other, back and forth, twisting until it came to rest in focus. He sucked in a quick breath through tight teeth. "No sir," he whispered. "Cannot be, cannot be."

But it was, and he knew without doubt who it was, and Turk Mincher smiled like he did when he'd liberated Feeney's head from its body.

Yes, sir, Turk, he told himself, this day is turning out to be something to recall, after all.

CHAPTER SIX:
BACK IN THE SADDLE

The sun had begun its rapid dip toward the jagged tips of the Rockies, the teeth of some great beast hoping to take a bite out of the very sky itself. The orange sun was a skin-peeler no matter the time of year in the rugged country of Colorado through which the big man traveled. But Rafe Barr paid it little heed. He rode straight-backed, puffing a cigar, his horse making no effort to slow its pace. Man and horse journeyed northward at a determined clip, the West to their left, through terrain that held little surprise for either.

Rafe peered beneath the tugged-down brim of his fawn hat, squinting even though he didn't really need to — the sun was no longer a hindrance this day. He was vaguely aware of the waning temperature, glad only that it would require him to roll down his cuffed sleeves.

As he rode, Rafe mulled over his situation

for what felt like the hundredth time that day and came to no sharper a solution than he'd had ninety-nine times before. He hadn't wanted to ride north to Denver, but southwest to Yuma to confront Timmons, but that would be foolhardy, even for him. Rafe knew all too well that the likely outcome of being seen anywhere near Yuma would result in his being jailed again. And that was nothing he had interest in.

But sooner or later, everything seemed to happen in Denver. He had an acquaintance in there, a fellow who'd been quietly making a fortune for himself, one "Doc" Baggs, the gentleman swindler, as some folks had taken to calling him. Rafe was pretty certain Baggs owed him more than one favor.

They'd traded information over the years, to the point where Rafe wasn't sure how he'd left it with Baggs, though the man himself would surely know. Or at least pretend to know. *No matter*, thought Rafe. *I'm past the point of caring. I'll gladly owe the man if I can get some sort of start. Some scrap of information, anything.*

"Hell, Horse," said Rafe, suppressing a yawn. "We might as well turn in. You're more like me than you ought to be — you'll keep going long past the point of sense."

As if in response, the big buckskin tossed

his head and snorted. Rafe had gotten in the habit of calling him "Horse" since he'd gotten him on riding out of Yuma all those long months before, and didn't see any reason to stop.

Denver was roughly north of the ranch. It was a city like any other, in Rafe's estimation — bubbling with activity and loud people shouting to be heard over the din of everyone else around them looking to do the same. Rafe sighed, wished he could avoid anything resembling a city for the rest of his days, and squared his shoulders, resigning himself to the task at hand.

Find Baggs and pull information out of him. More than likely that would mean buying it from him, favors or no. But he was willing, for if anyone might know of a place for him to begin, it was Baggs. If not, he would move on. He still had old scores to settle, old acquaintances to track down . . . and shake upside down if need be.

The sun set a half-hour after he'd found a decent spot to camp, tucked in a stand of sparse aspen and tumbledown boulders. Rafe sat close by a small fire, his back to a broad, tall span of gray granite, crisscrossed with shallow cracks deep enough for finger-holds. He didn't much feel like heating food, but he'd have to be tougher to forgo a cup of hot coffee on a night that was turning nippy. He'd tugged on his short canvas jacket, and sat hunch-shouldered, hands held out to the small, tight-flaming fire, savoring the smells of the coffee beginning to bubble and pop in the battered tin pot.

Something was wrong, and he knew what it was. He was out here alone; he'd left Cookie and the others in a huff, like a big, ornery child.

Rafe sat back on the painful nub of rock on which he'd draped his horse blanket. An angry, low growl escaped his tight lips and he spat into the dark.

Horse stood silently behind him, one leg canted, the white blaze running the length of his face easily visible in the fast-descending dark.

"Could be I was hasty, Horse."

A low, chesty chuckle greeted the equally low words.

Far east, toward the narrow coursing river they'd crossed not two hours before, a lone coyote yipped. Another, some distance south, responded, and soon a proper chorus cut loose. The hard lines of Rafe's face softened, then he smiled. *Cookie would enjoy this,* he thought. And then something he'd not thought of before occurred to him. If the hints Jack had been dropping came to anything — the young man wanted to visit a city, needed to — Cookie was back at the ranch, tending to things, likely with more responsibility than ever.

Rafe understood a call such as Jack felt. Not necessarily where a town was concerned, but that deep-down gut feeling that begged a man, no, that demanded a man tend to it and soon.

But there was Cookie, doing something that until now Rafe hadn't given thought to. The old trail dog was stuck in a place wrangling cattle. Stuck in one place, something ol' Cookie hated more than anything. And all because of Rafe. All *for* Rafe.

"What have I done to that man?"

Again, Horse whickered.

But I've come too far, thought Rafe. *Another day and a half and I'll be in Denver. And closer to answers.* And that stiffened him. He clenched his teeth, nodded, and snatched up the scorched palm-size scrap of thick leather he used to handle hot goods on the fire.

The coffee was bold and good, bracing to his throat, burning a path through the chill night air. He looked around the small camp. Others had used the spot — the broad wall of rock behind him a poorly decorated thing chipped and pocked by riders and Lord

58

knows who or what else over the years. He'd not add to the collection of poorly rendered initials, but he would keep an eye and ear perked for any latecomers looking for warmth on a cool night in mountain country.

Rafe would not begrudge a fellow traveler a spot at his fire, but he would prefer to be left alone. Not only because he needed sleep. Should a stranger turn up, he'd likely not trust him and would get little or no sleep the night through. He'd forgone rest plenty in his past, but he was getting older, and the excitement of life on the trail had long since worn off. He wanted nothing more than to get to where he needed to be, unmolested and quiet. It was not to be.

The first sign something was off came about two, three in the morning. The moon was a fingernail sliver, pinned high and bladelike in a sea of stars in a black-ink sky. Rafe narrowed his eyes and squinted into the dark.

Something had awakened him. But what? He kept his breathing low, trailed the fingers of his right hand along the butt of his Colt revolver. He lay on his left side, back to the boulder, facing the dwindled fire. Rafe flicked his thumb, popping free the rawhide keeper thong. Little sound greeted him, a high-up breeze soughing through the aspen leaves, their slight rattle gone almost as soon as it came. Then a sound, as if a cautious step had pushed gravel. But had it? And how far. To the north? South?

Rafe knew he should feel what he usually felt at such times — anger, instant alertness, a sharpening of his sight and hearing. But he struggled now to find them, feeling instead shock at what he'd become, that he was more than anything else, tired. Plain truth of it.

There was that sound again — gravel grinding, yes that was it. But far off. He was grateful his coals were not giving off much in the way of light. Rafe licked his lips, dry. He'd slept deeper than he intended, that couldn't be helped.

He sensed something of potential size and menace out there. A wolf? Lion? Bear? Not likely. He'd had plenty of run-ins with such critters over the years, and his instincts told him no. This was likely the worst of all creatures of the night, vermin of the lowest rank — the two-legged kind. He had no proof other than the tiny fist tugging at his gut, attached to the string that chimed the brass bell in his head. Man, the one creature that could be counted on to hunt man.

A hot, prickling feeling jagged up and

down his spine. Rafe lay still, his hat tugged down toward his nose, hand on his gun, eyes slitted cracks, taking care to ensure his chest rose and fell at the same rate as it did before he awoke. Perhaps it was someone who didn't know he was there. Rafe hoped so, though, in his experience, hope was a fool's errand.

Maybe it was someone too skittish to hello the camp. He'd almost rather be stuck with a stranger than the specter conjured in his mind of what might be out there. Then he smelled smoke, but not campfire smoke, more like that of a cigarette or cigar. It was bitter and fleeting — a light breeze worked against him.

Rafe lay like that for another twenty minutes, then slowly pushed upright until he sat leaning against the rock. The fire was little more than a handful of embers that glowed like the eyes of a distant devil-cat in a fanciful tale. He doubted they revealed much of his position.

His eyes, adjusted to the near-black of the camp, roved the night. From his right came occasional low sounds from Horse, a snort, flick of the tail. Then he recalled the beast's odd whickering of earlier. He should have paid more attention.

Rafe would not enjoy sleep any more that

night. He eased himself to the right, away from where he'd been for hours, and sat once more. He laid his carbine across his lap, set a revolver on the gravel at his side, and sat cross-legged, wincing as each knee popped as he bent his legs. They sounded like rifle shots.

He pinched his wool blanket tighter around his throat. Long minutes of quiet let his mind stray once more. *Curse my hide for living this long,* he thought, trying and failing to tamp down memories of his wife. Unbidden thoughts tumbled into his mind, how he wished they could have grown old together, seen their son become a man. They'd assumed life would go on as they wanted. They were foolish. No, no, he was the foolish one, never Maria. And never again.

And not Sue.

He should have known life could sour, should have prepared for it somehow. Maybe if he had been more wary, he could have prevented them from dying.

Hoofbeats, slow and measured, sounded from below the trail, as if a rider were in no hurry, walking away from him. Within two minutes, the scraping, scuffing sounds dissipated. That didn't mean the rider was gone. Could be a trick.

The old Rafe, the Rafe of years before, heedless of harm, would have followed, tracked, relentless in his pursuit. But now . . . Rafe settled in for a long couple of hours until daylight, drawing slow breaths of cold air through his nose, down into his lungs, anything to keep his head clear until the morning sun rose.

Nothing more happened in the night. As soon as he was able to see a couple of yards ahead of himself, he worked his way slowly southward, back toward the direction he'd ridden, and walked a wide loop around the camp. He left the camp as it was, Horse still picketed, looking as if he could do with another day of rest — Rafe knew the feeling. Life at the ranch had been busy and filled with hard but good, solid work and he missed it already.

He cut the trail of his late-night watcher some hundred yards from the camp, down in a draw that looked as if it would run in season with spring melt, though now was little more than a grass-bottom ditch. It was a man on a horse, no pack animal. The shoes cut deep in spots, though didn't leave as much of an imprint as that left by a fat man riding.

In direct sightline with the camp, whoever it was had ground-tied the horse, walked several yards away, and urinated on a sage bush. Then he'd walked back to where he'd originally stepped down from his saddle. They were blunt-toe boots, solid heels, worn evenly all 'round. No drag marks or scuffs from lazy steps. This might mean he was a man of precision, or at least not tired from riding.

And there, three feet away, the remnants of several hand-rolled quirleys. That confirmed Rafe's fleeting suspicion of last night, though it bothered him he'd not seen the glow — easy enough to mask. But that didn't seem likely with this character. Rafe pinched up a butt, and sniffed it. The sharp, off-smell of old cigarette clung to it, riming his nose. He smeared the stump between his thumb and finger and dropped it, habit from his own cigars and matches. Then he stood and looked around himself.

The land hereabouts was wide open, low and rolling enough that a man could be camped in a gulley and not be seen twenty yards away. But somehow Rafe didn't think his man was anywhere about.

So what did he know? As he walked straight across the sage back to his camp, Rafe mulled over what he knew of the watcher. Whoever it was had known he was there, had seen him, watched for quite some time, was a smoker, wore a midsize boot with blunt toe, and rode a well-shod horse. Not a lot to follow . . . But whoever it was had headed roughly in the direction from which Rafe came.

Trouble for the ranch? He shook off that snag of worry. Have to trust that Cookie and the gang could handle it. Denver was calling.

CHAPTER SEVEN: LADY LUCK BECKONS

"Now, how do you suppose a black man such as myself ended up in the company of so many white folks?"

Cookie recoiled as if Jack had slapped him. "What makes you say that? I reckon you've been around white folks all your born days!"

"Oh, I left out a little word — nice white folks."

"Well, that's . . . say, what are you anglin' at, Jack? You saying we ain't been treating you square? A man's a man, that's all."

"I'm funning you, Cookie. You should know by now when I'm tugging your leg."

"You do that any more and I'm liable to walk funny." Cookie eyed him with suspicion and ambled away to the water trough, dunked his dusty broke-brim hat in the water, and set the sloppy affair on his head. He sputtered and blew spray until he could see again. "And another thing," he said, stomping back. "Might be courteous if you tell me a'fore you head on out. I like to keep on top of such affairs, the comings and goings of the place."

"Cookie, you shock me. As if I would light out and not tell you? You know I won't leave unless you give me your approval. If it helps, I'm not expectin' to be gone long, then I'll be back and we can top off the herd, get them ready to drive to the railhead."

"Oh, I know that. Don't you think I don't know that? I'm steamed is all, steamed because ol' Cookie's going to have to step in, make sure this place don't go belly up whilst you're off gallivanting, sporting, and cavorting down Santa Fe way, excusez-moi."

"Why, Cookie, I had no idea you knew French."

Again, the rangy rooster of a man looked as if he'd seen a mouse in his morning porridge. "I don't! Don't know a lick of no lingo but good old American speech. Good enough for my pap, good enough for ol' Cookie, I reckon." He shook his head with finality, as if daring Jack to challenge the notion.

The only thing he got for his troubles was the sight of Jack Smith slapping his knee and trying hard not to laugh. "Cookie, as Rafe says, 'Don't ever change.' "

"And I'll tell you what I always tell that lummox — what in tarnation makes you think I could? Folks don't change. Why, if they did, this world would go ass-over-bandbox! Think on that a minute, what if we all of a sudden decided we needed to change who we was? The streets would fill with crazy folks, the hills would be overrun with more of the same."

"Cookie, I appreciate you letting me head on out to this tournament. I expect it's something I have to clear out of my system, then I'll be back, you can bank on it."

"Don't expect there to be any work here for you. Ain't like I can't fill that position, you know. I got me a good mind to save the money I been shovelin' your way and do all the work myself anyway!

"Here." Cookie jammed a knobby balled-up hand toward Jack, knuckles up.

"What's this?" Jack reached with a tentative hand.

"Got me a whole wad here, you'll need both them mitts of yours." And he deposited a sizable cluster of federal bank notes and gold and silver coins in the gambler's outstretched hands. "Bet with it. Bet it all. And if you win, we'll both be happy."

"And if I don't?" said Jack, looking at the cash with trepidation.

"Well, make sure it's fun in the doing, that way at least one of us will have enjoyed it."

Jack shook his head and pushed the cash back toward its owner. "Cookie, I can't take this. It's your savings."

"Yep, all of it."

"No, no way, Cookie."

"Ain't yours to refuse, mister. Way I look at it you ain't in a position to refuse me now, are you?" Cookie pinched his eyes tight and wagged a long, bony finger at Jack. "Besides, that stuff ain't no good settin' in my pocket, is it? Needs to be exercised like anything else of worth, elsewise it's useless."

Jack looked down at the money. It was bent and wadded and crumpled and from the heft of it, coins were jammed in the ball of cash every which way. "Cookie, this is putting mighty faith in my abilities."

The old codger held up a paw to silence the younger man. "Man's got to believe in something in this world, don't he, Jack? I reckon you already know that."

"So you're saying I can go to the poker tournament? Even though it's going to leave you with a powerful load of extra work to do?"

"Jack, you're a grown man; what's more, you're a free man, and you should grab hold of the chances life doles out to you. They wither as you age, so grab on now, boy. Don't wait."

"Cookie, I don't know what to say. I won't let you down. And I'll be back as soon as it's over."

"Do what you want to, but don't feel like you have to. You always have a home here if you choose to swing back by this way, no matter if it's next week or next year. But live your life, will you? Too many folks don't. Now, if you'll excuse me, seeing as how you'll be lighting out of here in the morning, leaving me holding the bag, I feel the need to set a spell, take down the jug, and calm my jittery nerves. A man has to take his pleasures where he can get them."

He winked at Jack and chuckled as he headed to the stable to retrieve the jug of bold liquor he kept tucked in the back corner, under a mound of chaff. He didn't think anyone else knew of its location, but everyone did.

CHAPTER EIGHT:
WHAT'S THE MEANING
OF THIS?

Warden Timmons blew a thick cloud of cigar smoke at his office ceiling at Yuma Territorial Prison. Soon, he would find out what the cryptic telegram meant. But soon was not good enough. He lifted his custom brogans from the corner of the desk and slammed them down. For a moment he all but bellowed for Feeney before remembering with a chuff he'd sent the man away to track down Turk Mincher.

He thought it might not be too difficult a task, given that he had a rough idea of where to find Mincher. Not that Feeney was a dolt, though Timmons had never actually held a conversation with the man. He'd lost his tongue at some point before Feeney came into his employ. Timmons had gleaned from other sources that Feeney and Mincher had had past dealings together, which included something to do with Feeney's lack of a tongue. No doubt it was a topic

71

Feeney would be touchy about.

Timmons detected nothing nefarious, at least toward himself, all the years Feeney had been in his employ. But this telegram, blasted thing. Something about it didn't sit right. Timmons snatched it up again, flipped his coattails, and rested a fist on his hip. Squinting through curls of cigar smoke, he read it again, hoping to glean details he may have missed on his previous half-dozen reads of the yellow paper.

found your man stop not fond of being summoned stop old friends will drop by soon to discuss business stop feeney and tm

"Bah," he spat, hooking a long finger around the cigar and jamming it into the pewter ashtray atop his desk. Cold ashes spilled out and annoyed him further. He had hoped to convince Mincher from a distance to do what he required of him. That's why he'd sent Feeney. On their meeting, the man had been instructed to hand a simple note to Mincher, written by Timmons, telling him he wished to talk with the hired gun. Should the note find its way into nefarious hands, Timmons could claim he was merely hiring a known mercenary to track down a fugitive prisoner. Simple and straightforward enough, and the truth.

Rafe Barr was a wanted man, a killer, and now, he would have little problem painting him with the escapee brush. Top it off with the horses and gear the man "stole" on his exit from Yuma Territorial Prison, and you have the mixings of a batch of woe for that bastard. Now he had to convince Mincher to do the job he'd only half-begun nearly six years before.

Timmons sighed. "Why do I put up with these insufferable subordinates?" He looked up at the ceiling. The whitewashed beams were still there; water stains and smoke stains and flaking paint stared back, nothing more. No sign from the Almighty.

"Hellfire and damnation," he muttered. The same thing he'd muttered for years, ever since he was a boy and had heard his father say it as he tugged on the secret party's robe, tucked the black hood under his arm, and kissed his mother on the forehead.

"Don't stay awake on my account," his father would say, "we'll be a while. Got lessons to deliver, so Colonel Dawkins says. Me, I don't know. I'm tired, I reckon." His father, one Ezekiel Timmons, would then hang his head like a whipped hound and his mother, Clara, would pat him and tell him

73

all would be well. That he was doing the Lord's work.

And off in the corner, young Talbot took it all in, delighted that his pappy was a soldier in the army of Christ, as his mother would tell him when they heard old Clem's hooves pound out of the yard and down the lane.

"Your pap's a good man. Needs a guiding hand is all. Like we all do, from the Lord himself." Then she'd nod. Talbot would, too. It seemed like the thing to do.

"Mama," he said one night. "What does Pap do, I mean, with his hood when he's out doing the Lord's work?"

She'd looked at him that night as if he had sprouted a new set of ears. "Why, son, he's burning the very souls out of those who would see us perish ourselves. The Negroes, you see. There are certain evil folks who want to give them freedoms that cannot stand. The only people who stand between us and certain ruination for the very soul of the South are men, good men such as your papa. He is delivering hellfire and damnation to all who would stand in the way of the cause."

There had been so much in that speech by his mama that Talbot had lain awake on his little trundle bed for the better part of an hour thinking on it and puzzling out what he thought she meant. The only thing he came to land on with any firmness to it was that the Negroes, like his friend, Jamesy, were doing something that folks like his mama and pap knew to be wrong.

Talbot knew whenever he did something wrong, Pap delivered unto his backside a righteous whuppin'. Must be that's what Pa and the Colonel Dawkins were doing — out there in the dark, a-whompin' on the backsides of all the Negroes doing wrong-headed things. Talbot pictured one of his father's hands as "Hellfire" and the other named "Damnation," flailing the badness out of all them folks. Might be he'd try it himself one of these days on his chum, Jamesy.

All these years later, Timmons stood in his office, a thumb tucked in the watch pocket of his gray brocade vest, striped serge frock coat riding over the crisp, white shirt and pressed trousers, black, with the thinnest of gray piping along the outer seams. His black leather brogans gleamed.

What Timmons could not understand from the telegram was who found who? And what did "found your man" mean? Which man? Did Feeney find Turk? That, of course, was the objective, but Timmons doubted the telegram had been sent by Feeney.

On the other hand, he knew Turk Mincher to be an odd duck and he wouldn't put it past the man to have somehow commandeered the situation. Mincher had come highly recommended six years before as someone who would see certain tasks done, no matter the dicey, unsavory nature. It occurred to Timmons later, too late to change his mind — not that he would or could have — that he suspected it had been Mincher who had posited the recommendations, via a telegram or two. And now here he was again, sending a telegram telling him . . . what? That Mincher had gotten the drop on Feeney?

What's more, the newest missive made it plain that Mincher did not appreciate being sought by Timmons. "How in the hell does he think I'm going to find him? I warned him I would be in touch at some point, dammit." He smacked the desk with a flat palm, if only because the offending telegram still sat atop the desk, staring up at him like an unblinking eye.

He knew his last statement to his empty office was a lie to himself, to make himself more confident of his standing with the ruthless bastard Mincher, who was the one to have told Timmons he would be in touch should he want to work for Timmons again.

Not the other way around. The truth made the warden's teeth grind together hard. Then the damned telegram went on to say how despite being "summoned" by Timmons, these "old friends" were nonetheless glad to spend time getting reacquainted. As if they were enjoying each other's company! The warden could picture them making their way toward Yuma "to discuss matters in further detail." Indeed, Turk Mincher was one smug bastard.

The entire affair left Warden Talbot Timmons unsettled, a feeling foreign to him. Not something he liked and not something he intended to become comfortable with. If only El Jefe and his damnable Hell Hounds had been up to the task. They had certainly looked unsavory enough when he hired them.

"Should have known better," said Timmons. "Nobody's as good as Rafe Barr, dammit." Wondering if even Turk Mincher was up to the task.

CHAPTER NINE:
BACK WHERE I BELONG

"Ahhh," said Jack Smith aloud, indulging in a broad smile. He shifted in the saddle and straightened his shoulders. Felt good to be out and closer to a bustling burg with each step the horse took. He could almost taste the fine whiskey, the cigars, hear the clink-clink-clink of the poker chips, see the pretty late-summer glow of the green baize surface of the games tables, the thick scrim of blue smoke hovering lower with each hour that passed, each bet placed.

The pretty smiles of the paid-for women leaning over close, letting you get in a long, close look at their bursting top-heavy gowns, whiffs of cheap perfume masking lack of regular visits to the Chinese bathhouses. Ah, he missed all of it, the good, the worse, and the downright foul, yes, even that. The point in the evening when the white men he sat across the table from looked at him through rheumy, boozed eyes and snatched at their thick, smoldering cigars from their fat, pooched lips.

They'd fix him with hard, squinty stares, and that began the hating period of the evening's performance. It usually slumped into anger that a "darkie" could be bold enough to steal money from them. No matter the fact that they were drunk, overconfident, and sloppy. They were no challenge.

But all that headache was worth it when Jack tucked into a solid game with players who were good and knew it. They played with confidence and kept on and on, not once regarding him as ill-suited to sit at the table with them, not once paying attention to the hue of his skin, merely enjoying the game for the beauty of it. That's when it was good, that's when all the hate he had to put up with paid off.

He shifted once more in the saddle, rubbed his bum leg, and eyed the road before him. Poorly built huts with sagging ramadas gave way to grander adobe homes in the past mile, a sure sign he was drawing closer to Santa Fe proper. He urged the horse into a trot, eagerness causing him to smile through the trail dust riming his face and the bone-sore throbs from his leg. He surely was looking forward to revisiting his gambling glory days.

Those were fine years when he became a better poker player than most men he sat across from, when he had a reputation that arrived before he did in gambling towns all over the West. It seemed for a time as if people knew he was on his way to their gaming halls before he knew himself he was bound there. They were heady, good times. But his skin color never left him. Truth be told, he liked the difference it afforded him.

If he had one hole in his life, it was in not knowing what had happened to his sister, Mala. They'd been ripped from each other's lives as youngsters. He as a worker in the fields, she as a housemaid. But she had been a pretty thing and could speak English, French, and some Spanish. Jack felt sure she'd landed on her feet, if she could escape the foul, sagged mess the war left behind.

Jack tried for years to find out where she was, who she had become, but traveling the South, where he would likely get information about her, was to beg for a quick death. A black man with fine clothes and cultivated speech would earn him nothing more than a short rope ride and a hard jerk at the bottom. So, Jack stuck to the West.

He'd not much regretted it. The riverboats, the roaring coastal cities, the cowtowns and railheads brimming with flush-faced drunken cowhands flashing more money than sense. And cranking out more bullets than was good for him. Jack learned when, where, and how to shy from such locales. Didn't stop him from going back, though.

And now here was this, the perfect excuse — not that he ever needed one — at the perfect time. Was there ever a bad time to gamble?

The Tournament of Kings, the poster had called it. Made it sound like something out of Ivanhoe, thought Jack. Hell, with the purse expected to rise above $10,000, every two-bit ranch hand with a snoot full of liquor and a notion that he was handy with the pasteboards was bound to show up for the first week's worth of activity — the qualifying rounds. The play was to take place at allegedly sumptuous digs known as the Santa Fe Grand Hotel.

This late in the game, Jack suspected the rooms at the venue would be booked, but figured by the time he upped his winnings enough to afford to stay there, some rooms would open up. In the meantime, he would find digs wherever he could within walking distance. His coin purse, while not empty, was not yet heavy enough to indulge in fine rooms.

The qualifying rounds would separate the wheat from the chaff in quick order. Though Jack wasn't foolish enough to think that a rich man who was a poor poker play would not be considered "qualified." Not that Jack minded such underhandedness. The more fresh money, the better.

It seemed as if the very heart of old Santa Fe sat before him. Jack guided the horse into the funnel end of a long, broad lane and angled diagonally toward a side street. Eager as he was to settle in and explore the offerings, Jack wanted accommodation for the horse, and a room, bath, and meal for himself. In that order would do nicely. And maybe he'd have enough stamina left over for a drink.

If he recalled correctly, the older, quiet part of town would best suit his purpose. At least until a room opened up at the Santa Fe Grand. But come tomorrow, watch out. He smiled once more, touched his hat brim, and nodded to a pair of lovely señoritas strolling arm in arm along a boardwalk to his right.

"Yes, sir," he whispered to himself. "Black Jack Smith is back in town, and he is set on having a good time while he's here. And then leaving a wealthy man. Watch out, Santa Fe."

Chapter Ten:
Trouble at the Door

"Hey! Who let that mangy-hided critter in here?"

Here we go, thought Jack, tensing despite his innate sense of confidence, indispensable in his line of chosen work. But the speaker, a broad-shouldered, wobbly blowhard with a red face, a drink in one hand, and a cigar in the other, squinted past him toward the door. It seemed the man hadn't noticed him. Good. For the time being, anyway. Jack made mental note of the man's face, as well as those of the man's acquaintances hovering around him as if he might say something clever at any moment.

"I said, 'What are you doing in here, boy?' "

Jack looked over his left shoulder once more. That's when he saw the shuffling lump of flyblown clothing slump forward into the center of the barroom floor.

"I say we give him the heave-ho on out of

here, what do you say, folks? I say we teach that damn bean-eater a thing or three, huh? In Texas we don't put up with such critters. But we do put 'em down!" The man brayed like a donkey at his own wit. His fellows followed suit as if they'd never heard a thing more humorous.

Relieved as he was that the fool's remarks were directed at someone else, Jack despised such situations, no matter the recipient. He didn't want to draw unwanted attention to himself by helping the poor wretch, but he couldn't stand by and let this fool roust the old Mexican. He sighed and tweezered a coin from his vest pocket, then hung the crook of his cane on his arm.

"Sir," he said, approaching the bum. He tried to keep his voice low, though any attention he'd wanted to avoid was now directed solely at him. "A little money." He proffered the coin but held it out of reach. "Follow me outside and you can have the coin, with the promise you won't spend it in here tonight. You likely need a meal more than liquor."

"Sí, sí," the hooded head nodded vigorously, the voice a hoarse whisper. They moved toward the door.

"Good riddance!" shouted the blowhard. "Killed me two birds with one stone, and didn't have to break my drinking pattern, neither."

Had to be a Texan, thought Jack. In his estimation, there were two sorts of Texans, at least that he'd come across. Big hearted and big mouthed. This was one of the latter, and a backward glance showed Jack the florid-faced man had changed his mind and wanted action. He was rolling toward the door, smiling and smacking his hands together. Several of his chums trailed behind, sharing grins and conspiratorial looks. *Here we go,* thought Jack. *Not what I wanted my first, or any, night in town.*

As soon as he'd ushered the hunched form out the swinging saloon doors, he nudged the figure off to the side, into the shadows. "Here, take this money and go. Now! They'll be out here any second and . . ."

But that was all he had time for, as the batwings slammed outward, the left one catching him on the shoulder and nudging him sideways two steps. "Hey now!" he shouted, scrabbling for his cane and silently cursing his game leg. Could have been worse — could be one-legged, or dead. But that thought was a fleeting thing, as the red-faced Texan and his devilish friends were upon him, one snatching handfuls of his black, rough wool coat, while another cuffed

85

his hat off his head.

"Where you headed, black boy?" The voice was low, slurring, and intended for Jack, no one else.

Jack regained his footing and, wedging one boot against a porch post, brought his hickory cane up hard and fast, feeling a meaty thunk as it connected with a body. It wasn't enough to slow down all four or five of them. Honeyed light spilling out of the smudged bar windows did little more than cast sharp shadows, splitting the faces of his attackers into leering masks, their arms arcing wide and lunging at him.

Any second now, he thought, *and this bunch of grunting men will commence to driving knives into me, filling me full of holes, leaving me leaking everything I am onto the wooden porch in front of this damn bar.* He heard the boot steps of several figures walk by in the dark street, snickers and outright laughter from them.

Jack whipped the cane upward again, landing another solid smack; this time it was followed with a wheezing groan, and he saw a dim shape double up. Jack knew he'd connected with the man's tender *huevos.* He indulged in a brief grin before a meat-fisted punch, thrown sloppily, caromed off his temple, and dragged down along his jaw.

Starlight bloomed behind his eyes.

He recoiled, felt the buzzing in his head, and saw clear now the bursting stars that let him know one more knock and he'd be out cold. He set his teeth, growled, and swung around hard, hoping to connect with anything flesh and Texan, anything but a big knife blade. That's when things began to change.

He heard a soft, high-pitched shout, saw movement off to his right in the shadows, heard the fluttering of cloth as if a blanket were being whipped and tossed, and then the sound of something hard hitting something soft. It connected once, twice, thrice, the following groans shrinking away with each blow.

"Hey! What's all this?" The red-faced man, who'd backed from the initial dance-steps of the fracas, growled as his companions, one after another, dropped, groaning and moaning, at least one of them sobbing, all clutching various parts of themselves. "Boys! Get up! Get on up, I said!" The Texan waved his arms upward as if trying to rally a summer-swelter crowd at a tent revival. "Come on now!"

But they were having none of it. The last of his chums still standing backed off, his boots clunking the wood floor. He turned and wobble-ran his way down the porch and off into the night, a string of whimpers trailing behind.

Jack, his head still flashing and ringing, saw movement to his right. A slender person bent to the floor and scooped up a bundle of rags. Light from the window wedged across the face. The eyes looked at Jack and his own eyes widened. It was a woman, a young Mexican woman, her hair long and straight and black, her eyes round and wide, her nose and mouth . . . perfect.

That was the word he would recall later, alone in his dingy hotel room, recounting the night's tirade, thinking of all the things he should have done, should have said. But right then, he found himself speechless.

But she was not. "Gracias . . . señor." Her voice was a husky whisper. She whirled the blanket around herself, and quick as a deer she bolted away.

"Hey!" shouted Jack, but she was gone.

A grunt from his left swung Jack back around. He found himself facing the wide-shouldered Texan. He'd think of the strange girl later. Just now, he had more important business to tend to.

"What was it you were so urgently trying to tell me, sir?" Jack worked to make his voice sound genuinely inquisitive. He knew

88

exactly what the man wanted. He was drunk and wanted to have fun beating, maybe even killing himself, a black man, do something foul to someone different than himself. Show he was one formidable fellow. But not this night.

Everything Jack had endured his entire life, everything he had seen, lived through, felt as the strap flayed the skin on his young back, the fingers and toes broken from beatings, the lashes and lacerations to his head, the beatings from men such as this, all his days. Seeing his friends, his family dealt the same . . . it all bubbled up in his throat, threatening to release in a spree of violence the likes of which this had rarely seen.

But no . . . Jack knew he could not give into that raw bestial urge, else he would be no better than this savage. He also did not want to spend this night, the night before the tournament opened, in jail.

He pulled on a broad smile, his eyes showing no kindness at all, and flicked his stout hickory cane upward. With a flip of his fingertips he caught it halfway up the shaft. The movement was enough to summon a gag from the Texan facing him.

"No . . . no, I didn't mean nothing, don't lay into me, darkie." As he blubbered, the Texan backed toward the bar doorway, now crowded with faces above and below the swinging doors.

Jack shook his head no.

The Texan said, "But my hat's in there, at the bar."

Jack shook his head no, popped up the cane a couple of inches, still smiling broadly.

"Okay, okay!" The Texan patted the air with his palms.

Jack took a step forward. The man squealed and spun and trotted down the porch. He missed the edge and toppled with a loud, sloppy thud. Jack heard a groan, then saw the man scramble to his feet and wheeze off into the night.

"Drunk enough to believe me," muttered Jack. "Thank God."

"That was impressive," said a voice from inside the bar, a voice with a distinctive southern drawl. As the other faces thinned out, one remained — a fat white man, on the tall side, with a dagger beard and a sharp look about himself. He wore a low-crown beaver hat canted to one side of his head. *A jaunty angle for a jaunty man,* thought Jack. He'd seen plenty of them. Had the look of a professional gambler.

The man pushed through the doors and held one open for a moment, as if to showcase himself for Jack. In the light, Jack took in a fine wool jacket, soft gray in the dim light, topping a purple-and-black silk vest. Beneath, he wore matching gray trousers and black boots gleaming in the dull light.

"Allow me to introduce myself, sir." The man tugged off what looked to be fine kid leather gloves, of a gray that matched his suit, and offered a hand. "Rufus Turlington. *Colonel* Rufus Turlington."

Jack returned a firm shake, the cane still gripped warily. Never failed. Every white southern man seemed to call himself "colonel," earned or no.

"I understand your reticence, my good fellow, but let me assure you," Turlington smiled warmly, still holding Jack's hand. "I am no threat. On the contrary. I could be your friend in this town." He released Jack's hand.

Jack straightened and looked askance at the man. "Well, Colonel, what makes you think I need a friend in Santa Fe? What makes you think I don't already have a friend, or several, hereabouts?"

"True, true. If your kind display is any indication, you do indeed have a friend here. Though one Mexican waif, even if she is a pretty thing, is hardly friend material, eh?" The fat man smiled. "Come, come, let us talk of finer things than waifs and beatings. Perhaps over a fine bottle of port? I suspect you are a man of the world, despite your obvious, ah, unfortunate situation."

Jack recoiled as if to he'd been smacked across the face.

"Oh, there I've put my boot in my big, old Georgia mouth. What I meant to say is that your unfortunate situation is only so according to our strange society. You can hardly help being born with the skin color you have, eh? The way I see it, you and I are more alike than not. I could as easily have been born as you, and you as me. But we are what we are. Come, come, I assure you I am no threat."

Jack's thoughts turned to Rafe Barr. The man was a walking example of caution. And he knew Rafe would tell him no, not in a hundred years should you follow this man for a drink or two of port or anything else. Something was, as Cookie says, hinky about Rufus Turlington.

Jack touched his hat brim and offered a quick nod and smile. "I thank you, sir, for the kind offer. But I am long on trail dust and short on sleep. I need to turn that situation around."

The fat Georgian shrugged, still grinning. "Suit yourself. If you are in town for the Tournament of Kings, then we will cross paths once again." He bent in a short bow. "I bid you a good evening, sir."

The man spun on his heels and strode down the porch, stepped down, and without once looking back, headed straight for the Santa Fe Grand Hotel, across the street and three buildings east. Jack watched him go, envy of the man's obvious wealthy situation nibbling at him. Jack's gaze trailed to the truly grand façade of the hotel itself.

It was difficult to miss. It offered everything the humble hole he'd found a room in did not — classy clientele, ample light spilling out the ample — and clean — windows, and no yowling drunks spilling out the doors every minute to engage in sloppy fisticuffs in the street.

Jack sighed and made for his own meager place of accommodation, some streets away, his thoughts still on the dust-up and on Turlington. Perhaps he ought not paint all southern men with the same brush? Tricky habit to outgrow, particularly given his dealings in life with that ilk. He sighed and thought of his more recently acquired friends, true friends in The Outfit, as Rafe and Cookie both had begun affectionately calling the gang.

Jack patted the left side of his chest, felt the wad of cash tucked and buttoned in there for safe keeping. His wages and what he chose to think of as Cookie's loan against winnings. Still there. Given the ruckus he'd half-expected to find an empty pocket. He'd count it out later. For now, he was content to dwell on what the southern dandy wanted from him.

CHAPTER ELEVEN: ODD, THESE CITY FOLK

Rafe rode along High Street, one of the mass of hundreds of people a-horseback, on foot, or riding in some wheeled conveyance, all moving with intent. He'd seen plenty of such activity in the past, spent his share of time in cities, never much liked it, but this time it felt dirtier somehow. As if they were all there for one reason — to take something from someone else. *All in the pursuit of money,* thought Rafe, a bitter edge curling around his words.

He shook his head and heeled the horse into a brisker walk while looking for a side street down which he might encounter less bustle.

Out front of saloons men loafed, hats tugged low over their foreheads, shadowing roving eyes. He'd seen their type too many times before. Coyotes starved for prey. Some of them wore fine clothes, but still carried the look of rapacious, foul thieves as evident to him as if they sported signs strung about their necks.

Rafe felt a twinge of longing for the ranch, for the company of Cookie, Arlene, Jack, Doc, and Sue. Sue. Where was she now? On her own. He half-hoped she'd changed her mind and would be there when he returned.

"Hey, hayseed."

The voice, Rafe realized with a jolt, was addressing him. He looked to his left and saw a blond man in a barouche with a fringed top. Next to him sat an equally blond woman in an emerald satin dress, a black feathered hat perched on her piled golden hair. Her dark eyes regarded Rafe through a scrim of black veil.

"Yes, you, plow-hand." The man's eyebrows twitched high. He jerked his chin. "You mind moving the nag along so we can cut down that street?"

Rafe was about to apologize and speed his own progress, but the man's attitude rankled too much. Rafe pulled the horse up short, leaned a forearm on his pommel, and in an exaggerated hick drawl said, "Well now, mister. I don't rightly know what to say to that. You are more familiar with this here busy place than little old me. Could be plain ol' luck that brought us to meet like this.

You see . . ."

The man cut him off. "That horse had better move in the next five seconds, you rube. I have important matters to tend to and you are preventing such. Now move aside." He waved a gloved hand at Rafe.

Rafe made a slow show of looking down the side street, then back to the man's reddening face. Several people had stopped their own progress to watch the scene play out. Rafe let a look of surprise dawn in his face. "That there road?"

"Yes, yes." The blond man sounded defeated, muttering something to the woman beside him, who covered her mouth with a lace-gloved hand.

Rafe straightened in the saddle. "Glad I could give you something to chuckle about, ma'am," he said, in his own resonant voice. Then he fixed the rude man with a hard eye. "As for you."

The man's head pivoted back on his neck out of instinct, his eyebrows rising, this time out of fear.

"Might I trouble you for a bit of information?" Rafe didn't wait for a reply. "I am looking for a fellow by the name of Doc Baggs."

The man's eyes widened even more.

Good, thought Rafe. *That means Doc's*

97

likely still kicking about town.

The blond man nodded and pointed down the street in a vague way. "The Golden Pearl. Can't miss it, the biggest place on the left. There's a dome atop. That's where Baggs is often found."

"Now that wasn't so tough, was it? Much obliged." He winked at the staring woman. "Ma'am." Rafe rapped a forefinger against his hat brim and dragged it downward in salute, then rode on.

The silly little episode pleased him more than it ought, but then again he had grown tired of this place and he'd only arrived. The kerfuffle had added levity to his afternoon, air in an otherwise dense, gray day.

It took him but a few minutes to locate Doc Baggs's favorite spot. Hopefully he'd find the man himself inside, plying his trade. *He'd better be,* thought Rafe. *I want answers.*

He tied his horse to the rail out front, well away from several others. He slid his carbine from the boot, cinched down and double-checked the buckles and straps on his saddlebags, and mounted the steps.

At the top, a mousy man in a tweed coat and black wool pants casually pushed away from a white-painted hexagonal column. He parted his short legs and thumbed back his coat to reveal a single, small revolver. He grinned and eyed Rafe with no sense of fear. "Ahem, sir. I am afraid I will have to ask you to hand over that rifle. You see, the owner of this establishment does not care for long guns in the place."

The man held out a pink hand, palm up, as if to receive the laid-out gun.

Rafe eyed the man briefly, then pushed past him. "Like hell I will." His voice was a low growl as he brushed the little man's squared shoulder. The move nearly knocked the mousy man over.

"Now see here," he said, dashing past Rafe. The little man once more tried to slow Rafe from swinging on through the saloon doors.

"I'm done talking," said the big man. "I need to see Baggs."

"Oh, oh." The little man wrung his hands together, and glanced without wanting to toward a smoky back corner. Rafe followed with his eyes, and saw a dark-paneled door at the rear of the room.

"Thanks." He pushed past the man and weaved through the milling gambling and drinking public. *Now we're getting somewhere,* thought Rafe with a smile. The sort of den of depravity Baggs would use as a base.

He knuckle-rapped twice on the door,

then grasped the knob and pushed on in — but the austere office was empty. Another door, set in the far back wall, seemed to be his only option. Perhaps Baggs had known Rafe was outside and had made his escape. Rafe strode for the door, eyed the alleyway up and down, then cut left and out onto a bustling side street. Cities — too damned many choices.

"Good Doctor Baggs."

The dapper man a half-dozen paces ahead of Rafe stopped walking, his silver-tipped ebony cane paused in mid-arc of its tight swing. The tip hovered, hitting the brick walk with a clunk. The man still did not turn. It was as if he was waiting for whoever had spoken to catch up to him. Rafe complied, walking up until he stood close by the dapper man's left shoulder.

Baggs cocked his head and eyed the tall man beside him. "Hmm. I should have known." His mouth twitched, and a clipped gray moustache bristled above pursed lips. He resumed walking, his left arm still held behind him, as if knuckling the small of his back.

"You know full well I am no doctor, Mr. Barr."

"I also know you like the title."

The dapper little man smiled. "Perhaps too much." He stopped again, turned, still smiling, and held out his hand for a shake. "How are you, then, Rafe Barr?"

Rafe offered a half-smile, his eyes indicating a guarded demeanor. He shook hands. "I'm not in Yuma, but I am in a city."

Baggs shrugged. "That is life, is it not? The bad, the good, blending from day to day, eh?"

"Ever the philosopher, Doc."

Baggs resumed walking. "I assume, given the weight behind the words you spoke, specifically about you being in a city, that you are here for one reason and one only. You want something."

"Yes. From you."

"I recall I am in no position to refuse a . . . reasonable request from you, Rafe Barr. Given the . . . delicate situation from which you assisted in extricating me some time ago."

"You recall correctly."

Moments passed; the men walked side by side. "I help you, we are even." The lilting, kindly voice had taken on a flinty edge.

"If you can help me."

Again, Baggs sighed. "Very well. If. But," he stopped once more, holding up a single gloved finger of admonishment that poked in counterpoint with each word he spoke. "I am not a man to be trifled with, nor a man who likes to have a debt hanging over his head."

Rafe leaned low, his nose inches from Baggs's. "Neither am I, Doc. Neither am I." The big man's voice came out low, stone ground beneath steel.

The little man's monocle trembled, dropped, and swung on its chain before the black-and-silver-brocade vest. He swallowed. "Very well."

Rafe smiled once more. "Now," he brought his big hands together. "Perhaps you can recommend a nice place where we might chat over a cup of coffee, a slice of pie. All this hubbub leaves me hungry."

Baggs nodded. "Follow me."

By the time they entered the brass-and-glass doors of Tillie's Café, Baggs had regained full command of his ramrod-straight composure and impeccable manners. He held the door and gestured with a nod of his head. Rafe replied in kind and resisted the urge to doff his big fawn hat. He took it off and stepped inside, followed by Baggs.

Despite its plain name, Tillie's was as far from a slop joint in a cattle town as a hungry hand could get. A tall, thin man in a white shirt, arm garters, and with oiled hair led them to a small round table in the middle of the half-busy room. Rafe wrinkled his nose at the scent of lavender wafting off the man. The big man stood over the little table, shook his head, and walked to a table not yet cleared along the wall. It was square, ample for four diners, and not in the midst of the busy room.

The waiter began to protest. Rafe made out a French accent — fake, he'd wager, if he were a betting man — but was cut off with a curt headshake from Baggs. The waiter cleared away cups and plates and crumbs of the previous occupants and hurried away, suitably if silently admonished by Baggs, likely a regular.

Rafe pulled out the second chair on his side of the table and plunked down his hat in the second chair. When both men were seated, Baggs spent a half-minute tugging off his gloves, one finger at a time.

"Still in the swindling trade, Baggs?"

The little dapper man recoiled, eyes wide. "I beg your pardon."

"No need to beg a thing from me, Doc. Let's get this silly game out of the way so we can enjoy our coffee and pie when Monsieur Lavender returns, okay?"

Baggs's eyes burned wide and bright like

diamonds, then a smile twitched a moustache corner and he nodded. "You are a refreshing sort, Mr. Barr. I'll give you that."

"Likewise," said Rafe.

"But you do not approve of my . . . methods of asset procurement."

It was Rafe's turn to nearly smile. "If that means bilking honest folks out of their hard-earned pay, then no, I definitely do not. And drop the look of shock from your face, Doc. I'm not telling you anything you haven't heard a hundred times from the law and the families of your victims."

"You sound as though you think what I do is little more than . . . than . . ."

"On par with the sleazy tactics of your compadre, Soapy Smith?"

At the mention of the name of that well-known con artist, Baggs's face took on a deep crimson tinge. "How dare you!" he spat.

"Pull in your horns, Doc," said Rafe, looking around at their fellow diners who were making little effort to hide their curiosity about the two ill-matched men conversing in their midst. "You might well be recognized."

Baggs leaned forward and spoke in a flurry of words, "I'll have you know what I do is an art, I'd even go so far as to say it is a vital service to this community. Mark my words, someday they'll . . ."

"Yeah, yeah, someday they'll erect a statue in your honor, new parents will name their babies after you, and we'll fly the flag at half-mast every year to mark the day of your passing. Look, Doc, I didn't mean to rile you but I don't much care. I am here for information. And if anyone has his ear to the pulse of this city's seamy side," he held up a big palm to ward off another tirade from the little man. It worked, though Baggs chewed his words back. "I figure that's you."

"Then we are even?"

"Then we are even," Rafe nodded, leaning in. "Provided you can help me."

"Naturally," said Baggs.

"Naturally," said Rafe.

The waiter wheeled a silver trolley to their table and made a long show of draping a towel over his arm, displaying each item before he filled their cups, fine chinaware, with steaming black coffee. Then he lifted a silver dome off a selection of powder-sugar-topped confections, each more elaborate than the previous.

"They are all toothsome, I assure you," said Baggs.

Rafe eyed them as if he smelled something off. His stomach gurgled, but only because he was thinking of Arlene's apple pie, with its toothsome, flaky crust. "Don't you have any pie?"

The perfumed waiter stood straight, his eyes wide, the dome in his hand. "But monsieur . . . These tarts, they are . . ."

Rafe sighed. "Never mind. Coffee's enough for me."

"But . . ."

"Go away, Miguel." Baggs dropped sugar cubes with tiny silver clawlike tweezers into his cup. "When his mind is made up, it will not budge."

The waiter, managing to look both affronted and defeated, replaced the silver dome on the platter of confections and wheeled it away.

"Cities," mumbled Rafe. "Everything's so . . . complicated here."

"And isn't it grand?" Baggs smiled, stirring a hint of cream into his cup. "Now," he said, tapping the dainty spoon against the rim gently. "What might I help you with?"

"You going to drink that coffee or build it to death?" Rafe sipped again. "Good brew, though. I'll give them that." He sipped and sighed. Not as good as the stuff he made on the trail, but he reckoned it was as good as he was going to get in a city. He leaned forward, fixing Baggs with a hard glare. "I need to know who did it."

The dapper man sipped his own coffee, pausing his cup halfway back to the table, confusion raising his eyebrows. Then they smoothed. "Ah, yes, your family. When we first met on the street, I suspected it might have something to do with that."

"Then you can help me?"

"You'll have to be more specific, Rafe."

"I'm starting with next to nothing. I need to know who did it, who told them to do it, why they did it, why they pinned it on me." As he spoke Rafe's voice grew tighter, his teeth clenching, jaw muscles bunching.

"I see," said Baggs, setting down his cup in its saucer. "The sort of people who would do such a thing — and I was so sorry to hear of it, no matter what you think of me, Barr — they are not good men."

"You think I don't know that? I don't need platitudes, Baggs," he said. "I need names."

"If I knew those names I would tell you here and now, and with no notion of recompense. But I do not know the names you seek, none of the answers you seek. In all honesty, which, I realize, must sound rich coming from my lips," he smirked.

Rafe leaned back, feeling ten years older than he had when they walked in the place. He nodded. "It must tell you something that

I came all the way here to see you with nothing more in mind than a hope that you had some . . . connection."

"No notions as to demons from your past? Men who believe you have wronged them somehow? I know in the war you were . . . ah, not popular on either side. And then the government's abandonment of you after the festivities."

"Don't remind me," said Rafe, sipping his coffee.

Baggs sat back, uncharacteristic for him, sort of relaxed in his chair. He crossed his arms, ran a finger along his groomed dagger of a beard, and regarded the big brooding man across from him.

Rafe looked up. "What is it?"

"Might be little, or nothing at all."

Rafe leaned forward, his eyes alight. "Anything," he said.

The dapper man leaned forward as well, looked left and right, then in a low voice said, "There are two men, the worst sort. I do not employ them personally, but I know others who have. They are foul, I tell you, but they may well run in the same pack of vermin as the people you seek. This is a long shot, mind you," he wagged a finger.

Rafe nodded and gestured with his fingertips. "Come on, out with it."

"Okay, their names are, and I kid you not, Knifer and Plug. They work together. An odd pair, but they will do about anything for money. And word is that occasionally they do it for fun as well as profit. They have also been known to kill their own employers, assumedly after they have been paid, that is."

"Knifer and Plug." Rafe nibbled his lower lip. "Sounds nefarious enough. How do I find them?"

"As it happens, I received word they are back in town. Something to do with that foul Soapy Smith, no doubt. Say, why don't you go bother him, anyway?"

Rafe rose, picking up his hat. "Because he doesn't owe me anything." He plopped his hat on his head, Tillie's be damned. "Yet. Thanks, Doc, for the tip." He walked a few feet, then stopped. "And for the coffee. Oh," he snapped a finger and in a loud voice said, "And I'll be sure to tell Soapy you said hello."

Once more, Doc Baggs reddened.

CHAPTER TWELVE:
THE STINK OF MONEY

A soft knocking sound came to Warden Talbot Timmons from the other side of his office door. "Who is it? What do you want?"

The thick wooden door creaked open a hand's width. The barest shadow poked in, a bit of hair, a nose. "Pardon me, sir. I'm so sorry to bother you, but . . ."

"Is that you, Winkler? What's wrong with your voice? And why in God's name are you simpering outside the door? You're the clerk here, aren't you?"

"Yes, sir, ah, there's a man here to see you, I told him to wait in the antechamber, but he's . . ."

A low, gravelly murmur of a voice sounded behind him; Timmons couldn't make out the words. "Who's there? Winkler, who is it, for heaven's sake? I have important matters to attend to."

The door swung open wider, emitting a slow squeak. The shadow of the door widened and lengthened to reveal a tall, thin stranger, dressed in black, smoking a cigarette. "Howdy, Warden."

Timmons forgot for a long moment he was the warden of Yuma Territorial Prison. Forgot he was much of anything. Certainly forgot all of the things he had told himself he was going to tell Turk Mincher once the man stood in front of him in his office.

Here was a man who received cash money for shooting, stabbing, burning, cutting, Lord knows what, but the stories were too frightening to forget. The warden slowly regained his composure; the room's light faded back to him from a dim, shadowy mass at the corners, the edges sharpened, all in focus on the face of that killer man before him, standing in his doorway.

Timmons cleared his throat. "Ah, Mincher." The warden pulled in a quick breath through his flexed nostrils. He began to cross his arms, gave up on the foolish movement, and stepped behind his desk, remaining standing.

Mincher stepped into the office, looking to his side at the small man standing in the shadows behind. He said nothing but Winkler squeaked like the mouse he was. The warden heard his footsteps as he scampered down the stone-flagged hallway. Why didn't his staff respond that way to him?

A cloud of god-awful stink reached his nostrils. He gagged, tried to control it, and nearly threw up on his desktop. "What . . ."

Turk Mincher let out a sharp bark of laughter, tossed the half-smoked quirley to the floor, and ground it out with his boot. "I see you have detected the presence of my trail mate."

Timmons only half-heard him as he rummaged in his breast pocket for a handkerchief. He jammed the white cloth against his nose and mouth, blinking his eyes rapidly to clear the tears forming.

It was then he saw the soiled sack Mincher held up before him, the top gathered in a tight fist. "Funny, I don't much smell it anymore. I know, I know," he nodded. "I am as surprised as you. But I tell no lie, I've gotten used to having ol' Feeney around."

"Feeney? Wha . . . what are you saying?"

"Warden, you'll have to take that rag off your mouth if you want to converse with me. I can't make out a word you said."

Timmons would not allow himself to believe what he was hearing. He shook his head, backing up a step until his legs clunked into his pushed-back chair. He held up a hand as if to ward off the approaching man.

"What's the problem, here, Warden Timmons? You don't want to see your old pal, Feeney? Hold on a minute there, Warden." Mincher opened the end of the sacking and put an ear to the hole. A half-dozen bluebottles flew out, buzzing heavily about the room. "Okay, okay, I'll tell him." He looked at Timmons. "Feeney here says after all he's done for you, you not wanting to see him makes him about want to lose his head." The man's raspy laughter echoed through the room.

"Okay, Warden." Mincher's smile dropped, and the sack hit the floor with a dull thunk.

Timmons winced, eyes wide.

"You won't laugh with me, I reckon that means you are more of a man of business than I gave you credit for. So let's get down to it, Warden." Mincher's voice was a low, hard thing, reminding Timmons of stone scraping stone.

"I know you hired that cut-rate gang of idiots, El Jefe and his Hell Hounds, to do a job I have waited and deserved to do for a long time. What's it been? Knocking hard on six years now, isn't it?" He nodded, agreeing with himself. "Yep, six. Killing Rafe Barr, slow, as is my way, is something I have long considered my special appointment."

"Then . . ." The word came out thin, dry. Timmons tried again. "Then dammit all, man why didn't you do it?" He tried to convey a sense of outrage, but it wasn't in him.

Mincher smiled, only with his mouth, and leveled a snake-eye gaze on the warden. "I did the job party-way, didn't I? Told you my rates for the full deal. I was waiting on you to respond. I don't work for free, Warden Timmons. Any man who does is a fool. You're not about to call me a fool, are you . . . sir?"

"No, no, of course not. But Barr was . . . It was necessary to jail him. For reasons that shall remain my own."

"Fine, fine," Mincher dipped his head in agreement. "Might I suggest, Warden, that you should have kept him behind lock and key and hired me to retrieve the girl? I wonder how come it is you didn't do that, eh, Warden?"

"You . . ." the warden groped for words, hitting on a notion. "You are difficult to track down. Yes, that's it, you see. Too blasted difficult to find. I am a busy man. I don't have time for your games."

"Oh you don't, eh? Then why send Feeney after me? Could it be you took a liking to my games?"

114

"No, I mean, well to be plain about it, Mincher. You have a reputation, Mincher. I wasn't certain the girl would have been safe in your company."

Mincher nodded, a clown's frown pulling his mouth corners down. But he nodded. "It is true, I love women. Then I leave them . . . dead." His cackles of laughter filled the little room, echoing around them in the small, tight office.

The warden shuddered, his shoulders twitching with the thought of the madman's comment. "Look, Mincher. You are here at my behest, are you not? So, let us dispense with the small talk. I wish to hurry along the proceedings as I have a train to catch."

"Oh? Where are you headed, Warden? Might be we could share the journey!" He smacked a hand on his thigh. "Now that's a solid idea. Where are we headed?"

"None of your business, Mincher."

The outlaw's face sagged into a stony mask.

"I've been thinking about it and I realize I don't need the girl after all. I would still very much like to see Barr dead. I will need proof, of course, and not merely a finger or some such freakish artifact. I will require full proof, full body, or at least a . . . head." The warden did his best to look commanding, flicking at imagined crumbs on the lapels of his jacket.

"Or what?" said Mincher.

"Pardon?"

"I said, 'or what?' You going to have me killed?" Mincher smiled.

"You judge me harshly, sir."

"I do not judge you because I can barely stand the sight of you, Warden." This time there was no hint of a smile in the voice or on the face.

Timmons tugged his lapels and tried to not look frightened.

Mincher laughed a quick, sharp bark. "Thought so." He stepped forward, said, "Boo!" and laughed again when the warden jumped. Then he flipped open the richly carved box atop the desk, revealing rows of cigars. He scooped up a handful.

"Oh, no need to pay me in advance. Unlike that El Jefe fellow, I know you're good for it. When the time comes, I'll expect full payment. However, my fee has gone up, Warden."

"How much?" the warden's voice came out as a whisper. He said it again, louder.

"I'll let you know when the time comes." Mincher almost reached the door, then stopped and looked down at the sack on the floor.

Mincher picked up the loose end and held the sack up close to his face, his nostrils flexing. "Well, old buddy. Here's where we part ways. I wish you luck in your future pursuits. Might be you'll get ahead one of these days." Mincher's eyebrows rose high and he smiled. "Here you go!" He swung the sack, and let go. It landed on the warden's desk with a dull thud, skidded across a stack of papers, sending them to the floor, and came to a rest before the mortified warden.

"You'll have your proof, Timmons. But don't ever sleep without a lamp burning low by your bedside."

"Are you threatening me, Mincher?" The warden's voice was barely stronger than it had been.

"Why, yes, yes, I believe I am, Warden Talbot Timmons. I don't go in for blackmail. I prefer direct dealings." He rested the heel of his free hand on a massive knife hilt partially hidden by his black vest.

"Well, well, hold on there, Mincher. I . . . I've had a thought."

"Oh, have you now?"

"Yes, what say you do accompany me on my journey. I'll be headed to Santa Fe in a couple of weeks and I will have need of someone of your specialized abilities."

Timmons warmed to his new line of thought. What was that saying? Keep your enemies close? Something like that. At any rate, he'd be able to keep an eye on Mincher. Maybe even figure out some way to dispense with him.

The killer smiled and nodded. "That sounds like a good deal all around. I'll make a little cash, you'll be able to keep me in your sights. Mm-hmm, I see it all."

Timmons shook his head. "No, no, it's not like that. I genuinely see the need for your assistance."

"Well, now, that's good of you. A man likes to be appreciated."

Timmons smoothed his vest front and tugged his cuffs. "Fine then, how will I find you when the time comes?"

Mincher turned in the doorway, looking back at the warden with one eye in shadow. "Oh, don't you worry your head about that, Warden Talbot Timmons. Ol' Turk will show up when you need him, rest assured." He walked out, closing the door behind him.

The warden stared at the door and thought he heard a light, dry chuckle recede with the man's footsteps.

"Oh, God . . ." moaned Timmons, the rank tang of Feeney's rancid head — and

all it represented — stinking worse than
ever.

CHAPTER THIRTEEN: HOPE IN ONE HAND . . .

Rafe Barr felt something blooming deep in his chest, something he'd long since forgotten about. What was that? Hope? Perhaps he was making headway. On to Soapy Smith's place. He found it within minutes; it seemed everyone in town knew where to find the famed huckster.

Rafe waited for his eyes to adjust to the dim room before him. The inside of the Tivoli Club, an establishment owned by Smith and his brother, Bascomb, looked at once fancier and much the same as every bar Rafe had been in through the years.

"Well, if it ain't a genuine war hero in our midst!"

The voice brayed up from the nearest end of the polished long bar. There stood a tall, lanky man with a full beard, mostly black, and wearing a straw boater atop his head.

Rafe walked over, resting an elbow on the bartop. "Afternoon, Smith," said Rafe.

"Don't mind me if I don't bow and scrape."

The man jerked his chin at the two men propped nearby on the bar. They found a table. Then he turned a hollow smile back toward Rafe. "You know me?" said Soapy.

"Apparently, I could say the same."

"Well," said Soapy. "I for one am flattered."

"Don't be. Your reputation preceded you." Rafe bit the inside of his cheek. He had to keep a tighter rein on his sarcastic responses. After all, he was here of his own choosing, in hopes of tracking down clues. Smith didn't seem bothered by Rafe's comment. He puffed on his big cigar and squinted through the smoke.

"You are curious about something, elsewise why would a man such as yourself risk being seen in here, eh?"

"What's that supposed to mean — 'such as myself'?"

Smith leaned closer. "It means that I happen to know you are not a free man, at least in the eyes of the law."

"That may well be. Then again, it might also be a fabrication. Depends on who you receive your information from. And speaking of information, I could use a little myself."

Soapy stood upright and smacked his

palms on the bartop. "Ah ha, I knew it. You are looking for a favor from ol' Soapy, eh?"

Rafe watched him, but didn't speak.

Soapy's smile faded. "Okay, then. How about you tell me what it is you need." As he spoke he drew a glass of beer, foam rising and overflowing the top. He slid the wet mess in front of Rafe.

Rafe looked down at the beer, then back at Soapy. "I expect the price of this beer hinges on the complexity of my request."

The bearded proprietor shrugged. "Something like that."

"A pair of men who work together, Knifer and Plug, they're called. I need to speak with them."

"Why on earth do you want to talk with those two?"

Rafe found the look of surprise on Smith's face telling. "So you know them?"

"Might be I do. Might be I have a bone to pick with those rascals. Might be I was fixing to deal with them soon myself. Might be if a person were to come in here, promise to . . . deal with the pair of them . . . might be this glass of beer would be on the house."

Rafe sighed inwardly. Why did all these city folks think everyone else were rubes? "Gee, Soapy, might be that sounds like a good deal to me."

122

Smith's eyebrows rose together. "I cannot decide about you, Barr. But I'll take a risk and trust you." He leaned down once more. In a lowered voice, he said, "Might be the men you are after are in town."

"That much I know."

Soapy nodded. "Yes, but might be I can tell you where to find them."

Rafe sighed again, audibly this time. "Smith, I know you're a big fish here in Denver. Everybody knows it. Tell me where they are or not. I have things to do."

"Okay, okay. Might be any time now they'll be getting a fix on a vault at the Denver Precious Metals Exchange. Second Street."

Rafe stood. "Now, see? That wasn't so difficult." He looked at the sloppy glass of beer sitting in its own puddle on the bartop before him. He tweezered out a dollar coin and tossed it into the glass. It spiraled to the bottom. "Don't like to owe a man." He ran a finger off his hat brim in salute. "Much obliged, Soapy."

"You son of a bitch," said the proprietor through gritted teeth. "I won't forget this, Barr."

But Rafe was already on his way out the door, bound for Second Street.

CHAPTER FOURTEEN: THIS CAN'T BE GOOD

Following directions given by a young Chinese man on the street, Rafe was a half-block from the Metals Exchange when a voice to his right curled out from an alley.

"Heard you been searching us out."

Rafe stopped. *That was fast,* he thought. He looked into the dim space, but saw only shadows. He sidestepped over to the mouth of the alley and leaned against the building. "That all depends on who you are."

A pretty woman in a tall feathered hat and a yellow dress cut a wide arc around him. He smiled, nodding. *Great,* he thought. *Now all of Denver thinks I'm talking to myself.*

Rafe held one arm across his chest, and tucked his hand under the other arm, keeping his right hand loose, the heel of his palm resting on the butt of his gun. He leaned into the alley and saw two shapes. The nearest was tall and thin, the other, less than half the height of the first, but wider, as if a full-size man had been stomped down. He saw no details of their faces or clothes, though. Only shades of black and gray. Light glinted off something shiny that turned slowly.

"Oh, we're who you want, all right. No worries there." The voice sounded deeply southern. Distinctive, though. Likely from the bayou swamp country of Louisiana.

"Then that would make you," Rafe pointed a finger at the tall figure. "Knifer. And you," he pointed downward, "Plug. Appropriate."

The shorter figure growled up a sound like a cross between a small bull and an angry dog.

"Them are names we don't much care for."

"Why go by them, then?"

"Don't. They was laid on us like a blanket some time ago and there ain't no shaking them. So, we wear 'em, like as not."

He was about to ask them the questions he'd ridden all this way to ask someone, anyone who might be able to light up his clouded thoughts, but the tall man stepped forward. The glinting item was growing more distinct. Rafe backed up a couple of steps, hands at his sides.

"We know what you want to know, big

125

man." Light fell across the man's face. It was long, with a jutting chin and four-day black stubble littering the pock-scarred cheeks and jawline. Rafe guessed the man to be thirty, maybe thirty-five. But a lack of teeth made him appear much older. His mouth was a sunken thing, cratered by puckered wrinkles. The glinting object, no surprise to Rafe, was a long thin-bladed knife polished to a mirror shine. Given the man's name and reputation, he wondered how many folks that blade had slipped in and out of.

Knifer was joined in the half-light of the alley's mouth by a short, thick man. The top of his head didn't reach Rafe's waist. Plug was appropriately named. Rafe had seen another such short, thick man during the war. He'd been relegated to rank tasks of cleanup in a field hospital, gathering hacked-off limbs, sopping up gore, wringing out bloodied rags and putting them back into the iron cauldron filled with bubbling crimson wash water.

The little man's face was a crabbed knob of crevices and craters, populated with paltry stubble and dripping brown lines where chaw juice leaked from the down-turned corners of his wet little mouth. He sneered and growled, revealing pitted, black teeth. Across his chest he cradled a sawed-off shotgun, twin barrels ready to lay someone low.

"You two going to answer my questions or not?" Rafe was tired of the day's foolish games.

"Yeah," said the tall man. "As soon as you pay us."

"Pay you first? I am not willing to be so foolish today."

"Maybe tomorrow then," said the man. "Come on," he said to the little man. "Time we moseyed. Got lots to plan out."

"Hold on," said Rafe. "I didn't say I wasn't interested. I said I don't want to pay for something until I know it exists."

"Sounds to me like you have trouble trusting folks." The two alley-dwellers chuckled together, the smaller offering up a snuffling grunting sound more appropriate of a pig than a man.

Rafe didn't move.

The tall man sighed. "Okay, tell you what. Meet us yonder at the Metals Exchange tomorrow and we'll tell you what you are looking for."

"I'd rather talk here, now. I'll decide what your information is worth."

Again, the small man growled and Rafe wondered in passing if that was all the man could say. Maybe he was a mute. At least Rafe wouldn't have to listen to him as well as to the tall swamp dweller.

"Nothin' doing, big man."

Rafe eyed them for a long, silent moment. A prickling warning, well worth paying attention to in the past, clawed up his spine, skittered its way toward his neck. He decided to heed it once again. "When?"

"Tomorrow, on them steps yonder, two-o'clock."

Chapter Fifteen:
And So It Begins

Jack felt good, better than he had in a damn long time. No offense ever intended to his friends at the Barr-McGee ranch, for he was thankful for Rafe and Cookie and the girl, Susie. They had saved his hide back in that dugout trading post from those two rough-cob bounty men, but since then he'd not had a decent game of checkers, let alone poker.

But now? Now he was dressed to kill, top to toes, and rested up, no mean undertaking, considering the funky little hole he'd been forced to stay in. But it was that or sleep in the stable, and that would not fly, not when he had a tournament to win. Besides, the money he saved went toward his entry fee — a steep $1,000 — as well as adding the little extras that made his entire ensemble that much better: Pearl cufflinks, silk string tie with matching hat band and pocket hanky, and to top it all off, a silver cigarillo holder.

It was true he enjoyed wearing finery and looking good, but he also knew the effect a black man sitting down at a high-stakes table had on white men, especially the sort who could afford to sit in on such a game themselves. They were often southern, often well-moneyed, and often far more than resentful of the fact that a man who they regarded as an inferior in every way should share the table with them.

What had always tipped the scales in Jack's favor, once they got over their foolish biases, was Jack's high ability to play a hell of a game of cards. Most of the time these men were far more in love with a good hand of poker than they were of their prejudices, at least while a good game lasted. In some cases, that only lasted as long as they were winning.

Jack had developed over the years an ability to read people, not only for what they may or may not have working in their hands, but long before that, for what sort of folks they were. Usually men, his adversaries at the table often split into two groups: Those who would not, could not tolerate playing against a black man, and those whose love of the magic of the game overruled their innate hatred of his skin color.

They were the ideal ones to play with. For they loved the game as much as himself.

He'd even been complimented by several of them over the years, long after the game folded, and he'd raked the winnings in his direction. He could detect them from a distance, deflated from their loss but elated by the thrill of a high-wire chase in which no slips were tolerated.

That was what he hoped for when he entered the ballroom-turned-poker-fiesta at the Santa Fe Grand.

Jack paused at the top of the wide, broad steps, and surveyed the scene below. What he saw were dozens of tables, a sea of smoke, and green tables like low clouds over bright spring fields. He felt readier to sit down at a poker table than he could remember.

Yes, the buy-in was steep, but having strolled down this road before, he knew the wheat and chaff would soon separate. A number of hands would see the men who thought they could play, the farmers, the drifters, railroad men, vaqueros, all of them.

"Gentlemen! Gentlemen, please!" The voice was loud, and cut through the babble, the clink of glassware, and the occasional bray of laughter. The back-clapping and showy camaraderie so common before a tournament, and so obvious by its disappearance when play got underway, dwindled.

Jack looked up. The master of ceremonies was none other than the fat Georgian from the night before. What was his name? Colonel something . . .

"Oh, yes, my apologies. I have been told not to forget we have not one but two fine ladies who wish to test their mettle at the games tables."

That brought the remainder of the braying and guffawing to an end as jowly gamblers swung their bovinic faces, hoping to see the faces of the two daring women.

Jack couldn't help himself and also looked about the room. One of the women was easy to discover, a pretty dark-haired flower in a white dress with bold red-painted lips beneath a crimson silk hat with a small wing of black feathers adorning the side.

She looked innocent and wide-eyed, but if she was who Jack suspected, Lottie Deno, then he felt sure he would be facing her one of these days soon over a baize table. She was anything but innocent, at least where cards were concerned. Lottie had carved a reputation for herself as one sharp character, cooler than winter ice under pressure, and unruffled in any situation, even when it appeared she was far behind the rest of the table. That, however, rarely remained the situation for long. She was a high-money earner, as the trail of penniless, lovestruck buffoons across the West readily told.

As to the other woman, she was more difficult to pick out, but he found her. It was who he thought it might be — Petula Hart. Now beyond her wild youth, this woman still showed signs of the prettiness that had wowed men all over the frontier. He'd heard the cigar-chomping woman had recently lost another fortune — a high-class bordello in Tulsa — in a five-day, no-sleep game of chance. She must have had a recent streak of luck, or a deep-pocket backer to buy her way into this tournament.

All too soon Jack felt eyes turn to him, much the same as they had focused on the women. Other than white-coated servants hustling through the crowd with silver trays mounded with hors d'oeuvres and clinking champagne glasses, he was the only black man in evidence.

The speaker continued: "As many of you know, I am Colonel Rufus Turlington the Second. I dare say most of you knew my pappy as well. He's gone, rest him, but I'm here, and this tournament, what I call the Tournament of Kings, is my idea. Sort of a charity event, you might call it."

"Aw, get on with it, Rufus!" shouted a voice from the far side of the room. More laughter followed.

Turlington didn't seem to appreciate the interruption. He scowled as color rose in his cheeks. Then he cleared his throat and spoke. "Rules of play are as follows: Don't cheat. If you do cheat, don't get caught. If you do get caught, you will be arrested, maybe hanged. That's not up to me to say. But cheating is not encouraged. Beyond that, play fierce — fortunes depend on it — yours and those of the people you win or lose to!"

Rousing shouts volleyed throughout the massive room, then the speaker held out his hands and, smiling, quelled the voices. "Now, now, as to the picayune points, we shall begin when I give the nod to a colleague who nods to another, and so on until we hear a gunshot out in the street. That will be the signal to begin. Before that glorious moment takes place, let me point out that you will play hard for two hours, take a ten-minute break for refreshment and other duties, then set yourselves down again until luncheon. At that time, we'll have a one-hour break. The afternoon's play will be divided up much the same. This is the only day when such breaks will be as regimented. This, as you all know, will be the day we weed out the less fortunate among you. Winnow the field down to the truly desperate!"

The room bubbled with predictable laughter. Even Jack, who normally preferred less talk and immediate action, found himself smiling. He was excited, but counted on the fact that he would soon enough settle into a comfortable place at the table and in the game.

"Please, please. Attention once more. Good. You should all have an envelope. Does everyone who has paid their entry fee have an envelope in their hand? Yes? Make sure it is still sealed, don't open them. Even though you're gamblers, we're trusting you!" Chuckles rippled through the room. "Okay then, open your envelopes — inside you will find which table you have been assigned to."

For the next five minutes, much jostling and shouting and confusion filled the room. Jack found himself halfway down the east edge of the room. A decent enough spot in that he was able to select a chair with his back to the side of the room, no other tables behind him. That made him feel less jumpy, and he was happy with anything that would not cause his innards to dance more than they already were.

He took his seat, choosing to offer a polite smile in return for the sneers from some of the others at the table. His eyes passed over one of the men, then back to him. The red face bore bloodshot eyes and a look of mixed surprise and anger. Great, it was the broad-shouldered Texan from outside the bar the night before.

"Now, we all seated?" The plump master of ceremonies raised his hands and his eyebrows. "I trust you all approve of the seating arrangements. If not . . . that's too damn bad!" Another round of laughter, though more subdued than before.

Before Turlington could give his nodded signal to his cohort, the Texan squawked his chair back. He squared his broad shoulders and stood facing the room and the emcee at the top of the stairs. He thumbed his silk vest and cleared his throat. All eyes turned to him.

"Colonel Turlington. I appreciate all you and your friends have done to put together this fine event." He looked around himself, smiling at the folks in the room. It was obvious from the casual nods and smiles he received he was well known among the gathered players. "But!" here his red face lost its jovial expression. The extended digit that he held straight up in the air for emphasis he rammed directly at Jack's face.

Oh, here we go, thought Jack. He gritted his teeth and willed himself to remain calm, to maintain a benign expression.

"I was not told, nor would I guess was anyone else hereabouts, that we would be forced to sit down with a . . . a damnable darkie!" The man's face took on an even deeper florid hue and spittle flecked his pooched lips. His comment generated loud murmurs of agreement; other voices bubbled up, overrode the murmurs until the room once more swelled with shouts.

"Now, now, Horace, everyone!" Turlington spent the next thirty seconds quieting the room. "If you are so all-fired bothered by the presence of that man in your midst, Horace, why don't you up and outplay him? Surely you are capable of that, aren't you?"

"But . . . but . . . This is a gentleman's game, dammit! I paid my fee! I demand satisfaction!"

"Well, now, Horace, the only satisfaction I can offer is your money back should you want to bow out. At that, I am going against the rules we set down well before this day, as you know, seeing as how you helped draw them up."

The Texan turned his shaking face from the man across the room to look down at Jack. "I . . . . Faaah!" He yanked his chair and sat down. It creaked and squawked as he scooted himself up tight to the table. He rested an elbow on the table and pointed at Jack. "Don't think I don't recognize you from last night, you . . . you uppity trouble-maker! You give me any cause at all to regret my decision, I will . . . ."

Jack's eyebrows rose up. "Yes? You were saying?"

"Enough of this," said another man at the table. "Let's get on with the game." And so, they did.

For the next two hours Jack labored to work out the wrinkles of his long-dormant skills. He made foolish blunders, caught himself contemplating judgments of his fellows, of their possible hands, that a green-horn at five-card draw would have laughed at. And the clock ticked on.

The Texan smacked his hands together and raked in his winnings. "You keep that up, Darkie, and we'll get along fine."

"The name is Jack. Jack Smith." Jack didn't bother looking at the man as he said it, but concentrated on shuffling the deck. He cared far less about the foolish flare-ups of prejudice at this moment than he did with why he wasn't performing as he demanded of himself, as he wanted to. Hell, as he needed to. If he kept this up, he'd be out of the running by the first break.

Concentrate, Jack, old boy. Focus your thoughts like Rafe's fancy brass spyglass. Bring the game in close and personal. At the thought of Rafe and the rest of The Outfit, Jack felt a glimmer of confidence — good people, strong people, and not one would tolerate such waffling.

"Hey," said a thin man across the table, pulling a green cigar from his mouth. "I heard of you, didn't I? Yeah, you're Black Jack Smith, from Kansas City way. The one who duped old man Jasper out of his winnings."

Jack shrugged, shuffling the cards. "Could be. Lots of folks with my name."

"Yeah, but not a black gambler decked out in finery such as yourself. No, you're him all right."

Jack paused in dealing. "That going to be a problem?"

"Hell, no," said the man, rolling his cigar around between his lips. He smiled. "I only wish I had been there to see what you did to Jasper. He deserved it. Man was an asshole."

Jack nodded to acknowledge the comment, and allowed himself a slight smile. Something at the table changed then. The mood grew less somber, less angry. The remark even had a quieting effect on the seething Texan.

Jack could care less what his opponents thought of him in any way except his poker-playing abilities. What he did care about was getting a leg up and over his poor performance thus far in the game. Before he knew it the morning flew past and luncheon had been laid out on long tables lining the perimeter of the great room.

It was a tasty though awkward affair, balancing a plate and a cup of piping hot coffee and his cane all the while searching for a place to perch so he might take nourishment and get back to concentrating on his afternoon strategy.

After minutes of fruitless search for a quiet place away from the rest of the gamblers, none asking to share a table with them, Jack settled for a quiet spot along a wall, and leaned close by a window overlooking the back alley. He gazed out at two Mexican serving boys horsing around. The fun of youth and fine friends . . .

He had just spooned in a mouthful of a spicy frijole concoction when a voice piped up beside him. He turned and there stood the soft southern master of ceremonies, Colonel Rufus Turlington. Jack saw the edge of a pretty blue-and-white dress behind the man.

"Well, I'm pleased to see you made it," said the colonel, his drawl stretching each word long and slow. "I thought for certain I was merely humoring you last night with my talk about seeing you at the tournament. But," he looked Jack up and down, nodding with approval at Jack's finery. "I see I was wrong."

Jack nodded, working to chew and swallow the mouthful of food.

"I have someone I'd like for you to meet. Jack, was it?" The man turned. "Honey, here is a fellow gambler, but I think you'll find you have something in common with him." He chuckled as he said it.

Jack nodded again and held up a finger and reached for his coffee cup resting on the windowsill. As he turned back, his mouth full of hot coffee, his eyes popped open wide and he almost sprayed coffee straight at the woman standing before him.

She held a leather-gloved hand extended, the strap of a purse hung from the crook of her other arm. She was a black woman, but beautiful in a way that few women the world over ever became. She was tall, slight, with eyes that, on seeing him, widened in as much surprise as Jack felt.

It can't be, Jack thought. *It cannot . . . cannot be her.*

CHAPTER SIXTEEN:
WITH FRIENDS LIKE THESE

Rafe leaned against a wood-sided survey and assay office, across the street from the bulky brick façade of the Metals Exchange. He checked his pocket watch, a hefty nickel-plate piece similar to one that had been a wedding gift from his wife. That one had long since disappeared, the day he'd been thrown into Yuma Territorial Prison six years before, stolen, no doubt, by any one of a number of filching bastards in Timmons's employ.

Quarter 'til the hour. He was early. He would wait.

He clicked the watch face shut and slipped it back into his pocket. Dredging up the past was no way to live in the present, he told himself, even as he ground his teeth together. Then why come to Denver? To chase fools who may or may not know something that may or may not help you? Who is the fool?

He didn't wait for long. The two men he sought ambled along the sidewalk from the opposite direction. That they drew outright stares from their fellow strollers made no discernible difference to the odd pair.

He saw them in full light, and they were no less strange than what he'd seen in shadow the day before. The tall man was made even taller with a narrow brim, tall-crown hat the likes of which Rafe had not seen before. It looked as if it were a top hat with a bubbled peak, or a ten-gallon topper with a hacked-back brim. The effect was, as with everything about the two, odd.

The little man wore what looked to Rafe from his distance across the street to be an assortment of necklaces looped and looped again. Feathers, bone, beads, bullet brass, and what appeared to be teeth from a variety of critters clanked and jostled as the short man walked in a hurried shuffle-step to keep up with his long-legged, unhurried partner. The little man rested a wrist on the stock of that short, double-barrel shotgun, now draped over his shoulder. As for the tall man's weaponry, he wore no guns, but around his waist rode all manner of blades.

At the base of the steps they stopped as if cued, and the tall man, Knifer, gazed straight at Rafe, who had taken no pains to hide himself. Plug's gaze drifted from his partner's face over to Rafe. Both strangers smiled at him and Knifer beckoned to Rafe with a long, exaggerated wave. He said something, but the resumed din of the street drowned out the words.

Rafe pushed away from the building and crossed the street. "Good day, men. Let's make this a plain business proposition. I ask you a question, you answer, I pay you money, we each go our merry way. Sound fair?"

Knifer scratched at the spidery hairs on his long chin, his brow furrowed. "No, no, that won't do. No, not at all." Then he snapped a finger and pointed skyward. "See, now here's an idea!" He looked down at his companion, who smiled and nodded, his black stubby teeth biting his own bottom lip.

"You do a little something for us and we can palaver all you want. Heck, we'll tell you everything you wanna know and them some. And believe me, we know exactly what you want to know. The who, the why, and the when." He nodded as he spoke. "We'll sing so much you will be tired of hearing our voices. Hoo-eee!"

Before Rafe could protest, the two mounted the steps. The tall man looked over his shoulder. "Come on, don't keep us waiting." A snag of cackling laughter trailed over his bony shoulder.

Rafe hesitated, knowing with each step bad things were about to happen and he was about to help make them happen. He knew he was fast losing whatever clawhold he had on his life, on reason and goodness. But dammit, man, the desperate voice in his head shouted, howling in anger. *These two killing thieves know something! They know something about it . . .* A voice deep in his tired mind told him this, chanting over and over again that they knew something.

Bright and clear and fresh in his mind flashed the faces of his wife, his son, alive, smiling, then washed over with mud, smudged with grime from his own useless hands as he'd buried them in the rain, buried them deep . . . dead and deep.

He mounted the steps two at a time and made it through one of the big wood-and-glass doors. Then Plug stepped behind him and tugged at the door, waiting for it to click. From around his neck he slipped free a length of chain. This he strung twice though the ornate brass loop handles and clicked shut a padlock, turning a small skeleton key attached to another of his many necklaces. He smiled up at Rafe, who realized he'd been used by the little man as a barrier to prevent his chaining action from being seen by patrons inside.

Rafe looked around the room, but met no glances from any of the dozen or so customers. The tall ceilinged space, marble floor, wood counters, and steel cages beyond looked to him very much like a fancy bank. And that's what it was, though instead of cash it dealt in far more precious commodities. Silver, gold, jewels, and lord knew what else.

Whatever Knifer had in mind would happen fast now as customers would soon want to exit or enter the building. And happen they did. As he watched, Rafe saw the tall outlaw climb up on a thick wood-top table. He waved a long-bladed knife with a gleaming cutting edge nearly as deep bellied as a man's forearm. "Gentlemen, ladies, if I might have your attention. That's right, I am standing up on the counter. I know, if this does not mark me as a heathen and a savage, I do not know what would." He flashed a wide, toothless smile.

"You see, I have the pleasure of introducing you to that man right there." He pointed his long blade's tip at Rafe. "None other than war hero Rafe Barr. Plus, there's me, I'm known as Knifer — wonder why that is?" He waved that menacing blade again. "And that little man behind Barr there? That's my trail pard, Plug. Plug, take a bow, will you kindly?"

The little man kept his shotgun draped over his shoulder, but held his free arm about his middle and folded himself in a neat little bow. He ended up smiling at the bewildered assemblage of customers, who were only then beginning to look worried, backing away to the outer walls of the cavernous room.

"Plug there will relieve you of your weaponry. Don't try anything offhand, as he's a nasty little thing, all grit and no nonsense." Knifer chuckled. "And when he's done with you, one by one you will kindly lay down on your bellies. You too, ladies. Ain't no call to worry. We're not bad folks. Following orders in life, same as you all.

"And speaking of the man giving the orders," he continued, "that man, Mr. Rafe Barr, has informed us that if we do not relieve this fine establishment of a couple of satchels full of precious metals, oh, dust and the like, why he's going to go loco and start filling you all with holes."

"Not true!" shouted Rafe, feeling more out of control of his life than ever before. He held up empty hands, hoping that might convince the terrified customers.

"No," Knifer shook his head solemnly. "I swear it's true. My sainted mama did not raise one liar out of the entire brood of eleven of us."

The threat of violence brought two screams, one from a man, one a woman. The man fainted, his fine suit of burgundy and black wool looking stark and wrong stretched out on the cold, creamy marble floor.

"Now, now, now," said Knifer in a soft tone, his palms patting the air before him with each word he spoke. "Barr is not as ruthless as that sounds, for he has also promised that once we do what we need to he'll personally see to it you're not attacked, but left well and unmolested."

A scuffling sound arose from behind the counter where clerks, Rafe had counted at least four of them, had been staring as confused as everyone else, at the blossoming scene on the other side of his wrought cage. The clerk was making a play for something, perhaps a weapon under the counter, or an alarm of some sort?

A new motion flashed out of the corner of his right eye — Knifer had whipped himself snakelike behind the counter. Before Rafe could shout, "Get down!" the clerk stiff-

149

ened, his gartered arms whipped akimbo, and he slammed against the paneled wall behind him, sliding down it. A red smear followed him to the floor.

Fresh screams rose up from the thronging clot of customers.

"Now that there was a poor choice, wouldn't you say, Mr. Barr?"

"You savage!" Rafe clawed at one of his twin Colts, and had it nearly clear of leather, his eyes set on his target, the sweaty, lined span of forehead below that Knifer's silly hat brim and above his beady rat eyes.

As quick as was the big man, Knifer had already palmed a gleaming blade from somewhere, his belt? His sleeve? And whipped his arm back to gather momentum enough to deliver the silvered missile straight into the meat between Rafe's right thumb and palm, pinning the thumb open and sending a flash of hot pain straight up his arm to explode in his jaw.

"Gaaah!" he growled, recoiling and cradling his wounded limb. He dove for cover behind an oak bench.

During the commotion, he caught a glimpse of the midget lurching in his strange gallop toward the end of the counter. He waited there, flashing a black-tooth smile at the crowd, the snout of his double-barrel shredder leveled on the room, scanning from side to side like a serpent deciding where to strike.

A rattle and clunk, the half-door swung inward as Knifer let Plug in behind the counter. "Anybody moves and every one of these stretched-out folks behind the counter will be gutted and shredded, likely in that order, or maybe the other way around. We ain't rightly decided yet. We kind of like to make that up as we go."

Rafe tugged the small gleaming knife free. It wasn't much longer than a finger, nor any wider, and had no handle save for a nub of steel. But it hurt — and bled — like hell. He gritted his teeth and wrapped the bandanna tight, tucking in the ends. That hand would be near-useless for now. But Rafe was long adept at shooting with both hands, and though his left was a close second, it wasn't his preferred gunhand. Perhaps that would be different from here on out, depending on the damage the nasty little blade had done.

He peered around the bench, but couldn't get a sightline on Knifer. But he did see the cluster of patrons, arms held high, and saw shadows of people outside trying to look through the pebbled glass. Presently someone jerked on the door handles; the chain binding them closed inside rattled. Someone out there muttered and Rafe heard his boot-steps fade away.

"Now, Barr, time for you to drag your sorry backside on in here. We have need of your services."

"Go to hell!" barked Rafe.

Knifer smiled and dropped out of sight behind the counter. Within seconds a strangled cry bubbled up and the tall man popped up again, still smiling, but holding aloft his big gleaming blade. Hot blood streamed down its length, strings of it slid off the blade as he turned it.

"God's sake, do it, mister!" hissed a red-faced fat man who glared at Rafe from his awkward spot on the floor.

"Wise man there," said Knifer. "Hurry up, Plug. Them bags won't fill themselves."

A growl boiled up from deep within the vault.

"Okay, okay, Plug. I'll help you in a minute." Knifer's voice rose. "Waiting on Rafe Barr, who don't seem none too concerned that I have, oh," he looked around at the floor, up and down the aisle behind the counter, "another four or so folks who ain't yet tasted steel in their guts."

"I'm coming. But if you hurt another person, I'll . . ."

"Ha! What are you going to possibly do, boss?"

Rafe had thumbed back the hammer on his revolver when he shouted earlier, hoping to mask the sound.

What were these idiots hoping to do by wrangling him in on this crime? Hoping he'd shoulder enough of the blame that they might make a quicker disappearance? And how were they going to get out? Back door? Must be, the front was not a quick possibility.

Rafe low-walked toward the back of the room, angling in a wide arc toward the wall where the counter and clerk cages stood. He kept his eyes on the spot where he thought Knifer was standing — the man had a disturbing habit of dropping out of view and reappearing feet away, not in any spot Rafe would have guessed. As for Plug, he was too short to be seen over the counter.

He did his best to keep quiet as he peered around the end of the oak counter. Not but four feet from him sat the flopped body of Knifer's first victim of the robbery, propped but otherwise sagged and lifeless against the wall. Red-black blood leached out in a slow-growing pool beside the man.

Jutting from the wall to his left Rafe saw the big steel door to the vault, its star handle and three other, smaller mechanisms gleaming silver, all manner of gold scrollwork and fancy lettering adorning the otherwise black door. Beyond it, sprawled on the floor, the body of the second clerk. Even from his awkward spot, Rafe saw the brutal gutting the poor young man had taken. A long wound, from waist to chest, brimmed with fresh blood and glistening innards. They welled out and down the man's torso, startling red against the white of his shirt.

Knifer had tromped through it, painting brutal bootprints on the marble floor. And there, visible beneath the open vault door, the side of one of the bastard's boots was visible. Rafe aimed, squeezed, and though the gunshot boomed loud, echoing in the stark, vaulted room, the tall swamp man's screams grew louder. He screamed and yowled, hopping, but not close enough to the bottom of the door that Rafe could get another shot.

He hoped the killer would fall backward and give him a clean shot, but the man had dropped forward into the vault. There was an idea — if he could get over there he could slam the door shut on the pair of them.

He had to holster his gun in order to vault the now-closed half-door, but snatched it free of the holster once more as soon as his boots landed, one sliding atop the first dead clerk's leg. He dropped in a crouch, whispered, "Sorry," to the dead man, and barreled forward, shoulder set to ram the vault door closed.

Rafe shoved the heavy door with all his bullish strength and in a loud voice bellowed, "Kick out the glass door! Get out of here! Get off the floor! Get out!" Rafe shouted his commands, hoping the hostages had enough wits about them to follow through. He had this one slim chance to trap that tall bastard and his midget partner.

To his relief, Rafe heard scuffling and sobs and frantic, whispering voices from the front of the great room — the customers were going to try for the door. He had to distract the killers. No more need die.

Rafe knew, wounded or no, the tall man would slice him up quick and deep should he show any part of himself around the side of the vault door. He didn't feel like bleeding all over again, and from a different limb. Or worse, stuck in the gut. He'd never seen anyone as accurate with a knife. Guess he earned the name.

The door whammed to a stop, though far short of sealing closed. On the hinge side, he saw a tight cloth knob — someone on the other side had stuck what looked to be a full canvas sack of gold dust in there, preventing the door from closing.

The front doors rattled, rattled — didn't they see the chain? — then he heard the hard, quick kicks of several boots against the glass, he hoped, and was rewarded with shattering sounds. They were leaving, shouting, screaming as they bolted out into the fresh air. Go for help . . .

Now he was in a pickle, a standoff with someone inches away but not easily got at. He was all set to spring, run low past the door to the other side of the vault, firing into the vault as he scampered, when he heard a low growl behind him.

He turned his head and saw the leering, stump-toothed, chaw-stained, pockmarked face of Plug staring at him from under the counter. Both killing barrels of the little man's shotgun jutted, daring and steady. Rafe guessed, not for the first time in his life, that he had about run out of choices.

"Well, now." Around the vault door peered Knifer, his long, homely, toothless face drawn longer and uglier with pain. "Who in the hell shoots a man in the foot? I ask you." He grunted, dragged himself into view, hobbling upright on his good leg. The shot foot looked to be a bloodied mess, drawn up, with blood streaming from the ragged boot.

"Should have been your head, you worthless bastard." Rafe was about to say more when, in a blur of movement, the tall man snatched something gleaming from his belt, another knife, and held his arm poised. His face shook, one eyelid twitched, and droplets of sweat slid down his face, slipping off the end of his long, bony nose.

Plug grunted, breaking the momentary spell.

"Yeah, okay, you're right," said Knifer in a low voice, almost a whisper, not taking his eyes from Rafe. "Got to go." Then he smiled. "But not you." He jerked his head once toward the little man, still half-hidden beneath the counter.

Plug shuffled forward.

Rafe moved his gunhand, but Knifer drew back more on his knife. "Go ahead. Do it. It was my foot you shot, not my hand."

Plug grunted around behind Rafe.

Rafe flinched and began to spin. A quick shadow appeared by his right ear. He clawed for his Colt, but too late. Sudden bolting pain bloomed up the side of his head. Black flecked with pinheads of stars burst before his eyes. He felt himself fall, fall, never seeming to stop.

From his stupor, Rafe thought he heard

screams mingle with the blast of a shotgun, followed on its heels with a second *ka-blam!* Shouts and more screams. He pictured people running down the broad steps of the tall brick building, other folks paused on the street, hands to mouths. He heard whistles, then closer, by his face, grunting, smelled the mingled stink of old food, booze, tobacco . . . .

"Nah, leave his pockets be, Plug! We got to go — or I'll leave you here, dang it!"

A loud slamming *whump* echoed in his head. Then all went black.

Chapter Seventeen:
You Seem Familiar

"Yes," said Colonel Turlington. "She is a pretty thing, now, ain't she? My little sweet potato pie. Goes with me on all my trips." The southern gent rocked back on his heels, hands rubbing together. "Say, you two aren't going to give me any trouble now, are you?"

The woman shook her head so slightly he wasn't sure she had. But she had, and Jack understood — somehow it would not do to let her white man know that yes, indeed, they knew each other.

Jack broke his gaze away from her. She must have reason to not want this secret revealed. He looked at the man. And that's when he saw something had changed, hardened about the man's face. His friendly gaze had firmed, tightened.

"No, no," said Jack. "I have something to attend to before play resumes."

And then it was gone, the look of recognition, of defiance, of something . . . was gone as soon as it had appeared. But Jack knew better. You didn't reach his age at the poker table of life without a solid grasp of reading people's faces. And this one told him the man had seen the exchange, however slight, between Jack and the girl.

"I understand, understand completely," said the southern gent, as if all was innocence. "When nature calls, we best answer the door."

Jack walked stiffly away toward the nearest door that would take him outside.

The man shouted behind him. "We shall have a drink together later on."

Jack glanced back, nodded, and smiled weakly. The girl was staring as hard at him as he had at her.

He pulled out his pocket watch, checked the time, saw he had roughly twenty minutes before play resumed, and decided he needed fresh air. Jack hit the steps, stomping along the boardwalk, his cane tip smacking counterpoint to his steps. Without thinking about it, he stepped down to the dusty street as a clot of saddle tramps walked toward him. Last thing he wanted was trouble. He edged by them, not looking up.

This day was not working out as he had planned. Soon enough he found himself at the end of the street gazing out at a bleak vista, haggard adobe ruins dissipating with the long road out of town. A dust devil kicked up, skirted a bone-rack burro, and moved on.

Jack looked down at his new suit of clothes. The fine black trousers were dusty; the boots, a-gleam only hours before, were now so powdered he could write his name on them. He knew that no matter his mental efforts of concentration, the best he could expect of himself for the remainder of the day was to hang on and try to forget her. For now.

Not possible, he told himself, shaking his head.

He hoofed it back to the Santa Fe Grand, hands in his pockets, dust clouding around his boots, the image of the girl he'd told himself had died long ago. The girl who was the plaything of a braggadocio white plantation-owning southern colonel. The girl who, without a doubt, was his own sister, Mala, full grown and very much alive.

CHAPTER EIGHTEEN:
OH, WHAT HAVE I DONE?

Voices came to him as if he were hearing them underwater. They bubbled up close, retreated, then light did the same. Something nudged him, and again.

"Hey!"

He felt a stinging, someone slapping his face.

"Hey, you! Get up . . . now!"

A kick this time, then a slap. Barely thinking about it, Rafe reached out with a steel-band grip, managing to snag a tight grasp on the offender's wrist. At the same time, he struggled to open his eyes. When he did, the light stung like the slaps, his eyes felt filled with sand, and his ears echoed and tolled like the sound of dozens of far-off church bells.

"Let go of me, you son of a bitch!"

Another kick, this time in his side. He loosed his grip on the man's wrist and tried to focus his sight.

"Clem, you and Horace grab this big bastard by the feet and yarn him on outta there. I have had about enough of him. Leastwise we know he ain't dead. Lock up his wrists and lug him on down to the jailhouse. And if he still looks this groggy once you get there, you go ahead and toss a bucket of water on his kisser."

As he felt himself dragged in quick, rough jerks, Rafe understood that voice had been talking about him. He tried to move his arms but they wouldn't obey. That hand had worked, why not now? Legs, the same. Useless. Oh, but his head hurt something fierce. Tried to put together what had happened, where he was. "Hey . . ." he said. Or tried to. But he heard next to nothing.

His voice sounded strange, tinny. "Hey!" He shouted it, and though it hurt his head, which felt as though he had thunder cracks throbbing inside his skull, at least the voice sounded like his own.

"Hold on, boys. He's yammering. Best let him speak."

Rafe squinted upward, and saw a round red face looking down at him, a big dragoon moustache drooping with the effort.

"You got something to say, mister?"

"Yeah . . ." He licked his lips and tried again. "Yeah. Two that did it . . . got away."

163

The round-faced man nodded his head. It looked to Rafe as if he'd been inflated, like a pig's bladder, the way it bobbed.

"We know all about them two. We'll get your pards, don't you fret."

"No, no, killers! Not my friends . . ." But they were dragging him again. As they dragged him fully out of the vault, his head clunked down the six inches to the hard marble floor. Once more, with a flashing deep inside his head, and a groan that wheezed out, Rafe Barr lost consciousness.

A cold stillness woke Rafe. Shivers coursed through him, from head to foot, rattling his teeth like pebbles in a gourd and throbbing his head. Even before he opened his eyes he knew where he was. Same smell, same sound, same feel to it. Prison. In Denver. But it didn't matter where, it was the same as Yuma. Prison is a prison. He'd let himself become a caged beast once more.

He let slip a sigh of disgust and made to push himself up off the steel cot, the thin mattress and thinner wool blanket providing little in the way of comfort. What was it now, four, five days? Each the same as the one before. He swung his feet down, settling his boots on the stone floor. Murky gray light made its way through a high

164

window at the far end of the central walkway between cells here in this basement of the jailhouse.

Rafe sat on the edge of his cot in the near dark and touched fingertips gently to his head. The doctor they'd fetched when they hauled him in here had been thorough, he'd give him that much. The man had washed his head, cleaned the wound, then swaddled the entire affair with thick wrappings of gauze. Rafe imagined he looked like a swami from the old book, *Arabian Nights.*

He'd learned a bit since coming here, none of it of much use to him. The head lawman, a Marshal O'Dowd, was a decent sort, friendly, maybe too much so. Always whinnying at his own jokes and one of those fat men who can't help but make a lot of noise. Even walking the man was a rolling arsenal of sounds — farts from his backside and belches from his frontside and janglings from his massive key chain and squeaks from his boot leather and gunbelt and soft clinks from his various badges that he wore like a field-title general. Top all that with his soft mutterings and whispered whistles to himself and you had a man who would live but two minutes in Apache country.

But it wasn't Apache country, it was Denver. A city. And no matter how many

165

times Rafe had explained his situation to the man, how he was not in league with the two who robbed the Denver Precious Metals Exchange, no matter how many times he urged the fat lawman to re-interview those folks who had been in there, ply them with questions about the event, he would say the same thing, in that same, slow, patient, cud-chewing tone: "We done that, son. Them first two days you were out to the world. They all say what you say, that you did your level best to protect them, and that will count in your favor."

"Then what's the trouble?"

"Trouble is they also say you come in with them two, Knifer and his tiny pal, Plug, as you called them. That's another thing, you know their names, but no one else did."

Rafe had sighed, his head thudding with the effort such thought required. "Like I told you, I only wanted to talk with them. They may have information I need."

"Like what?"

Rafe shook his head, once more, at the same question the lawman had asked him earlier in the day.

"Well, son." The fat lawman pushed himself up out of the wooden chair he kept in the hallway. He grunted to a standing position, adjusted himself, then grasped the bars of Rafe's cell. "I am willing to listen to whatever it is you have to tell me, but I'm here to tell you that now that you're up and blinking like a beached fish, Judge Emory-Wilkes wants you in his courtroom to open the ball on this thing. Townsfolks are crying for blood. Them men who were killed were well liked, you know. Had families."

"But I didn't do it. I tried to save them." Rafe held his swaddled head in his hands and held his tongue He hated the way his voice sounded, almost as if he were begging, something he'd never done in all his days. Damned if he was about to start down that path now.

"Truth is, you pulled through with that nasty knock on the bean, even though the doc said your skull was likely split and gone for good. I'm surprised you have your wits at all, given what he told us often happens to folks who've been walloped like that."

"I'm still here," said Rafe in a voice nearly a whisper. "Though my wits I'm not so certain about."

The fat man chuckled, then grew serious. "One more thing, son." He leaned in tight to the bars. "We all know who you are . . . Mr. Barr. We know what you did in the war. Lot of us are mighty impressed with you being here. But the fact remains that the last time your name was in the news, it was in the news in a big way. About five or six years back, as I recall. And it wasn't good. You get me?"

Rafe said nothing, but listened. He knew where the lawman was headed with his conversation.

"Now, I'm no judge, and I do my best not to judge others, but a man accused of what they say you done —" he broke off, seeing the sudden glint of anger in his prisoner's eyes, even in the low light of the cellar cellblock.

"Now, now, as I said, I don't judge. Don't pay me enough for it." He smiled at his own joke. "But as I was saying, you are wanted elsewhere, by some other lawman. I'm speaking of Yuma, you see. Elsewise why would you be out?"

Rafe was silent a moment, then said, "There was an arrangement."

"An arrangement, you say. Good, well that's good. For you, anyway. Though, with all that, ah, happened, if I was you I'd keep my sniffer clean. If you take my meaning."

Rafe nodded, and said nothing. Round and round, nothing new was said, day after day. And now the judge wanted to see him. They'd contact Timmons in Yuma, unless they already had. Wouldn't surprise him if there were dodgers on him on every law-dog's desk west of the Mississippi. It would never end.

"Okay, Mr. Barr. I reckon that's enough of our chatting for now. Enjoy the silence, 'cause it's Friday night and the cowboys will be coming into town, drinking themselves full up and then some. And you'll have plenty of neighbors down here. Heh, heh."

The fat marshal squeaked and clanked and farted and belched his way down the long stone hall, huffing on up the steps. Presently Rafe heard the thick oak-and-steel door open, squawk on its massive hinges, then squawk closed and slam. Jangle of keys, click of the lock's oil-needy mechanism, and he was doubly secure. With nothing before him but time, plenty of time to think about the past, the same things over and over. And over.

Rafe Barr held his aching head gingerly in his hands and tried not to think. Not to think of his wife, his son. That day he found them. Tried not to.

It didn't work.

CHAPTER NINETEEN: PROVING UP ON THE CLAIM

Jack's afternoon at the poker table did not go well. He lost hand after hand, dollar on dollar, sometimes a little, more often a lot. As the late afternoon break approached and the latest hand wound down for them — each table's break came according to their game — Jack sighed, sat back, and ground his fingers into his weary eyes. He longed for a long nap under a shade tree with a tall glass of spring water and maybe a slice of Arlene's berry pie. He missed the ranch. What was happening to him?

He almost smiled, but the sudden jag of memory of his sister's face, that of a full-grown woman, came back to him. He looked around the room, but did not see her. He didn't even know where Turlington was seated, assuming the man was still playing.

He shook off all thought of her. He'd have to talk to her soon, but right now he had a more urgent matter to attend to. If he didn't tighten his poker playing, he'd lose everything, his entry fee, the money he'd carefully saved, the money, the money Cookie had trusted him with.

Oh lord, he groaned audibly. All that money he'd spent on his clothes. He looked good, true, but a glance at his ensemble made him wince. He'd been so cocky, so sure of himself, and now look at him. A hollowed-out dandy, a tinhorn, a card sharp in name only. Not worth the paper he wrote that name on.

Snap out of it, Jack, he told himself, ignoring the stares of the white gamblers. He had to snap out of it.

A voice close by his right side snapped him from his reverie of self-pity. "Why are you playing so poorly, son?"

It was the friendly gambler who'd sat across from him the entire day.

"What do you mean?" Jack tried to make himself sound miffed by the comment, but the man was right.

"I mean I know you, at least by reputation, more so than I let on at the table, and I expected a hell of a good time playing against you. But so far all I've barely seen are the efforts of a raw amateur." He shook his head, his lips pursed with the pitying effort.

"I appreciate your concern, mister," said Jack.

"Say, you look like you've seen a ghost, son."

Jack sighed, nodded. "Might be I have."

"Well, see to it that you don't let it interfere with your God-given talent as a gambler. You owe it to yourself — and maybe to me, too." He smiled. "I have a feeling I could learn from you if you tightened your game."

Jack forced a smile. "Thanks, I'll be all right." As he watched the man amble away, Jack thought, *if I don't get my mind sharp and play tighter, I won't make it to tomorrow, ghost or no.*

CHAPTER TWENTY:
ILLEGAL MIND

"Hostetler Rawlins . . . the Seventh."

The marshal looked him up and down and sniffed, as if his nostrils could detect what sort of critter this man was. "Seventh what?"

The attorney's face reddened and veins stood out on his bald temples.

"Now, now, no need to get your suitcoat in a knot, mister. I'm funnin' you."

"Well it's not likely funny, is it, now?" The man crossed his arms.

"Where are your papers and books and such?"

"Huh?"

The lawman nodded. "Your lawyerly satchel. I've met plenty in my day and they all lug around more paper goods than any five men would in their right minds."

"Oh, yes. Well they are back at my office. This first meeting is merely a . . . a . . ."

"Yes?" The fat marshal's bushy eyebrows rose like birds taking flight.

"A first meeting! Now can I see my customer or not?"

"You mean your client?"

"Yes, for heck's sake!"

CHAPTER TWENTY-ONE: JINGLE, JANGLE, JINGLE

Two days after Marshal O'Dowd told him he would have to appear in court, Rafe had that moment. He'd stood in the bright white-and-wood-panel courtroom with too much light slicing in through tall windows. Judge Emory-Wilkes banged that gavel too loud, too hard, and for far too long, and told him he was waiting on certain replies from certain people at certain places far outside of Denver, and that Rafe would have to wait in the basement cell of the Denver City Courthouse.

Now he was back in the cell, relieved to be in the dark and quiet once more. He was alone, other than the drunken man two cells down who didn't appear to be sobering up, despite the fact he'd been there more than a day. *Maybe he was crack-minded. Maybe that's what I sound like,* thought Rafe. *Maybe being off the beam in the head means you think you sound fine in your own mind, even if others hear you yammering, not making any sense.*

He stretched his long, lean body on the cot and closed his eyes. Better to listen to the drunken fool than to hear the same sounds in his own head, a bubbling stew of shouts, of victims of bad men over the years, from the war's battlefields — all the way through the robbery with Knifer and Plug. Where did those men go? The marshal had said his men hadn't caught them. Probably hidden in the city, likely by Soapy Smith or one of the other thieving brutes that suckle on Denver's raw underbelly.

And then he heard the upstairs door unlock, heard the keys clank and clink, heard the door swing wide, heard heavy steps descend the stone steps — Marshal O'Dowd — followed by a second set of feet. Another prisoner? No, they wouldn't follow, they would be in front. So who?

"Mr. Barr? You awake? You got yourself a visitor." The lawman walked up close and stood by the cell door. "Mr. Barr . . . you awake?"

Rafe was already sitting up, letting his swimming head catch up with him. "Yes, who is it?"

"Says he's your attorney. Fancy man from . . . where was it you're from?"

A small figure stepped into the thin patch of light beside the marshal. "Originally from Kentucky. But my people are scattered to the far winds like seed on the prairie."

"No, I mean where you practice your task. Lawyering and all."

"Oh, yes, well, let's see. Mostly I am a traveling sort of lawyer. I go hither and yon, helping folks who are innocent, making sure the law don't railroad 'em too hard."

"Well, now," said the marshal, hooking thumbs under his braces and puffing out his ample sunken chest. "I don't think we been treating Mr. Barr here too awful, have we?"

Rafe stood, walked over to the bars, and peered through. "My lawyer? What's your name?"

The small lawyer fidgeted with his tweed jacket's lapels, patted his pockets, and made a show of looking for his spectacles. "Can't seem to recall where I placed them."

"Man only wanted your name, Lawyer Hostetler Rawlins . . . the Seventh." The marshal snorted, then turned to go. "You lawyerly types. You amuse me to no end."

"Oh, marshal?"

The lawman turned. "Yeah?"

"Might I be allowed to enter my customer's cell? Can't very well discuss important matters out in the open like this, can we?"

"Mister, you can't get much closer than betwixt them bars. You're fine on that side of the locked door, believe me." He turned and padded his way down the hall, then called over his shoulder. "Shout when you want to leave."

"What is that accent you have going, Mr. Hostetler Rawlins the Seventh?"

"It's my own concoction — sort of Australian and Irish, with a dash of Boston snootiness stirred in. Say, you remember that Australian fella we come up on that time who . . . hey, wait a minute. How'd you know it was me, Rafe?"

"Cookie, anyone who has ever met you could pick you out at ten paces. Took me four."

The wiry older man hung his head like a snoozing bird. "Aww, Rafe. And here I was thinking this was a corker of a disguise." He edged closer to the bars. "Rafe, you don't mind me saying so, but you have looked better."

"Felt better, too, Cook. How'd you find me?"

"Don't take a scholar, Rafe. I know what you're after and I know a couple of folks in this town owe you. Plus, a fella at a stage stop south of here said someone told him

178

they had an old war hero in the lock-up. I worked it out from there."

Rafe nodded. "Glad you did. I really stepped in it this time."

"Yep, yep you have." Cookie gripped the steel straps of the cage tight in his hands, wedging his bony face between them. "But I got me a plan."

"You're not going to cook up a hot batch of dynamite, are you?"

"Naw, naw. Not yet, anyway . . . say, you funnin' me? I about had enough of that for one day from that fatso lawdog. And now you?"

"Easy, Cook. Is everything all right at the ranch?"

"Yeah, it's still there. I ain't set nothing on fire, if that's what you're getting at."

"You are a touchy one today. How's Arlene?"

"She's fine, fine, cooking up a storm." There was a pause, then Cookie said, "Ain't you going to ask about Sue?"

"Of course, yes, how is she?"

"She's gone."

"Gone? She really left?"

"Course she did. You drove her out, didn't you?" Cookie rasped a hand across his freshly shaved face, then spun in a circle. "Don't know why I bother with you at all,

179

the way you treat us."

"Look, Cookie, I had to do it."

The older man held up a hand, shaking his head. "I don't want to hear it, Rafe. I got enough on my mind. I got in here and I have a rough idea on how to get out again — but the tricky part of the plan is getting you out with me."

"I can't leave like that, Cookie. They already hauled me into court once, they have notices out, waiting on contact from Yuma, I expect. And besides, there's no way out of here that won't risk you ending up in the cell next door. I appreciate the thought and the effort, Cook, but I'm done."

"What? This ain't the man I know. Why, they must have really walloped you on the bean, Rafe Barr, to stand there all locked up and tell me you're giving up."

"Not giving up, Cook, giving in. For now, at least. Big difference."

"Nah, no sir. No difference at all! Why, I don't know why I wasted my time coming down here to bust you out —"

"Cookie, keep your voice down, will you?" Rafe gestured with his head to his left, toward the line of cells. "We're not alone down here."

"Oh, well," said Cookie in a lowered voice. Silence hung for a moment, then a slight scuffing sound rose from a cell down the hall. "Pardon me, gents."

It was an English accent. Cookie and Rafe traded silent looks.

"Couldn't help overhearing. You are in a bit of a pickle."

They said nothing.

"Hello? Mr. Barr and the, ah, if you'll allow me to say so, unlikely sounding name of Hostetler Rawlins . . . the Seventh, was it? If you permit me, I may be of assistance to you."

"Who are you?" said Rafe.

"Ahh, that is the great question we all face at one time or another, is it not? I suspect you mean by what name do I exist under. What guise do I pull on like a sheer suit each day when I awake."

"Sounds loopy to me, Rafe," said Cookie, squinting into the shadows of the cellblock.

"As to that, my good man, I am as apt to be, as you say, loopy, as I am quite in control of my faculties. Time will tell, time will tell. But what you really need to know are three things."

"Now hold a minute there, mister fancy talker . . ."

"No, sir, there is time enough for one of us to talk and you, sir, are not that person. I am. You must listen to me. The first thing

181

you need to know is that our robust jailer, one Marshal O'Dowd, did not lock the great door at the top of the stairs when he last ascended on his overworked legs. The second is that he hangs that very sizable key ring on a hook to the left of the same door at this time each day when he, as he calls it, 'chases 40 winks with an eye toward catching a few.' This, I take it, is his jovial way of saying he naps of an afternoon. By my pocket watch . . ."

They heard a click and a snap.

"He has, by now, caught himself a handful of winks."

"You said three things."

"So I did, Mr. Barr. You are as astute as I was led to believe by my . . . but I have said too much. Now, as to the third thing, there is a door at the end of this cellblock. Far to my left in the inky depths of this stony dungeon. It is largely unused, yet serviceable enough to permit anyone exiting to find themselves in an infrequently used alleyway. From there, as someone with a knack for something once said, you, sirs, are on your own."

"I understood about half of what that crazy man said." Cookie's whisper was none too quiet, and the Englishman chuckled. "You are as promised, Mr. McGee. The genuine article."

"What? You know who I am?"

"Indeed I do. And much more. But if you do not retrieve those keys you will be known as the man who allowed his bosom friend to wither in a Denver jail unjustly." The man sighed, then continued. "From here I am told it is a long yet direct trip to Yuma Territorial Prison."

"Cookie, I know what I said before, and I'll understand if you don't want to risk your neck, but I won't go back to Yuma."

Cookie smacked his hands together, and both men winced at the echoing sound. "I'll be right back!" He scampered down the hallway; they heard his feet scuffing slightly up the stairs.

Rafe licked his dry lips. "Whoever you are, my thanks to you. The same goes to your friend . . . Doc Baggs."

Again, the Englishman chuckled, neither confirming nor denying Rafe's guess.

They heard the big door emit a long slow, low squeak, and all held their breath. Then light footsteps trooped down the stone stairs.

"Ah, here comes your amusing friend," said the Englishman. "Good luck to you both."

"Took me longer than I expected, but I

seen these hanging on a peg over the fat man's head, thought I recognized them." He hoisted Rafe's two-gun rig, the worn brown leather creaking slightly; the twin nickel-plate Colt revolvers glinted dull in the low light, their bone grips seeming to glow.

It took him but a brief moment to find the correct key, then twist it home. He sighed when the mechanism's throaty *click-click* yielded.

The men walked down the hall, but Rafe stopped at the cell in which their benefactor stood. Rafe eyed him, a medium-height man, short dark beard, wavy dark hair, wide smile. He wore a rumpled light-cloth suit and on the little finger of his left hand a gold signet ring with a diamond.

"No, Mr. Barr. We've not met before, but I know of you. Both of you. And I have reason to be able and willing, most willing, to lend a hand in this matter."

"Well, thank you, even if I don't know your name. It's much appreciated."

Cookie leaned in, jangling the key ring. "You'll want these." He thrust them through the strap-steel.

The man backed away, smiling and holding up his palms. "No, no, thank you, all the same. I will do my time. I am here on charges of conducting myself in a drunken and disorderly fashion and I will pay the piper his two bits. I expect I'll be out by tomorrow. Besides," he said, jangling something in the dark. "I have my own keys should I feel the walls close in on me."

"Well," said Rafe. "Tell Doc Baggs I said thanks."

The Englishman chuckled. "Good luck, gentlemen. Oh, one more thing — your horse, Mr. Barr, has been retrieved from the livery where you boarded it. It is waiting in the alleyway. Now go, go."

As Cookie fumbled in the dark for the keys, they heard their English friend whisper, "Not to alarm you, gentlemen, but I believe I hear a certain puffy man of the law aroused from his slumbers."

"Aww, hell . . ." Cookie mumbled and dropped the key ring. The clattering sounded louder than a cannon fusillade.

"Let me try," said Rafe, snatching up the keys. A brief wave of dizziness swelled, and receded through his head. He jammed a key in the lock, but it would not turn.

"Gentlemen . . ."

They paused, heard the big lawman yawn, far-off, but any second, they knew, and he'd see that the key ring was among the missing.

Cookie grabbed the keys once more and stuffed another into the lock. It turned, clicked, and he grasped the latch and thumbed it down. The door squawked inward.

CHAPTER TWENTY-TWO:
THE LOOK OF REVELATIONS

Jack made it back to the flea-trap hotel room and leaned against the closed door. It had been a damn long time since he'd had a day as trying as this one. His sore leg throbbed — he begrudgingly admitted that while it always felt a little rough, it fared better day to day on the ranch than it did in town, sitting all day at a poker table.

He'd squeaked through the last hands today, ending with enough points to enter play in the morning. But that wouldn't carry him far if he didn't get serious.

"All I want right now," he said, slow-stepping across the room toward the bed, "is to lay down and get me a good night's sleep."

He sat down on the bed, but knew he had to stand up again and take off the nice clothes, make sure they weren't a smelly, wrinkled mess for tomorrow. Gone were the days when he had a fine wardrobe of freshly laundered clothes. If he could pull all the loose strings in his life together again, he'd be able once more to have handsome possessions.

"Tall order," he said, loosening his blue silk string tie. That's when someone knocked on the door.

He slicked out his two-shot derringer, and held it in his hand inside a coat pocket. It never paid to answer the door in a strange room in a strange town empty handed. Especially when he'd already caused such a ruckus today.

"Who is it?"

The pause was long enough that Jack's finger tensed around the little derringer. He wished he had his six-gun on him, but it was in his luggage beneath the bed. He must be tired; he didn't even check it when he came into the room.

"Hello?" he said, standing to one side of the door. If they were to shoot through the flimsy door, he didn't want to be in harm's way.

"It's me," said the voice on the other side of the door. It was a woman. For long moments Jack had no idea who "me" might be. A prostitute knocking at the wrong door? The girl from the night before?

"It's me," said the woman. Then, in a

quieter voice, said, "Mala."

His sister. He hadn't heard that name in so long. Not since they were a family, him, Mama, and Mala. As much of a family as he had ever known — until recently, anyway.

Jack reached for the doorknob, pulled his hand back, and wiped it on his trouser leg, then opened the door.

Though she stood in shadow, a lacy shawl over her head, he knew her immediately. Same dress as earlier, but something was different about her now, something had changed.

"Mala," he said.

They stared at each other once more, brother and sister, then she broke the spell, looking left and right along the darkening hallway.

"May I come in, Jack?" Her voice sounded muffled, clouded.

"Of course, of course." He opened the door wider, and held an arm out to usher her in. "It's not much, I'm hoping to improve my situation tomorrow," he said. She still said nothing, so he kept talking, half-afraid if he didn't, she might vanish. "How'd you find me?"

She walked straight into the room, her back to him, and faced the single smudged window. Scant light glowed in from the set-

189

ting sun. "I kept an eye out. Followed you."

"Mala? You okay?"

She turned and faced him, arms hugged tight about her chest. That's when he saw her face fully in the oil lamp's light. Her left cheek, from below to above her eye, was swollen, purpled, painful to look at. The right side of her mouth likewise was swollen, the corner split where knuckles had driven her lip against her teeth. Jack saw the remnants of a trickle of blood trailing down from one nostril.

"What happened? Who . . . did he do this to you?"

She looked away, but that only boiled Jack's blood all the more, for it fully showed him the right side of her face, a near perfect brutal imprint of fingers on her cheek.

"Mala." He stepped toward her, then stopped with his arms half-extended. "Why?" Then he remembered the man's look of hardened suspicion. "Did he think we knew each other?"

At first she didn't respond, then nodded slowly, still not looking at him. "He thinks that because we're the same color we naturally like each other. I guess."

"What?"

She shrugged.

"Did you tell him we are brother and

190

sister, long lost to each other?"

"No, he wouldn't believe me. He is jealous, thinks you're out to steal me from him," she said. "It's not the first time this has happened."

The gambler flexed his fists, shook with rage. He might not know his sister any longer, but he'd be damned if he was going to let that savage get away with beating on women.

Jack had too many questions, but first he needed to help her. He splashed water from a chipped jug into an equally chipped bowl, and dampened a washcloth.

"Why didn't you tell him we are related?"

She turned to face him. "I didn't dare, I didn't want him to hurt you. Not when I found you again, Jack." She rushed at him and nearly knocked him over as she hugged him.

"I don't understand," he said, hugging her and patting her gently on the back. "How could you be with him — a white southern man? What is he to you?"

She pulled away and looked hard at him. "You think you've had a tough time of it in your life? Try being a former slave and a woman. I'm lucky to be alive at all."

"But —"

"No," she said, pulling away from him.

191

She dabbed gingerly at her face with the washcloth. "I don't want to hear it from you. I don't have the time. Listen to me, dammit."

She walked to the bed and sat down with a sigh. "I didn't want to get you involved, but I have no one else to turn to."

Jack slid a chair over toward her and sat facing her, taking one hand in his. "Tell me what's going on. I can help, Mala. I promise you. You won't ever be treated this way again, you hear me? Take a deep breath and start at the start, as Mama used to say."

She smiled weakly, then nodded. "About two months ago, he took me on a trip, a gambling junket, he called it. That time on a riverboat on the Mississippi. Wasn't the first time I'd been on one, but it was the first time treated as a lady, well, near as I'd ever been, anyway. That was the third such gambling tournament, as he calls them, put on by friends of his. Sometimes he's involved in planning them. But I've come to find out something about these so-called tournaments."

Jack sat up straight. "What about them?"

"That's just it. They're not really about the gambling at all. They are a way for his group to raise money, but more importantly for them to attract investors as he calls them. 'Luring right-thinking men to the cause.' That's the phrase he uses."

"What's this group he belongs to, Mala?"

She sighed again. "They call themselves 'The Brotherhood of the Phoenix.' That mean a thing to you?"

Jack shook his head, puzzled.

"Me either, until I read a letter he received by courier."

"You read his mail?"

She nodded. "You bet I do. More and more lately. I figure if I can learn something I can use against him on down the road some time, well, that can't be a bad thing for someone in my position, can it? But until I saw you today I had nobody to turn to, no one I could tell about what I learned a number of days ago."

"What did you learn?"

"First things first; the Brotherhood, as they call themselves, use the slogan, 'The South Shall Rise From the Ashes, Reborn!' "

An icy finger raked up Jack's spine. "Hence the reference to phoenix, the famous bird that rises reborn from the ashes. Aren't they clever boys."

"Yeah, well, you won't think so when I tell you what they're about to do —"

"Let me guess, they want to turn back the

193

clock, make slavery legal, squash the life out of the North and all who sympathize with the cause."

She nodded. "He says they are about to become the dominant political force in the country, and that they will have the top army, too. More powerful than ever before, if he's to be believed. He's a braggart, but he has powerful friends, Jack. And they're gaining more money and influence with each so-called tournament that takes place. Up to now, though, they've been small time. But they have been calling this one their coming-out party."

"Like a southern belle's, eh?"

"Something like that. But this one will be celebrated in blood."

"What?"

"The last day of the tournament."

"What happens then?"

"That's the thing, I don't know yet, but when he talks of it, he gets all worked up like a kid given sweetmeats. Not acting like him at all. He and his friends get together, they get all liquored up on their bourbon. Few days back they talked in front of me even more than they usually do, especially him. They think I'm dumb and pretty, that I don't care a whit about what they're saying."

"Can you find out what's going to happen on that day, Mala?"

"This morning I thought maybe I could, but now . . . he's so angry. He's hit me before but never this bad."

Jack rasped a hand across his stubbled jaw, feeling the sudden weight of the day's dismal dealings warring with the excitement of finding his sister. But this news, could it really be more than drunken rants of a bitter southerner?

"Mala," he said, already feeling guilty about what he was set to ask. "You think you could give it one more go, find out what it is they're planning? Don't risk your life, but any scrap of information might be helpful."

She shrugged, looking so tired and thin and despondent in her pretty dress. "I don't suppose it could hurt at this point. I don't have a damn thing to lose anymore."

He knelt before her, held her by the shoulders, and looked into her eyes. "Yes, you do, you have me now. You have your brother, Jack. And I'm never going to lose you again, you understand me? We have each other again. We're family. And I want you to meet my new family."

"You're married? With babies?" She looked suddenly hopeful, brighter.

He smirked. "Not exactly," he said, images of Cookie and Arlene, of Doc and Rafe and Sue flashing through his mind. "But they will be mighty interested to hear of this Brotherhood of the Phoenix. Mighty interested."

The next day saw Jack play hard, half-distracted by the appearance of his sister in his life, and more than bothered by the state of her when she came to his room at the hotel.

His abiding thought was that he had to get word to the ranch. Cookie and Rafe would know what to do. They'd send help, likely in the form of themselves, and come on down there to Santa Fe and help him prevent what sounded like the biggest calamity to befall the barely healed union.

"You going to play or pass?"

It was the fat Texan who hated him. He was still in the running and didn't appear to have any lack of funds or ability. He was, Jack had to admit, a damn good poker player. Even if the man was a holy nightmare.

Now that Jack was armed with the information about the Brotherhood of the Phoenix from his sister, every face in the room looked to him like it could well belong to such a nasty organization. And top of the list of likely candidates was that no-good stumblebum who whomped on his sister.

He'd go to the law, but first he had to get word to the ranch — in case the law decided he was suspicious. He didn't trust any lawman any time, that's the way his world worked.

Too bad he couldn't send a telegram to the ranch. It was all but hidden from most folks, a fact Rafe was happy to promote.

"What day is today? Day of the week, I mean?"

The fat-faced man looked at him as if he'd spit on the table. "What sort of a question is that, you damn . . ."

"Never mind, I see it's Wednesday. That makes tomorrow Thursday, fourth one of the month, by my calendar." Jack tapped his temple and grinned at the table for the first time since play began. He'd recalled that the fourth Thursday of each month was the day that Doc "Deathbed" Jones pulled teeth and tended to any other ailments the townsfolk in Dibley were saddled with. Doc didn't mind, as it helped cover his bar tab.

Jack would have to wait until the midday break to send the telegram. He only hoped the message would make it to the saloon in time to reach Doc. Even if it did, he hoped the message would reach Doc before the medical man became too inebriated to get word to the ranch. He also had to word the note with care, lest someone in Santa Fe get wind of his attempt to bring help and kill the note — and him — before it got sent.

By the time midday crawled its way onto the clock face, it felt to Jack as if it was never going to arrive.

CHAPTER TWENTY-THREE: TRUTH'S HARSH STING

"You know, for a man who was swinging by the short hairs, you got the look of a glum fella all about you. All hangdog and sort of mopey." Cookie glanced at Rafe out of one eye.

"Yeah, well, I feel worn down and rode hard and everything else in between." Rafe's reply came out low, little more than a mumble.

Cookie decided not to say anything for a spell. This was mighty odd behavior from the man he'd come to know nearly as well as he knew himself. Despite the fact they'd been separated for five years by Rafe's stretch in Yuma Prison.

"You look like the fella I know, but you sure as hell don't act like him nor talk like him. The Rafe Barr I am acquainted with has more fire in one tiny finger than most men you are likely to meet." He glanced once more at his companion and saw the big man's mouth twitch up a slight smile.

"That's more like it, by God!" Cookie slapped his leg and made a big show of carving off a thumb-size nub of plug tobacco and jamming it in his cheek. They rode in amiable silence for a few minutes more, each man apparently buoyed by the brief exchange.

Dust curled up and away from the horses' stepping hooves and a mass of cloud made its slow way southward, revealing a wavering early afternoon sun, bright and pinned high.

Rafe spoke. "Listen, Cook, I am sorry you had to break the law on my behalf." He tugged the brim of his hat lower on his forehead, and looked at his trail partner.

Cookie glanced at him and sighed. "Hell, Rafe. Wasn't the first time, as you'll recall. And I'll wager it damn sure won't be the last. We're lucky we made it out of Denver with so little foofaraw."

"Mmm," said Rafe, scrunching his brow. "Doesn't that seem odd to you?"

"How so?"

"Marshal, he's shrewder than that. If I didn't know better, I'd swear he let us go."

Cookie shrugged. "Yeah, could be, I guess. I try not to think too hard on the wonders of providence. Might foul it up next time I need a helping of it on my plate."

They rode for a while in silence. Then Cookie said, "I know how you feel about the ranch, about being there and all. But that's where we're needed."

It was Rafe's turn to sigh. "I have nothing against the ranch, Cookie. About that — any strangers show up lately?"

"No, no, and I would know if they did. Why?"

Rafe shrugged, making light of it, though his thoughts had turned back to the trail to Denver, and the person who'd watched him in the dark. Likely it was no one of importance. He hoped so, anyway. "You might not think it's important, Cook. But I have things I need to do, questions that need answering."

"Yeah."

"Cookie, I had to go, had to try something, anything."

The old man shook his head. "Yeah, that worked so well for you, didn't it?"

Rafe could think of little worth uttering. Now or ever — what a mess it all had become. Maybe he was better off in Yuma. No, that was too dark a thought.

"Ever occur to you I could have been useful to you in Denver? Aside from dragging you out of there? Ever cross your mind we been through a pile of scrapes together over the years and we're both here to yammer about it? Hmm?" Cookie spat, dragged a grimy cuff across his mouth. "Course not. You're so worked up about your own problems, and selfish to boot."

Rafe looked at him, eyes wide, nostrils flexed.

"Yes, I said selfish, by gum. And I'll say it again any blamed time I want to. 'Cause it's the truth. And while Cookie McGee might tell a windy now and again, he don't never, ever tell a lie. Least not about his pards. I tell you what you need to hear right to your homely face, you got it?"

Silent minutes passed, then Rafe said, "You done?" and plucked out a nub of cigar from his shirt pocket.

"Near enough. For now."

"Good." He set fire to the cigar. "And Cook?"

"Yeah?"

"Don't ever change." He shook out the match, and stuffed it in his pocket.

"What makes you think I can?"

They rode the rest of the day in silence. That night they made a cold camp, each man chewing over his own thoughts. But something had cleared between them and while they weren't quite back in their old

202

grooves, might well never be, it was close enough for now.

CHAPTER TWENTY-FOUR: THY NAME IS HUMILITY

Thanks to the largesse of Rafe and Cookie, and from the thin but steady vein of gold Doc had found on ranch property, Sue Pendleton now found herself in an upscale millinery and dress shop on Dwight Street, Chicago. A covey of plainly dressed young women attended her, fluttering about with pins clamped between their lips and cloth measuring tapes draped about their necks. They in turn were overseen by a broad-hipped woman, similarly attired in dark, subdued tones — so as not to outshine the fine clothes being tried on by their customers.

"Girls, if you do not finish the hemline in less than one minute I will hand you your final wage packet as you leave . . . by the back door . . . this evening. Do I make myself heard?"

Sue could not help but smile. This was the world in which she was raised — a privileged girl with the means to have clothing tailored to her whims. Her smile faded as one of the girls fumbled the heavy steel scissors. The girl glanced up at Sue, eyes wide, as if Sue was about to light into her for being an oaf.

The girl was obviously new to the job, and though she knew how to wield a thread and needle with a quick, adroit hand, Sue noted the boss woman's demeanor and lingering presence terrified the girl.

The game was not as fun as she had expected. It had become wrong, somehow. And it made her sad for the shop girl, sad that Sue herself had once been little more than a society snoot who looked down on shop girls. She who had been the lowest of the low, a prostitute. Hell, not even that if she was honest with herself. She'd been a drug-addicted whore chained to Al Swearengen's bed, craving nothing in life save the next hypodermic needle filled with whatever drug that pig had jammed into her over and over, days, weeks, months — she wasn't sure how long.

At some point Rafe Barr had stormed in, larger than any man she had ever seen, risking his life to save her from Swearengen. He, along with Cookie McGee and the others in "The Outfit," had saved her from herself.

And she was repaying them how? By reverting to snobbish ways, by adding misery on the head of this poor girl fumbling with the hem of the dress.

Sue cleared her throat. The woman who ran the shop bustled over. "Yes, madam?"

"I . . ."

"Yes?" The stout woman inclined her head and forced a smile.

"I will take the dress as it is, thank you. And I will also need gloves and boots, and a hat besides."

The shop lady's smile widened and her eyes twinkled. "Of course, madam, you shall have my personal attention."

"Ah, perhaps this young lady might assist me?" Sue nodded toward the girl at her feet.

"Surely not . . ." said the shop lady. "Tillie is not experienced. She only began working here a week ago."

"I see," said Sue. "Be that as it may, we have hit it off swimmingly. I would be grateful if she could attend me. She is very kind and is a natural at her job."

"Oh, I see, yes, well . . ."

Sue watched twin urges of haughtiness and greed war on the woman's stern face.

The woman nodded to Tillie. "See that

you attend the lady well." Her last word snapped out of her mouth as if bitten.

Sue decided the woman was bitter and cruel and she wished she could escort the girl out of the shop and give her employment elsewhere. Anywhere so long as she wasn't subjected to the woman's sharp tongue.

As they perused items in the shop, Sue tried to engage the girl in conversation, but the most she could drag out of her were nods, followed with "Yes, ma'am," "No, ma'am," and "I'm sure I don't know, ma'am."

At a display in the far rear corner of the shop, well out of hearing range of the grumpy boss woman, Sue held up a boot that had far too many buttons and too small a heel for practical use. My my, how her tastes had changed since she went out on her own what seemed like years before.

"You know, you could do better than work here." She spoke in a low voice, to be sure. "I know enough about dresses and dressmaking to guess you are smarter than you let on."

A quick light shone in the girl's eyes and she began to smile, then glanced toward the front of the store and cast her eyes down again. "I'm sure I don't know what you mean, ma'am."

"Oh, you know," said Sue, grinning. "You need to believe in yourself. Maybe I'm stepping way out of line here." She turned the homely boot as if admiring it. "But perhaps you think you need to get the experience this place will offer you, then you can set up your own shop. If you do, I'd gladly be your customer."

"You would?"

It was the first the girl said that didn't end in "ma'am." It sounded good to Sue. "You bet I will. Now, what's say you help me find a pair of boots that aren't so . . . ugly." Her eyebrows rose with the word.

The girl nearly giggled, but kept her composure.

Twenty minutes later, laden with several parcels, including a hat box that dangled by red strings from her newly gloved hand, Sue made her way back toward the Hotel Charlmont, where she'd taken a room. She had decided to make a day of it, the only one she dare indulge in on her way to her new career. A career she hoped would involve much excitement and that would provide her with the ability to prove to her father, and to Rafe, that she was capable of taking care of herself. Not surviving, but thriving. And certainly not with Daddy's money.

She would only visit her father when she had established her own successful life. And not a day before.

The doorman doffed a small blue cap, offered a quick smile and nod, and held the door for her. She returned the smile and continued on into the lobby. She gazed about her at the richly carved and polished wood, the pretty glass chandelier casting slivers of dazzling, dancing light even in the midafternoon. Yes, she missed the finery of a life of money. She would miss it even more when she had to move out of here and take a room at a boarding house to save money.

But not until tomorrow, she told herself as she set her purchases down on the brass four-poster in her room. Tonight I dine, perhaps even dance, in my fine new clothes. Then I sleep well and luxuriantly in this fine big bed. And tomorrow?

"I will worry about that when it comes," she said to the tall mirror, tilting her head and admiring herself. The healthy pink of her cheeks, the shine back in her hair, the strength she felt in her arms and legs, the fact that she no longer needed anything unhealthy to sleep through the night, she owed all this and more to Rafe Barr.

And she would one day, hopefully sooner than later, visit him in style and show him what a woman she was, what a woman she could be . . . for him, with him?

"But first," she said to her reflection, not even daring in private to smile. "I will become a detective for the Pinkerton Agency."

CHAPTER TWENTY-FIVE:
PARDS IS PARDS

Rafe toed his companion's leg.

"Cookie, we have to get our backsides moving."

The old man on the ground opened one eye, blinked it a couple of times, then groaned. "Knew I shoulda left the jug alone last night. Hell, I shoulda left you in the pokey a little longer, let that rock-hard knob you call a head heal."

Rafe stared down at the man.

Cookie sat up, stretching his neck. "You know, I don't half-wonder that you have been permanently affected by that blow to your bean. Might be you will never be the same again. What do you think?"

"I think you better get up. My horse is saddled and ready to ride. I would have rigged up yours, but Stinky is feeling cantankerous this morning. Not unlike his owner. You two share more than horse-headed stubbornness."

Cookie scrabbled on the ground, doing his best to get to his feet despite the cracking and popping sounds his knees emitted. "You best run, Rafe Barr. 'Cause when I get hold of you there won't be much worth saving. You hear me?"

Rafe stood well back from the flailing older man and grinned as he sipped his coffee.

"Yep," he said, rocking back on his heels. "It sure is good to see you again, Cookie McGee."

"You won't think so when I . . . oh, never mind." Cookie leaned over, his hands on his knees, his braces trailing behind, and his chest heaving. "I'll get you when I see fit. And not a minute before."

Rafe handed Cookie a cup of hot coffee. It soothed the ruffled man, at least for the moment. He smiled, poured himself another splash, and waited for his old trail pard to get a leg up on the new day.

CHAPTER TWENTY-SIX: SO, WHAT'S THE PLAN?

"I need to stay with him, Jack. Believe me it's not something I want to do any more than you want me to." Mala sighed, her shoulders slumping. For the first time since they met on the tournament floor days before, Jack saw not only the long-buried little sister he thought he'd lost forever all those long years ago, but also the look of exhaustion their mother had borne at the end, before their lives had been hacked apart by foul circumstance.

"Turlington did this to you. Again." Jack held her chin in his hand. She didn't have to tell him. "You look tired," he said. Another waste of words. Of course, she was tired. She was a white man's plaything, risking her neck to bring her long-lost brother information that neither of them knew what to do with.

Worried and weary.

But there was something else there, too.

213

That other thing their mother had had . . . determination. The woman had never given up. Not even when they took her man from her, when they took her babies from her, when they peeled her dignity and carved away at her body, whip lash by whip lash. Try as they might those white owners could not really own her, for they never laid claim to a single speck of the woman's spirit. That snapping flame of defiance that guttered in hard breezes never blew out. Jack now saw that was what Mala had, too.

And he knew he, too, had some of that spirit. But it wasn't a sliver of his mother's grit.

As if they had been talking, Mala turned to him. "You remember much of Mama?"

Jack nodded. "I do. I do indeed. Kind of figure she's here with us now."

"What do you think she'd say if she saw us?"

"You all bruised up as a . . ." Jack scrunched his face. "And me as a gambler?" He shrugged. "She'd light into us. Swat us up one side, then the other. Then she'd hug us, tell us it hurt her worse'n us, and tell us to walk straight, stop playing games."

Mala nodded. "That sounds about right." Her smiled faded and she looked at him. "I found out something else. Rufus, he likes to talk when he's had a couple of drinks and, well, afterwards. And he said some things."

"Like what?" Jack poured water into the basin, and tore a scrap of rag from a clean undershirt. "Here, you need to wash your face, get that dried blood off your lips and nose. You can use the mirror at the wash-stand."

She sighed, closing her eyes. "There's not much. He got all riled up when I asked him when this group of his planned on doing its rising, you know, like the phoenix. Then he grunted and . . . well, he took what I said to mean something else, if you know what I mean."

"No, no, I don't want to hear any of that business." Jack put his palms to his ears and shook his head.

Mala smiled. "I have to get back. But he did say one more thing, Jack. He said there would be a reckoning and that it would hap-pen right soon. Said something about show-ing that bastard Grant. I assume he means the President?"

Jack stood motionless, staring ahead, but not at her.

"Jack? You okay?"

"Mala." Jack's voice was little more than a whisper. "You sure he said 'Grant'?"

She nodded.

"You know who's coming here to Santa Fe to play the last big day of the tournament?"

She shrugged. "I try to block all this gambling business out. Not my idea of a good time, if you know what I mean. Oh no . . ."

Jack nodded and paced the small room, covering it in four stiff strides, his game leg's boot heel clunking softly in time with the tapping of his cane. "The man you mentioned."

"President Grant?"

Jack stopped and faced her.

"Then that means . . ." Her eyes widened.

"Yep. Might be your colonel is more than a fat good ol' boy who likes to run his mouth when he's drunk. You know anything more, Mala? Anything at all?"

She shook her head, eyes on his.

"Okay. Where's his office?"

"It's on Blossom and Nino, one block down from the square. He rents the space from someone. Said he used to own the building, but Rufus is a gambler. Only not so good at it sometimes. I have no idea where he keeps getting all his money."

Jack worked his tongue between his teeth. "Well, right now I need to find out what he has planned for the President. Hopefully we're wrong and there won't be more to it than a drunken man running his mouth in bitterness."

"But if you're right?" she said.

"If I'm right, Colonel Turlington is planning a welcome party President Grant might not want to attend."

"I better get back there, see if I can find out something . . . anything else. But what can we do about it?"

Jack shook his head. "No, no, no. First off, you cannot go back to him. Not after this." He gestured to her face. "That isn't right, Mala. You know it."

"Jack." She hugged him and stepped back. "I appreciate your concern. And I know you're my big brother, always were, always will be, even when I thought you were dead. But this," she touched her bruised cheek lightly. "This is nothing new. He still looks at me as a possession, and treats me in kind."

"Nothing kind about it, Mala. You can't go back to him. You have to lay low — I'll find a place for you. Right now." He reached for his coat on the back of the chair by the door.

She put a hand on his arm. "Jack, listen to me for once, stop acting like a bull-headed man. If I don't go back he'll get even more suspicious than he is. He already thinks there's something between you and me. I can't give him any more fuel for that silly little fire in his mind. I'll go back and he'll be fine like he always is after he hits me. For a day or two, anyway. That will give me time to find out something else. Anything I can learn might be useful for whatever it is you think we can do. There's two of us, though, Jack."

"No, there isn't," he said. "I already contacted my friends. Friends who won't stand for this. I only hope my telegram gets to them before it's too late. But we need to figure out a back-up plan, in case."

Chapter Twenty-Seven: Home Again, Home Again . . .

As soon as Rafe swung wide the kitchen door, heaven-sent succulent smells of bubbling beef stew with dumplings — about right, with a hint of chewiness — at least that's how he imagined the dish — clouded in his face in a most pleasurable way. He peeked around the corner of the tall sideboard.

There stood Arlene, as always, before the stove. Slightly stout — Rafe pitied the man who called her plump — and forever swaddled in a flowered apron of her own devising, a bib front and pockets in which she kept hair clips for herself. Her silvered chestnut hair, pulled back in a loose gather at the back of her head, was forever slipping down in her perpetually red face as she leaned over her stove, the largest cast-and-enamel brute they could order from Robeson's Mercantile in Stukerville, some fifty-seven miles northeast of the ranch.

It had fortunately arrived in four crates, each piece carefully wrapped in canvas, then cradled in shredded fiber that Arlene had insisted on using to stuff an extra mattress for the bunkhouse. The horses had earned their feed those two days it took to haul the stove back to town.

"Miss Tewksbury, as I live and breathe." Rafe smiled at her from the doorway. As he expected, he had startled her.

She looked up from the bubbling stewpot as if someone had touched off a cannon beside her. Then the cook and unspoken ramrod of the ranch squinted her eyes and pursed her lips in mock anger. She wagged the massive wooden spoon, the woman's only necessary weapon, at him with each word she spoke.

"You have a lot of explaining to do, Mister Barr. And don't tell me you are a grown man and all that blather. You . . ." Her eyes widened as she saw the bandage on his head. "Oh, what's happened to you, Rafe?"

He grinned and shrugged. "No problem, really. A little dust-up with bad apples, but it's all resolved."

"But your head . . ."

Rafe forced his smile wider, though in truth his head still ached. Over the past days on the trail with Cookie, the throbbing behind his eyes had lessened, and while it still felt as if it had migrated on nail-sharp teeth to the back of his skull, it had been worse. There was no fooling Arlene Tewksbury, though. She squinted and scowled up at him once more.

"Rafe Barr, you ought to be in bed. I have seen plenty of ailing heads in my time and yours is worse than you let on. It's all in the eyes, and yours look addled, if you don't mind me saying so."

"Somehow, Arlene, I don't think it would matter if I did mind." Rafe smiled again to show her he was kidding. All he really wanted to do was crawl into his bed and sleep for about a week. But he'd never been much of a hand for admitting weakness to anyone, and he didn't feel like starting now.

Then Cookie clumped through the doorway, mumbling about Doc and the ranch and catching up on all his work. He caught sight of Arlene and fell silent, snatched off his hat, and worked the brim, stammering and reddening about the face. "Good day, Miss Tewksbury. I . . . I have to go check on Doc." Cookie turned and clomped back down the front steps.

Rafe and Arlene traded quick laughs. "That man," she said, shaking her head and smiling. "His stomach is like a clock —

221

knows exactly when it's time to eat. I'll have lunch ready soon. I believe Doc has something in the barn he'd like to show you both."

"Sounds good," said Rafe. "And whatever you're cooking smells mighty good, too."

"I'll ring the bell when it's ready. Now get along with you!" She playfully waved her spoon at him.

Out in the barn, Doc, with all the puffed-up pride of a strutting tom turkey, tugged the edge of a stained canvas tarpaulin. Beneath stood a chuckwagon . . . of sorts.

Cookie and Rafe stared at it a moment. Cookie said, "Ain't that the work wagon? What'd you do to her?"

Doc smiled with the indulgent look of a patient man who knows something others don't. "You are an observant man, Cookie. This, gentlemen, is no longer an ordinary work wagon. It is now a war wagon. Or it will be. I haven't quite perfected it."

"It is, eh?" said Cookie walking around it. "Kind of looks like a gussied-up version of a chuckwagon. Except different somehow. Wait . . ." Cookie walked closer, bending low. "What have you done to it? That work wagon didn't need nothing done to it — I greased the hubs before I left."

"That is where you are wrong, sir. Allow me to show you the modifications I have made thus far to Ethel."

"Ethel?" said Cookie. "Who in tarnation is Ethel?"

"I believe Doc is telling us he has christened the work wagon."

"That's not all I have done, my good sirs."

"Why you talking all fancy anyway, Doc?" Cookie kept circling the wagon. "And why Ethel?"

Doc, who had climbed inside the wagon, poked his head out a hatch in the roof. "She is named for the most beguiling yet fickle woman I ever had the distinct wonder to have met. Alas, that was a long time ago and I am still not certain if I am lucky to have lived through the ordeal through which she dragged me. Perhaps it might have been better for all involved if I had perished those many years ago when my heart was freshly stomped."

"Ah, Doc," said Rafe. "What say you show us what it is you wanted to show us. We promised Arlene we'd not be late for lunch."

Doc beckoned the two men to the interior with a curled pudgy finger. "Once you see what I have to show you I believe you will want to take Ethel with you on your next adventure."

"Now hold on, Doc," said Cookie. "We ain't got time to ramble all over creation in a rickety old wagon."

"I think you'll agree, Cookie, that Ethel is no longer a rickety old wagon, as you so insultingly put it. Instead she is on her way to becoming a finely tuned, tight conveyance that will only slow down the concerned parties if they happen to fall asleep at the reins."

Cookie's eyes narrowed. He didn't like where this chatter was headed. So what if he had a habit of dozing off on his supply trips to and from town. Especially from town . . . after a visit to the Lucky Lady . . . and then Jimbo's.

"Now, let me show you some of the finer attributes Ethel has to offer." Doc grunted to his feet and waved them over to stand beside him. "Here," he said, pointing to the underside. "Rap your knuckles under there." He nodded, smiling at Cookie. "Go ahead."

Cookie looked from Rafe to Doc back to Rafe, taking no pains to hide his scowl. But he gingerly extended a gnarled callused hand and gave the spot a hard quick rap. Immediate curiosity knitted his brows. "That metal?"

Doc nodded, smiling. "It is indeed. Where it will do the most good, bottom and four sides, Ethel has a skin of thin sheet steel to help lessen if not eliminate the more disastrous effects of explosive projectiles."

"He's got more two-dollar words than you, Rafe," said Cookie as if Doc wasn't standing right there beside him.

"He means it will help slow down bullets."

"I know what he means, confound it!"

Rafe ignored the flustered Cookie, and said, "What else can she offer us, Doc?"

"I'm glad you asked, Rafe. Keep in mind this is a work in progress, but if you'll follow me to the rear where the chuck box is located, you'll see." Doc tugged open drawers and bins and cupboard doors well beyond their normal capacity. "She has ample storage, false bottoms, and all manner of hidden compartments suitable for storing ammunition, assorted bits of gear, explosives . . ." He nodded at Cookie, who with mention of one of his favorite words showed more interest.

"But that's not all — the inside of this rolling brute, equal parts vault, gun cabinet, and protective bunker, offers a number of features you won't find on your average chuckwagon." He winked at Rafe who nodded.

"By all means, enlighten us, Doc. But keep in mind that Miss Tewksbury doesn't suffer malingerers to her table."

"Not to mention I'm more peckish than a hydrophoby wolf in a hen house," said Cookie, rubbing his grumbling belly.

Doc nodded. "See that ring in the floor? Tug on it and you'll find it's a convenient escape hatch should you need to . . ."

"Escape?" said Rafe. But he wasn't smiling. He was running his hand over every angle and inch of the well-rendered interior of the wagon. "It looks a lot smaller on the outside than it really is in here. If that makes any sense."

"I wish someone would say that about my belly," Doc giggled. "But yes, that was part of my intention. I wanted to make the entire affair seem unobtrusive and anything but a chuckwagon. You'll note there are a number of compartments in here, as well as those two fold-down cots for sleeping, and ample storage for gear. I've included a drawer with up-to-date maps of all major regions you are likely to find when roving the West."

Rafe whistled. "You have been a busy man, Doc. What prompted all this?"

"It began as a mere flicker, a thought, if you will, something of a whimsy. I soon realized if I could make real even half of the ideas I have for this wagon, it might actually be useful on long treks where saddlebags prove a limitation."

Cookie snorted. "You can't take this thing to half the places we go, Doc. Too big, too wide, too slow . . ." He shook his head knowingly.

Doc nodded in agreement. "While that is true, according to your math, I believe that leaves roughly half of the places you do go on your various dangerous ventures."

"Got you there, Cook," said Rafe, not even trying to hide his grin.

Doc shrugged. "Even if it is rarely used in the manner to which I have rigged it up, I have learned valuable lessons in the construction of it. For instance, my notion of devising self-greasing hubs for the wheels, while thoroughly attainable, will have to wait. There is only so much a man can shoehorn into a prototype, after all." Still, the Doc seemed pleased as he ran a hand lovingly along the smooth edge of a dovetailed corner. "Gun cleaning station," he mumbled.

The clang of Arlene's dinner triangle cut through the momentary quiet as each man, even Cookie, had fallen silent admiring the various knobs and chains and shelves.

"As you say, Doc, she's more a war wagon than a chuckwagon," said Rafe. He looked up. "And if we don't get a move on, there'll be plenty of reason to use it when Arlene comes after us with that big spoon of hers."

Doc and Cookie both reflexively rubbed their heads, evidence of past run-ins with the spoon.

"Heck of a job, Doc. This really is impressive and will no doubt prove mighty useful. Really." Rafe stuck out his hand. "A job well done."

Doc puffed up and offered his own grease-smeared hand for a shake.

"Oh for heaven's sake," said Cookie. "Let's get a move on before we all end up bunkin' in this here rig of yours."

"You two go on ahead. I'll be there momentarily. I have to close up compartments, put away my tools."

Cookie and Rafe legged it toward the ranch house. "Why would we need such a contraption, Rafe?" Cookie whispered to the big man. When Rafe didn't respond, Cookie looked at him, then stopped. "Oh, now don't tell me you're actually thinking of dragging that thing along behind us whenever we take to the trail, are you?"

The big man shrugged. "Certain trips, it's not a bad idea."

Cookie groaned and climbed the two steps to the porch of the ranch house, his thoughts already on lunch.

"Won't take them long to find me here, you know. And you'll be identified, too, sure as the sun rises each day."

Cookie said nothing. He reached for another biscuit from the half-filled platter before him. For once, Arlene didn't playfully chastise him for hogging the biscuits. A somber mood had descended on them.

No one, it seemed, had anything to add to Rafe's statement. Perhaps something would occur to them once they'd finished their meal. At least that's what they hoped — the lack of the usual banter and ribbing, coupled with the obvious foreboding of Rafe's plight as a fugitive twice over, made for a long, silent meal.

Rafe felt badly about it, especially considering Arlene went to so much trouble as she did with each meal. Yet the usual toothsome flavor of it was compromised.

Added was the fact that Jack and Sue were not among them. The gambler's easygoing, unflappable demeanor was missed, as were Sue's twin moods of nervousness around Rafe and wise-cracking jokester around Cookie.

With Cookie's help, Arlene cleared the

table of the plates and bowls and platters. She chastised Cookie more than once for being an oaf and ham-fisted with her crockery. He took it with red-eared goodness, like a dog who can't help but stick tight to its stern master.

Arlene set out a huge apple pie, still warm, and as Rafe sliced it, the quiet mood of the meal lifted. Arlene set out cups and poured hot black coffee for all. Cookie dolloped plenty of sugar into his cup, stirred it well, then dumped it several mouthfuls at a time into his saucer and slurped as the others watched on. The man's odd ritual never failed to mystify and amuse.

As she sat down herself, Arlene said, "Doc, I don't mean to pry, but I assume you told Rafe and Cookie about that telegram you received?"

Doc held up a finger. "I knew there was something I'd forgotten! Yes, yes, well, I was at the saloon in Dibley last Thursday, you know . . ."

Rafe nodded. "Pulling teeth and pulling corks."

Doc nodded. "It is thirsty work, this doctoring business." He winked and took a bite of pie.

"Doc? The telegram?"

"Oh, yes, yes. I received a telegram, of all

things. Yes, me. Odd I know, but interesting. It was delivered right to me in the bar by Ferd."

Again, long moments passed before Rafe cleared his throat. "So . . . what was in this telegram? Who sent it?"

Arlene sighed. "I haven't seen it myself, but I believe he said it was from Jack."

Rafe set down his fork. "Is he okay?"

"Oh, yes, I believe so," said Doc. "Still, it is a most mysterious missive."

"Missive? There you go talking hoity-toity again." Cookie shook his head and looked away, as if disgusted by the absentminded Doc.

Doc slapped himself as if he felt a bee beneath his shirt. "Ah ha!" He held up a finger as he pulled out a sloppily folded piece of yellow paper and handed it to Rafe.

"Once you read it, you'll agree it is most cryptic indeed."

Rafe read it twice, then handed it to Cookie.

Doc's smile faded when he saw Rafe's face settle into a hard line.

The big man stood, his chair squawking on the plank floor. "Doc, why didn't you give this to me earlier?" He turned to Cookie. "We have to go."

Arlene set down the coffeepot. "What's

wrong?"

"Jack's in danger — or will be soon. He wouldn't ask for help unless the situation was dicey."

" 'Bout what I'm thinkin', too," said Cookie.

"Be ready to ride in ten minutes."

"But Rafe," said Arlene. "Your head — you're not well."

"Doesn't much matter how I feel," said Rafe. "We need to get to Santa Fe. At the very least we might be able to prevent bad things from happening."

The older man nodded grimly. "What's the plan?"

"Like always," said Rafe, from the porch. "Make it up as we ride."

Cookie sighed. "Here we go again." He pushed away from the table. "No matter that a man's half-starved to death."

"What can I do, Cookie?" Arlene's eyes were wide.

"Oh, Jack'll be fine, like as not," said Cookie. "Still, it's best to make sure." He sighed and headed for the door. "Looks like we got us some cogitatin' to do," said Cookie. "How's that for a fancy word, eh?" He smiled at Doc as he passed by the hangdog man's chair.

Several minutes later they were both

nearly ready — Rafe's big buckskin was saddled and anxious to work, despite the fact they'd only arrived at the ranch hours before.

Cookie's mustang, Stinky, was less enthused and offered a half-hearted crowhop before dropping his head and eyeing Cookie out of one eye, in hopes of landing a quick nip to the cantankerous cowboy's backside.

"Not today you don't," said Cookie, landing a quick slap to Stinky's rump. "You mind your manners or it will be a long, hard ride to Santa Fe, you hear me?"

"Cook," said Rafe. "I hope you're packing your boom-boom sticks."

Cookie's grizzled countenance swung around and his clear-eyed gaze fixed on Rafe. The old buck was grinning. "What do you think?" He reached back and patted a bulging saddlebag, then thumbed his brown wool overcoat back to reveal his specially made holster, a tubular affair he'd recently altered to accommodate up to a half-dozen sticks instead of the two or three he usually carried at his waist.

"In case." He followed this up with a wink.

"Good man," said Rafe, then swung up into the saddle.

Cookie was about to reply with a fresh volley of complaints about missing out on his pie when he saw Rafe's face drain of what little color he'd built up over the day. The big man was still in pain, no doubt from that knock on his bean, but he was set to ride hard.

Arlene bustled out of the ranch house with two sacks bulging with food and fixings for trail grub. She handed them up to Cookie, who eyed them and licked his lips. "You happen to . . ."

"Yes, Cookie," she said. "I put in the last of the biscuits, and the pie, too. Take care not to squash it." She turned to Rafe, visoring her eyes with a hand, the other resting on her hip. "Is there anything at all I can do?"

Rafe wheeled his horse around. "Say a prayer we don't arrive too late." He touched his hat brim and heeled the big buckskin into a gallop.

Cookie winked at her. "Aww, Rafe is always funnin' like that. It'll all be fine, you'll see. Be back before you know it." He sunk heel into Stinky's ribs and the fleet-footed beast hit the trail. Cookie waved his hat. "See you soon, Miss Tewksbury!"

She watched the two men thunder out of sight, then sighed and walked back to the house. From the porch, she saw Doc, shoulders slumped, making his way slowly to the barn.

dors slammed, making his way slowly to the barn.

Chapter Twenty-Eight:
Strangers in the Night

"Now what in hell is this door doing open?" Punk Clements blinked back the whiskey-fired urge to not care. He shut the door and sat down in the chair he was supposed to be sitting in all night, "guarding" the boss's room, for whatever reason. "Boss don't care to share his secrets with me, hell if I am going to bust my hump playing nursemaid to an empty room."

A scuffing, squawking sound reached him through the closed door. Punk paused halfway down into the chair and stood back up. With a hand on his revolver he stepped once more to the door, paused outside, and gazed at the closed door. If it was the boss, why would he have left the door of his office open? And if it had been the boss, now it was coming to Punk, then he would have noticed Punk was not where the boss had told him to be — parked in the chair outside the office.

So, someone was in there? Maybe someone the boss was afraid of? A thief? Punk slipped his tongue over his lips and swallowed. *You ain't paid to stand here doing nothing,* he told himself. Maybe whoever's in there was climbing out the window at this very minute. Might be if Punk waited he would leave in peace. The idea had its appeal. Then two more notions followed right on its heels. What if it was the boss in there, testing him? Or worse, what if the intruder was waiting for him to barge in?

Punk licked his lips again, then muttered, "Hell with it anyway," and pressed himself flat against the wall beside the door. With his near hand, he thumbed the latch and shoved hard on the door. It swung inward.

No shots whipped out. Nothing happened at all.

Punk lowered himself to his knees, peering around the doorframe, but there was no light on inside the boss's office, so no way to see what was happening in there. But he realized that whoever was in there, in the dark, was likely looking out, and seeing him skylined against the low light of the hallway.

He pulled back and thought about it. Then he snugged his hat, pitched back off his knees, and squatted on his haunches. He bared his teeth, and with a growl, barreled through the doorway. Smack into a wooden chair. It scudded across the floor. He held still in the near dark and tried to get his bearings.

Could be the liquor he'd taken while in the company of the lovely Dee Dee Tulane was addling him worse than he knew. Punk could not recall the layout of the office. There was a big desk somewhere, usually covered with papers and decrees and documents and whatnot, all because the boss was an important man, at least that's what he wanted Punk to think.

Another sound, not one of his own making, came to him from the right, from the other side of the room. Someone was over there. It would be a race to get to the door, if it was an intruder.

"Boss? That you?"

He heard fast, low breathing. Someone was trying to hold in quick breaths. Wasn't working. Punk checked to see if it was himself. Nope. Someone else, and it didn't sound like the boss, who being a fat man was a heavy breather. Even his breaths sounded fat, sort of thick and huffy and puffy. "Who's there? Boss, that you?"

"No."

The voice was thin, raspy, and closer than Punk expected. He heard the quick, clipped word before he saw the face, felt breath on his cheek, and felt the hot flash of pain flowering up the side of his head. Punk grunted, and barely faltered before dropping to one knee. Before the attacker could strike once more he lurched to one side, slamming into the chair once more. He moved enough to keep a second blow from landing on his sore head.

The blow had knocked clarity into Punk's throbbing pate. He kept low and scrabbled around, fidgeting with the hammer on the revolver. Close quarters, and the sound would be foul, loud, horrible. Then what? People would rush to the scene, Punk would be out of his job, if not out of his life. No, no, he had to get the upper hand on this bastard, lay him low.

Even as he thought it — always a stretch for Punk Clements — he knew he had to subdue the intruder, lay into him, then let the boss see that he was doing his job. Of course, the fat man would want to know why an intruder had gotten into the office in the first place. But that was beginning to get beyond Punk's line of thinking. He had to get control of the intruder.

Punk squinted, and saw a hulking, low-walking creature. No wait, it was a shadow, nothing more. "Gaaah!" He hurled himself forward, managing to barrel directly into the legs of the attacker.

But the attacker moved, leaving Punk feeling little more than fabric as the legs whisked from him in the dark. "Damn!"

That's when he felt another club to the head, this time only grazing Punk's temple. That meant the attacker couldn't see so well either. Still, the blow sent a jag of hot pain down to his jaw. He rolled with it, then felt another solid hit behind his shoulders.

As he collided with something large and unmoving — visions of the big mahogany desk filled his buzzing mind — Punk kicked out and felt his right boot heel connect with a thin thing that sure didn't feel like furniture. A gasp and groan followed it. Whoever it was must have lost balance, because the next thing Punk felt was another damn knock to the head, but this one was wild-thrown, accompanied with a crash. Someone had fallen, and since Punk was already down, he guessed the odds were evening.

Still too dark to shoot, he swung his gun-hand hard outward, felt the revolver's butt connect with something definitely man and not furniture. Another groan. He repeated the move, but the attacker rolled away.

The scuffle thus far, grunts and groans and shoved furniture aside, had been a quiet affair, at least no gunshots. It was spooky to Punk that the attacker hadn't shouted in anger, cursed him, anything. Had only said the one word, "No."

In Punk's family, you shouted, you threw knives and chairs and oil lamps and insults at people you loved, and for the people who were trying to do you real harm? In the dark? You went all out, by God. *Time to do that,* thought Punk, thumbing back the hammer on his six-gun. The clicking was tonic to Punk's ringing ears.

But he had no idea where to shoot. He knew he wasn't getting paid enough by the boss to take a beating like this. His head was already fuzzy from whiskey and a quick romp with Dee Dee. And his nostrils were still filled with her damn fancy perfume that smelled like the ass of a dying mule, especially up close when him and Dee Dee were going at it hammer-and-tong like feral dogs fighting over scrap meat.

It was all too much for poor Punk, at least that's what he told himself. He was a hair of a second from giving himself the single-best sensation he'd ever felt throughout his entire body — even better than rutting with Dee Dee — that warm gush when he pulled on that trigger and a bullet burrowed deep like a tick's head into some asshole's flesh.

But it didn't work out that way. Reason, a near-stranger to the abandoned shack that was Punk's breeze-filled mind, took hold once more. *Son,* it said in a voice that sounded like his father's. *Son, you best think on what you are about to do, 'cause once you do that, a whole lot of things are bound to happen, and knowing how you lead your life, few of them will work in your favor.*

But he's a-whompin' on me in the dark, Daddy. That alone is reason enough to shine me up in the law's eyes.

Not with a record like yours, boy. You are on the losing end of that stick, and it's a short stick to start with. Looks to me you're headed for bad things. Take your boss, for instance. He's not going to look too keen on you if'n you drag the law into his office, all red-faced and pantin' 'cause they heard a gunshot. Sure, they might say someone was fixing to rob your boss. But then again, way your boss is a cagey man about his affairs, you ought not want to risk lawdogs rummaging in that there office.

All this conversation took place in Punk's head in the time it took him to ease a breath out of his mouth and relax that finger. He was shaking, tense; he heard a clanging sound in his head from that beating, like far-off church bells in the Mexican country-

242

side, maybe topped of with the screech of a train's wheels grinding and sliding, leaving smoking, sizzling silver-steel tracks behind on a July afternoon. Never a good sound. And, certainly, not one you want to hear in your own head.

"Where you at, stranger?" Punk's voice came out sort of windblown, like a hoarse cough through a cupped hand. Punk smelled something, and recalled how he'd wanted to head on back to the outhouse before coming in here, and had too, but someone had made it there before him, leaving something behind they ought not have eaten, from the stink of it. No way he was going back there.

Didn't matter now, as he seemed to have forgotten his need to urinate when all this happened. But now there was that faint tickle of smell, like someone had wet themselves. Odds were good it was him. He would check later. Not much to be done about it now. But next time he had to let loose, he'd damn well do it in the street if he had to rather than risk pissing himself like this.

What was the attacker thinking about him, a man who pissed himself? As if in response, a gurgling groan bubbled through Punk's muddy mind. Whoever it was he guessed was still on the floor. And from the sounds of it, he was worse off than Punk. That gave the stringy-haired hireling cause to grin.

"Hey!" He followed the barked shout with a quick kick to where he thought the man lay. He was rewarded with a solid delivery with the boot's toe and another grunt.

" 'Bout time you simmered down. I got Ol' Devil's snout aimed right at your mangy-ridden hide, you thieving bastard, so don't you move a pinch or you'll leak more'n groans. You hear me?" He kicked again and his wide smile drove his eyebrows high in surprise — he'd been tricked again.

The bastard had grabbed his boot heel and Punk felt himself lurch backward once more. His head hit something hard. Hot, sticky feelings washed over his head as if he'd pulled on a stocking cap of something that, though it hurt, also gave him a warm, comforting feeling. For a second he felt sure all this was a drunken dream, maybe he'd slipped down a couple stairs at Dee Dee's place, and hit his head. Been known to happen. With all the scars lacing his bean every which way, Punk reckoned if he ever went bald, his head would look like a map drawn by a blind man.

Fortunately, he still mostly had a head of hair women liked to drag their fingers through — why in hell did they like that, anyway? Not like he washed it all that often — but he could, by God, grow hair. It was about the only thing his pap ever give him that was worth a fiddler's fart.

"You son of a bitch, son of a bitch, son of a bitch."

The voice came to Punk over and over reciting the words as if the man were praying.

"Whaa?"

He heard the intruder suck a quick breath in through clenched teeth, like a man does when mighty pain has been delivered.

"That mean I got you good?" Punk's voice sounded stronger. He struggled to sit up, somehow not sensing any more danger from this man. He saw a dim outline of someone about five, six feet away in the dark. Must be a big moon or else light leaking on over from the bawdy house's front room.

Punk heard a bray of laughter from out on the street; a woman squealed as if she'd been goosed on the behind.

The shape made to rise to his feet, but slipped back down. So he had doled out a hurting to the thieving bastard. Punk got to his knees, his head fogged from the back now, too, where it felt cold and wet. He daren't touch there, likely he'd gotten a gash from the upending he'd taken. He wasn't sure if he was seeing double, then triple, then double, all glazed with darkness, from the whiskey or from the knockings his head had taken.

He rose; the man was still humped up, half-sprawled, hugging something down low. Must be really hurting to ignore Punk as he made his way half-dragging himself until he stood over the man. Still the man sat hunched holding himself, maybe a leg? Bent low, alternately sucking in breath and hissing it out again, blowing through his nose and swearing, too, noises like a human calliope.

"Get your ass up, damn you," said Punk. The man ignored him. He made to kick, but recalled the man's fast reflexes last time he did that, and caught himself.

"What in hell is wrong with you?" said Punk.

But the man stayed low, still obviously in a stupor of pain.

"Aw hell." Punk shucked his revolver from its holster and once more made to club the man. The man lashed out again and made a weaker attempt to snatch at Punk's leg. This time the bedraggled Punk managed to step back even as the man's fingers scrabbled against his pants leg. Punk swung low and clunked the man smack dab on the side of his head, right on the spot where a man will drop most every time, no matter how big and bull-headed. *There's that sweet spot,* thought Punk as the butt of the revolver smacked solid bone. Breath hissed out of the man in a quick burst, and he collapsed, Punk sincerely hoped, for the last time that night.

It took Punk a full thirty seconds before he felt safe enough and less addle-headed to grope in the dim light to find the desk. He recalled there was an oil lamp with a hammered-nickel finish and an ornate green glass globe. He hadn't heard any glass smash to the floor so the lamp might still be on the boss's desk. Then he patted his hands, gun still clutched in one should the demonic attacker come to life again. His forearm rapped into the lamp and he heard the glass globe totter on its wire cradle.

Lord don't break now, he thought. It didn't. He steadied the base of the lamp with one hand, tweezered a wooden lucifer out of his vest pocket with the fingers of his other hand, and scratched it alight on the backside of his denims. It flared; the stink of sulfur filled his nostrils and Punk fought the urge to sneer. Nobody in the dark to sneer to.

The match's orange glow lit the lamp that

would soon light the room. He found the wick wheel, raised it, lifted free the glass, and set the wick to light. He adjusted it, replaced the glass, and slid the lamp to the edge of the desk.

He looked down and a form lay on the floor, a white shirt peeking out from beneath a coat. Must have had black pants, for Punk could see no legs. Nor, for that matter, could he see a head or hands. "What in the hell?"

He bent closer. "Oh," he said as he squinted low. It was a black man he'd been fighting. And it came to him that that was the most he'd ever touched or been touched by a black man. He didn't know how he felt about that. What was the man up to? Punk looked around the honey-lit room. Nothing looked too upset, apart from the desk top's usual litter. The way the boss lived, he reckoned. The furniture was the only mess, and Punk had caused most of that. Not that he'd own up to it.

"Best stop wasting time, Punk," he said out loud, and looked about himself for something to tie up the man's hands and legs. He ended up using a spare set of leather shoulder braces the boss had hanging off a hook behind his desk. The boss didn't take chances, especially where his waist was concerned.

He slit the braces apart, used half for the man's wrist, and flipped him onto one side. He was about to tie the man's legs together at the boot when he noticed that one of the legs was bent all wrong. Nothing living ever bent like that. Except maybe a broken branch.

He leaned closer, prodding the odd-looking thing. Nope, the man's leg was snapped and Punk himself had done it. He beamed as he lashed the legs together, topping off his task with a wadded-up fancy snot rag he pulled out of the man's own breast pocket.

Speaking of pockets, he thought. *I might as well see what this thief has on him. Could be he's packing valuable items skinned from the boss's office.* Punk figured he'd be shirking his duties if he didn't empty the man's pockets. And so, he did, and came away disappointed. Not much more than a deck of cards, a small case with cigarillos and matches, and two poker chips not worth much, maybe a drink or two. He pocketed the lot and shouldered the man. He had a notion that getting the man out of the boss's office was a good idea. But where to lug him?

A horse whinnied out on the street and

Punk took it as a sign. "The boss's stable," he said and made his way out of the boss's office door, down the long hallway to the back of the building. He cut cross-lots to the livery. Grunting and whistling the entire time, doing his best to not attract the stares of curious folks.

"Get enough of that as it is . . ."

CHAPTER TWENTY-NINE:
SO CLOSE . . .

The clarity of sudden consciousness smacked Jack Smith across the face like a plank of green hemlock. It was dark; there was a jostling, thumping motion; he heard wheezing and grunting, smelled rising dust, dung, and heard far-off titters of laughter; a badly played piano hammered into helplessness by the fingertips of a drunk's ham hands. He almost could have smiled. Almost, had it not been for the vicious stabs of pain jolting through his head with each jostle he was given.

But that pain was sweet relief compared with the clot of agony he felt lower down. The leg. The same blasted leg that had been shot and smashed and trampled all because of El Jefe and his Hell Hounds in what seemed a lifetime ago back in Colorado at the ranch. So long ago . . . Jack gritted his teeth, tasting blood tinged with the salt of sweat.

And the night's events gushed back to him with the speed of a hard, fast fist. He'd been rummaging in Colonel Turlington's office, then the man in the dark found him. He'd tried to keep quiet, but his leg had pained him something fierce lately. Too many hours sitting at the baize bitch, the poker table, no exercise to stretch out the gimping muscles of his bum leg.

He was foolish enough to think he could slip into the office and find . . . what? Anything that might help him understand what the Brotherhood of the Phoenix was. Much of him did not care; he only wanted to help his sister escape from the foul life she was leading well off the path their mother would have approved of. But then again, he was one to talk. Then there was the Brotherhood's mention of President Grant and the worry and complications that brought to the table. What did they have in mind for the man?

The wheezing grew louder. *He was being carried — should have known that long minutes ago,* thought Jack. But he had no time to think any deeper on it, for he was slopped to the ground like a sack of wet cornmeal. Searing metal daggers ripped up and down his body, set his teeth tight, eyes rolling too high, eyelids twitching.

He vaguely heard a door being kicked once, twice, a grunt, then wood splitting, and the door spasming and slamming into something.

The wheezing and grunting grew louder. Jack felt himself hoisted up, the pain, hot and bad, so very bad. *Damn, why can't I pass out?* Jack cracked an eye, and light bloomed bright once more. The pain crested, rode high, stayed there. He tried to breathe, but the leg said no, no breathing, no nothing but pain.

Been better off if they'd killed me right there on the plateau above the ranch. Damn horse turned a leg, landed hard, somersaulted me, and now here I am, a young man in years, an old man in my head and body, leaning on a cane, nothing else in the world to cling to. Get the looks because I'm a black man, because I dress fine, because I use a cane and actually need it, not like the riverboat dandies who twirl them and whistle as if they hadn't a care.

Who am I kidding? thought Jack. *I behaved the same way for far too long. But now I let a drunk man get the best of me. And from the smells of him he'd pissed himself, too. All because my leg let me down. All too much.*

Such thoughts gushed through Jack's mind, setting his teeth tight with each step

253

the groaning, wheezing bastard took. Smells, dung again, more pungent. Heard a horse. Jack tried to see, forced his eyes open, saw a sunset glow in the air about him. A barn? Stable? Heard wood creak, slam, felt himself heaved once more off the man's shoulders, arcing through the air light, so light, but only for a second, then he felt uneven wads of something beneath him, not hard but not comfortable. His head caromed off wood. None of that mattered for his leg screamed for mercy, screamed with a voice Jack had never heard.

"Hush up your damn black mouth!" growled a voice from above him.

Would it end? Born a slave, beaten and beaten and kicked and gouged and whipped and beaten some more. Lied to and robbed and owned and sold and hated and trussed and beaten again, and here I am no further along the road, thought Jack as the light winked out once more.

He cracked his eyes open long enough to see the leering face of a white man, snag-toothed and foul, long, stringy grown black hair hanging like wet yarn about his face, a mashed nose, crusted blood and a purple lumped cheek, leering down at him.

Nothing changes, and it never will.

Chapter Thirty: Can't Get Worse . . . Can It?

"Why in hell did you take him to the stable?"

Punk shrugged. "Guess I didn't want him to rile up attention . . . or somethin'."

"And you didn't think that dragging his sorry ass across lots to the stable wouldn't attract attention? Hmm?" Turlington heard no answer and shifted his gaze to the closed lid of the grain bin in which lay the unconscious man.

Rufus caressed his chin with a fat, pink hand. "Punk Clements, you mean to tell me you nabbed him, but failed to ask him questions before you cold-cocked him on the head?" The colonel's red jowls purpled and trembled.

"I don't understand the problem, Boss. That bastard is the darkie you wanted, right? Caught him red-handed sniffing around in your office, I did. Must be he didn't know I was on duty to make sure no bad seeds get through." Punk lowered his voice, looking away. "Might be he slipped on through whilst I was engaged elsewhere."

"Punk." Turlington leaned close. "You were with a whore, weren't you? That's why you weren't watching my office."

Before the guilty underling could swallow and conjure up another thin excuse for his negligence, Turlington's meaty pink fist slammed down on the bow-planked feed bin. From inside a muffled groan rose up. "Simmer down in there, you son of a bitch."

Rufus smiled. "Least he ain't dead." He turned his gaze on Punk, his eyes hooded, and in a voice lower and meaner sounding than Punk had ever heard it, said, "This had better work out, Punk, elsewise you will pay the price. The Brotherhood don't tolerate shirkers, you understand me?"

"You mad, ain't you, Boss? I mean, I know you are, but I . . . I can make it up to you."

"Nothing to make up, Punk." Rufus slapped his hand on the bin's lid once more, and dust rose. "He lives and can talk, and has something to offer of use, then you are spared. He don't then you are . . . well, let's us cross that bridge when we get to it, okay?"

Punk swallowed and nodded, not quite knowing if he should speak, pray, or run.

"Funny, ain't it, Punk? Your future depending on this here slave. Might be you want to crawl right in there with him and kiss his black ass."

Punk's eyes grew wider at the thought of tangling with that man one more time. That black man was tiger-mean and snarly and quick with a fist and not afraid to use his own head for a battering ram, neither. Punk patted his lumping forehead, then his similarly bruised cheekbone. He didn't dare touch his nose, that thing had taken a thrashing worse than the rest of his head. He knew it was busted, maybe mashed beyond use.

He was still a little liquored up from the hooch he'd sampled to round off the sharp edges of the beating, elsewise he would be hurting a whole lot worse right now. Punk expected when the whiskey wore off, which it always did, that whistling sound his nose was making would be matched up with throbbing pains he might not be able to bear.

He sometimes wished he was in heaven. Punk nearly smiled, thinking of his idea of heaven — a bottle of booze that never emptied. Like that story in the Bible he recalled hearing when he was a kid.

"You listening to me, boy?" Punk opened

his eyes and the boss's jowly face was right in front of his own, those nasty wet lips looking like they was fixing to bite him or kiss him. Neither possibility made Punk happy.

"Yes, sir," he said. Though he couldn't remember what it was the fat boss had been telling him. Something about the slave saving his ass?

"Good, then let's hear what this fella has to say for himself." Turlington rested his hand on the grain bin and raised the lid a pinch. "You ready?" He was smiling.

"Yes, sir, ready as I'll ever be. So, you know, he's tiger-mean."

"Okay, then. You best get yourself ready to tackle him. In case he shucked his ties. And no shooting, don't want to draw attention. Besides, I have conjured me an idea that will please the boss man of the Brotherhood, the other boss man, that is, and it will require this here darkie to be alive and not full of holes."

The colonel lifted the grain bin's lid all the way. The rusted steel hinges squawked, rattling Punk's nerves something awful. Punk jumped.

Chapter Thirty-One:
Starting at the Bottom

Sue stood in the middle of the dank storage room in the brick basement of the Pinkerton building in Chicago. The oil lamp made the gloomy place worse than full darkness. Shadows twitched and jumped in the dim glow each time she held it aloft to look at her new surroundings. *So, this is what prison must feel like,* she thought. Her mind flashed briefly on the hellish time in Deadwood, before Rafe saved her, when she was Al Swearengen's personal drugged slave.

Sue breathed deeply, letting out the breath with finality. Her life now was measured along that very precise line, before Rafe and after Rafe. Would there be a time when it was with Rafe? She did not know. In truth, she wasn't certain that's what she really wanted. But she knew he wasn't ready for such a commitment with anyone, maybe never would be. She also knew she had to get out into the world and prove to herself she didn't need anyone other than herself anymore. And that had led her to the Pinkerton Agency.

Sue hadn't really figured out what she might do should she not get hired there. She assumed she would get hired — and she did.

She hadn't really thought she would start with her own case to solve, but she had hoped for something more challenging than cleaning up after the rest of the staff.

"Well, best get to it, Sue," she told herself, as she set down the lamp and thumbed the wheel. The war had been unkind to so many archives, these included. Not that from the looks of things they'd ever gone in for tidying up the place. And that was now her job. It was as if Allan Pinkerton had been waiting for her to appear.

She took note of the tall shelves housing sloppy stacks of papers, maps, several non-paper items, but those were in part why she was hired. Told to hoe out the files, keep interns busy while at the same time, if one of the agency's remembered cases from the previous years had reached the term limit, so to speak, Sue had been instructed to bundle it up for the incinerator.

"If you aren't certain what to do, opt for making room. You saw the office," said Mr.

Pinkerton. "It's become unbearably cramped. We need to get the most recent files out of there and stored in the archive shelves."

Thinking back on that unusual conversation, Sue should have sensed that throwing away files was a poor way to run a business. She moved to the nearest stack, laid a hand on the top, felt the paper, and sighed, despite her effort to maintain her resolve. All she had to do was plow ahead and make sure she impressed the man in charge.

She lifted the file, opened it, and held it close to her face. The paper smelled musty, but it was covered with tiny, tight writing, as if the person were cautious but concerned with not wasting paper. The script betrayed that notion with its jags, sharp points, and hastily dotted and crossed letters.

Whoever wrote this seemed to Sue as though they were in a hurry, perhaps because what they were writing was fascinating, perhaps because they were in danger of being caught. Sue smiled at herself: *look at me, making up tales. I sound like Cookie.*

Still, she slid an oak keg closer to the lamp and sat down. If she was supposed to use her best judgment, hadn't she ought to assess each file? What if in her haste to please her employer she tossed away a file that might prove of some future importance?

Despite her hopes that the file she had selected would turn out to be filled with salacious or bold acts of amazing courage and fortitude, recreated for the page, the file instead was little more than a poorly spelled, boringly rendered account of justification of one employee's expenses. From nine years before. The man's name had been Granville Borden. Even his name was snoozy.

Sue set it aside as the first in what she suspected was about to become a tall stack of boring reports. And for two hours she encountered file after file, report after report. She became dozy reading facts about towns, railroads, horse breeds, weapons, and figures pertaining largely to budgets, tallies of expenses accrued by operatives. It was, she decided, soul-deadening work.

She stood, regarding the steadily growing stack of files, loose papers, and curled sheets filled with neatly written figures, all destined for the incinerator. She heard her bones protest at the sudden movement, felt her legs throbbing from the long session of sitting, and for a sliver of a moment decided she would have been better off staying at the ranch, helping Arlene.

No! She shook her head, that was no way

to think, no way to stand on her own, no way to prove to the world, to Rafe, and to her father, that she was a modern woman, a singular and proud woman who could blaze her own road. And to prove it, she was going to pull this storage room into shape, far better than it ever had been. Then Mr. Pinkerton would see she was no laggard but a person, an . . . operative . . . who knew how to get things done.

She snatched the next file, the first she'd seen that bore a green covering — no matter — and smacked it on the stack to be discarded. There, it felt good to be so decisive, so in control.

She reached for the next file. But her eye caught the soft glow of the lamp's light on the green folder she'd set down.

Her shoulders slumped. There was no way around it — she had to read it, knew then that she would have to peruse each file, each scrap of paper, each note scribbled on train ticket stubs, on playing cards, on pages torn from books, in case they contained something important. How she would know if it was important was something she had not yet figured out, but she knew it would come to her. It had to.

But from what she had found so far, there was no importance to any of these files. Why would there be? It was a storage room that nothing good had been relegated to. She was being kept busy until some other distasteful task could be found for her.

In addition to its peculiar green coloring, unlike the other files, it bore no name, no brief description on the front page, faded green. Then she opened it and read the first words on the page. She bent her eyes closer to the script in bold black ink, printed in blocky letters, not in flowing cursive hand. And the one word there at the top in the middle held her gaze and made her heart beat a pinch harder, faster. It read: "Confidential." And centered under it, "A. Pinkerton Only."

What would it hurt to peek? Sue dragged her teeth across her bottom lip. No, she shouldn't. It must have inadvertently made its way down here. There would be some mistake behind the file being here amid all these old stacks of useless papers. But hadn't she been told to use her best judgment? Perhaps she should take the file upstairs right then and there and hand it to Mr. Pinkerton himself. Would he think she was admirable for being trustworthy and careful? No, he would think her a silly girl. After all, she reasoned, aren't being curious and taking chances two of the top requirements of being a detective?

Sue breathed out, licked her thumb, and slid the top sheet over. And was promptly faced with a blank sheet of paper.

She turned that page over and this time saw a page filled with writing not unlike the previous boring pages she'd been reading. She bent close to it, and rotated the brass wheel on the lamp, raising the wick and brightening the room. That was better. She didn't have to squint to read the type. And what she read at the top of the page quickened her pulse once more.

"Disrupted: Plot to Terminate." Sue's eyebrows rose. This sounded promising. The second line read: "the Following Individuals"; then a third line read: "for Posing a Threat to Pro-Slavery Forces."

A list of names in three neat columns filled the rest of the page. Perhaps thirty names in all. It became obvious the names were listed alphabetically by last name. The first, in the far left column, read: "Alphonse Aaron"; beneath that: "Raymond Andrewson." The third: "Rafe Barr."

Sue stopped reading, her blood chilling in her veins. She read the name again. Yes, it was Rafe's name. None other. In fact, she highly doubted there were any other Rafe Barrs out there. She trailed her index finger down the list, but the last name on the page ended at "H." She flipped the page over and found the second name she expected to find, "C. McGee," halfway down the third column, to the far right of the page. Had to be Cookie.

She flipped back to the first page, reread Rafe's name, then back to C. McGee, as if seeing them might confirm whatever suspicions were beginning to bubble in her mind. She flipped through the rest of the list, but saw no names she recognized.

Then she came to another blank page, flipped that, and once more was faced with a page of tightly written script. "The preceding names are those of U.S. Government Operatives and various associates, not all men, it should be noted, who were targeted for assassination by the now-defunct firm based out of Savannah, Georgia, operating under the name of Phoenix Shipping. More than half of the 196 names it will be noted bear the letter 'x' beside them."

Sue had barely taken note of that fact, but she flipped back through the pages of listed names and sure enough many of them did have a small, slight "x" preceding them. She flipped back to the page she'd been reading, scanning to find her place once more.

"Those bearing the 'x' were successfully

targeted by Phoenix Shipping, a now-known pro-slavery collective of wealthy southern gentlemen whose mutually beneficial interests led them to form said collective for the sole purpose of eradicating anything and anyone that might prove an impediment to their cause, namely preventing the eradication of slavery.

"It is my considered opinion, as well as that of the Secret Panel composed of various senators, judges, and highly placed merchants, that those individuals left alive by the end of the war would have little to fear from the defeated and disbanded dummy organization operating under the name of Phoenix Shipping. This case largely consisting of monitoring the progress of Phoenix Shipping's eradication of those named on the list. My own organization was ordered to monitor and behave in a hands-off manner, allowing the individuals to proceed with their various directives. Any interference by my own operatives would have been a breach of Official U.S. Government Policy. I am pleased to say we did our utmost to follow that directive and at the same time were able to provide information that assisted in the eventual disruption of the organization known as Phoenix Shipping."

Below that was signed, "A. Pinkerton."

Sue realized she'd been holding her breath. She let it out and breathed deeply. What did all this mean? She was unsure, but . . . surely this information might be of use to Rafe and perhaps to Cookie, too.

Yes, he would know, he was approachable. She would take it to Cookie. *And . . . what, Sue?* she asked herself. *What is it you plan on doing? Rushing up to Cookie and then Rafe, wherever he may be, and offering him stale information nearly ten years old, about an organization that, for all she knew, Rafe was largely responsible for removing from power?* She shook her head.

It all bore more thought than she could muster, but she knew one thing was certain: There was no way she was going to incinerate that file. Seeing Rafe's name and Cookie's, too, if he was indeed the "C. McGee" listed — and who else could it be? — gave her a warm jolt of familiarity she'd not felt since she arrived in Chicago.

CHAPTER THIRTY-TWO: TALK OF THE TOWN

"What's all this kerfuffle, then?" Cookie stood in his stirrups and surveyed the crowded scene before them.

"Looks like something's going on at the train station. Maybe a dignitary."

"Bah." Cookie spat. "Likely one of them politicians. A more useless breed you'll not find. And that's all I'm going to say on the matter!" He raised a long finger. "Spent enough valuable air on those rascals."

"You done?" Rafe puffed on his cigar. "Because we have things to do in Santa Fe and they don't involve politicians. At least I hope not."

"See? You agree with me."

Rafe puffed, nodded, then heeled the buckskin into a lope. "Can't say I don't."

"What's that mean?" Cookie's eyebrows pulled together like two caterpillars squaring off. "Hey, wait up."

As they rode into town, Rafe halted his

horse and nodded at a Mexican boy. "Que pasa, amigo?"

The boy smiled and took off his bristle-rimmed straw hat and held it like a bowl up before his chest. "El Presidente." The boy nodded in the direction of the crowd.

Rafe leaned forward, hands folded on his saddle horn as leather creaked. "Of Mexico?"

The boy shook his head, a stern expression replacing his smile of moments before. "No, no, señor." He nodded once more toward the throng. "Grant! Of the States!"

Rafe squinted in the same direction. Behind him Cookie said, "See? See? Politicians, showing up where you want 'em the least. Ain't that about something . . ."

The big man stuffed the cigar into his mouth, fished in his breast pocket, and flipped a coin into the boy's hat. "Gracias, amigo."

"Gracias, señor! Gracias, gracias!" He legged it between two sand-colored adobe huts, his bare feet slapping the hard-packed alleyway.

"It's generous souls like you that make it hard on frugal folks such as me to make it in this world without ladling out heaping handfuls of coins to every waif that comes begging along my path!"

270

"Frugal?" said Rafe, smiling. "More like scrimy." Before Cookie could cackle in response, Rafe said, "Let's get going, find Jack. Something's off and I don't like it that Grant's here at the same time."

"Well at least we agree about that," said Cookie, nudging Stinky in line with Rafe's buckskin.

"Yeah, but not for the same reasons," said the big man, eyeing the growing crowd as they rode forward.

"What are we looking for, besides Jack?"

"I'm not sure, so we should —"

"Look at everything all at once?"

"Yep."

"Figured so." Cookie nibbled his lower lip, then said, "I also been doing some figuring. Figure we might get more honey with vinegar than bees might like."

Rafe reined up, turning a confused stare at Cookie. "What in the hell did that mean?"

"What I said it did."

Rafe continued staring. A slow smile cracked his face and he clucked his horse forward. "I suspect you meant to say, 'We'll get more flies with honey than vinegar,' eh, Cook?"

"That's what I said, dagnabbitall!"

Rafe lit a cigar stub, and didn't look at his friend again for a moment.

Cookie said, "What I was getting at was we might want to consider dolling up in fancy duds, pretend we're gamblers, see if we can't get a fix on what's become of Jack. Could be he's holed up with gambling fever!" He licked his thumb. "Why, I recall a fella I knowed back on the Snake, above them treacherous falls, you know the ones I mean? Kilt more critters, four- and two-legged, than any fusillade you ever did see in the war."

"Who? The man or the falls?"

"Ain't you listening? Man or the falls, why I ought to box your ears for being thick."

"What's the upshot of this, Cookie? I have to get to a haberdasher and get fitted out for fancy duds if I'm going to infiltrate the poker palace."

"Don't you never mind about that. I still have my attorney-at-law togs rolled up in my traps." He patted the bulging sacks bouncing on Stinky's rump. "I'll mosey on in there, make like I'm a high-falutin' rancher come to inspect the doings."

Rafe blew a cloud of smoke. "Well, that would be about right, you being co-owner of the ranch and all."

Cookie puffed up his bony chest and nodded. "Hey now, that's right enough. And what's more, I am here on the scout, legit too. Protecting my investment, so to speak."

"True enough," nodded Rafe. "Jack is a trusted employee."

"Yep," said Cookie. "And he happens to have my life savings with him, too."

Rafe's eyebrows rose but he said nothing. He was hardly in a position to criticize his old pard for trusting a friend with money. For all his faults, Cookie had always been a prudent saver of cash. Rafe, on the other hand, had always done his level best to help out those who needed it by lending whatever money he felt he could afford at the time. The only time he'd invested in himself had been the ranch, with Maria. He bit down hard, flexing his jaw muscles, biting back the memory, a hard thing to do.

"While you're busy hobnobbing with the bigwigs, I'll scout around, see if I can come up with some trace of him on my own."

Cookie nodded. "Let's find us a stable close by the gambling hall — once we learn where the tournament's being held, that way I can change my clothes and slick up my hair."

"You bring scented toilet water for your hair — what's left of it?"

"What?"

"You heard me," said Rafe, taking care to keep him and his horse ahead of Cookie and his flailing wrath. "You might want to keep it down, you're attracting attention." He nodded toward the sidewalk where a woman hugged two little boys close to her skirts and regarded Cookie as if he'd blasphemed in church.

"Uptight lot here, ain't they?"

A quick question of a cowboy loafing out front of a saloon and they learned of the venue hosting the tournament. A half-hour later found them unsaddling their hangdog mounts in a stable further from the Santa Fe Grand than they would have liked, but the town was thrumming, like a midsummer beehive, with activity.

"Surely it's not all because of the tournament," said Rafe to the stableman, an old Mexican who walked as if he'd been kicked in the knees a time or three by ornery boarders of his establishment.

"Sí. Maybe no," he winked and went back to helping them arrange their saddles and blankets on the worn racks.

"What's that mean, fella?" Cookie squinted at the man, then sent a thin stream of chaw spittle into the straw at his feet.

"I theenk better when my pockets jingle, eh?" The Mexican smiled, revealing a nearly full set of teeth the color of brown river silt after a rain.

Cookie rolled his eyes. "Fella, you think we need an answer to that friendly question?"

Despite Cookie's groans of disapproval, Rafe handed over a coin. "What else do you think is going on in town this week? Anything unusual?"

The stableman's smile widened as the coin touched his callused palm, and it disappeared in a clenched hand as if to prevent it from running off. "I never see so many gringos in fancy clothes. And the buggies! Oh, I see them roll by, but they never put up here. Always with the fancy hotels where they stay. Me, I am a poor stable keeper, that is all."

"Hold on there," said Cookie, pulling out a faded blue bandanna. "Let me wipe away these tears."

"Cook." Rafe smirked at his friend, then turned back to the Mexican. "Any of these men say anything to you? What makes you think they're not here for the poker tournament?"

"Oh, I theenk they are here for that, all right, but they bring lots of others with them, and others, characters who scare away business, you know? They arrive later, after the gambling has begun. And now the great U.S. President Grant! These are big days

275

for us here in Santa Fe. But I can't figure out why." He shrugged and, muttering to himself, still clutching his coin, he shuffled in his painful-looking bent-kneed gait, back toward his quarters off the side of the eight-stall stable.

"There," said Cookie. "Feel better about spending your money? He told us next to nothing."

"Not so," said Rafe. "We learned that even the most humble of the town sense a change in the air. Couple that with an unexpected visit by the President, who we know is an aficionado of the pasteboards, and then top it off with Jack's odd telegram, you have more than we had before we rode in."

Cookie snorted, rummaging in his sack for his rolled-up suit. "I'd say not. Ain't nothing more than a feeling he had anyway."

Rafe crossed his arms and leaned against the wide-open frame of the big double doors, and watched the people roll, walk, ride, and run by, raising dust as they headed toward the depot, the gleam of excitement on their faces.

"Sometimes a feeling is enough, Cookie."

"Yeah, I reckon," said the older man, dancing on one foot as he tugged off his broke-down stovepipe boots. "Me, I'd rather have a glass of cold beer and a plate of Miss

Tewksbury's hot buttered biscuits."

Rafe turned around. "Cook, before you head on into the lion's den, something occurs to me . . . it's likely Santa Fe is filling up with folks who might recognize us."

Cookie stopped straightening his oddly tied cravat and eyed Rafe. "How do you mean? Like long-lost relations or some such? 'Cause I ain't got but one or two cousins, leastwise that I know of, and they're back East somewhere, no doubt hopping around some city wearing foofaraw like this damned monkey suit!" He clutched at the necktie, jerking it.

"Let me help you with that," said Rafe, hiding a grin. "No, I mean more like folks from the war, folks we fought against." He looked at Cookie sharply. "Folks who bought and sold people."

"Oh, that Phoenix mess, eh? I reckoned that's what ol' Jack was getting at in his note. Now that you bring it up, I have noticed a fair number of folks with deep-South accents. Didn't think on it much, passed it off as a gas bubble and moved on. Shoulda trusted my gut, eh?"

"Something like that. I'm not saying they're here or that it's anything more than coincidence —"

"But it'd be a mighty big one, eh? Rascals,

277

I hoped we'd wiped out that nest of them back in Savannah. Too good to be true. Should know better." Cookie stood straight, his shoulders popping and snapping with the effort. "How do I look?"

"Like a sack full of gold coins," said Rafe.

"I guess that's a compliment. I'll think on it some." He headed for the stable door.

"Um, Cook?"

"Yeah, Rafe."

"You sure you're going to need that dynamite?" He nodded toward the barely concealed specialty holster.

"Man can't never tell, can he?" Cookie winked and stepped outside.

Any confidence Cookie McGee had talked himself into believing he had leaked out as he set foot in the foyer of the vast and impressive foyer of the Santa Fe Grand. He didn't have to guess if he'd found the venue hosting the tournament. All about him stood gleaming brass kiosks sporting signs in bold and flowing script telling which rounds were currently in play, how many folks had thus far dropped out of play, and how big the stakes were. Cookie offered up a low whistle and shook his head on turning and taking in the gaming floor through the wide, propped-open glass doors. "Ain't

278

that about somethin' . . ."

"Yes, yes, it is," said a thick southern voice from behind him.

Cookie spun, eyes narrowed.

"I don't recognize you, sir," said the man, a jowl-faced fellow with pink cheeks and a light gray suit, a big belly, and a gold watch chain dangling off the face of the belly.

"Me, neither."

"Allow me to introduce myself," said the strange fat man, slowly edging around so that he stood between Cookie and the doors leading to the gaming floor. "I am Colonel Rufus Turlington the Second." He extended a pink puffy hand. "And you are?"

Cookie faltered and shoved a hand outward. Turlington! That was one of the men they'd nabbed at the docks during that night raid! But how could he be here? And so young? The years, in Cookie's experience, weren't kind to anyone. Not that kind, anyway.

The fat man grabbed tight and mashed down on Cookie's fingers. "I am in charge of this little fiesta." His smile sharpened and he pulled on Cookie's hand and leaned forward at the same time. "You look familiar, sir. Do I know you?"

Cookie was about to say the same thing when it popped into his head that it might not be wise to mention a thing about the past. At least not to someone who favored mightily a man Cookie had had a hand in apprehending years before.

Well I'll be, thought Cookie. *So Rafe was right.* Not that he was much surprised, Rafe was rarely wrong. Phoenix Shipping. But they'd all either died or been locked up, or so Cookie thought. Until now.

He reached for his hat to snug down low but found he'd gone topper-free. He dipped his bald head, hoping to hide further recognition. "Nope, your face don't ring any bells, mister. Me, I'm passing through."

"No, no, that's not it. I swear I've seen your face before. Memphis? Birmingham?"

Cookie managed to pry his hand from the death grip of the fat man's hand and backed away a couple of steps. "No, I ain't been in none of those places, wasn't me." He did his best to look anywhere but at the fat man's probing eyes.

"Savannah?" The fat man said it slowly, ignoring Cookie's protestations.

That jostled Cookie's apple cart, and his eyes widened as he backed further. "I'm here looking for a friend. Heard tell he was in the tournament. Don't see him, so I'll be moseying."

"Not so fast, sir." Turlington laid a fat

hand on Cookie's shoulder. Cookie wanted to sink his teeth into that plump hand and drive a quick couple of rounds into the balloon of a gut. He restrained himself — for the time being.

"Perhaps I may be of help to you. Tell me who your friend is and I'll see if I can't track him down for you, eh?"

"Naw, naw, thanks, all the same. He ain't here." Cookie jerked his shoulder and wriggled free of the fat man's grasp. He hotfooted it for the door, mumbling to himself all the while. "Didn't even make it through the big doors, some detecting type I am."

Cookie made his way toward the train depot where folks were gathered in hopes of catching a glimpse of President Grant. He didn't get far when he saw a sideshow of sorts attracting increasing attention. Voices, mostly those of men, were gabbling and barking, and a throng looked to be gathered around a fight of some sort.

"Uh oh," he said, stopping as he recognized the familiar fawn-colored hat jutting above the others in the crowd. "Rafe, you big galoot, what have you gotten yourself into now?"

Cookie made straight for the melee,

weaseling his way between tight-packed spectators. " 'Scuse me, pardon, 'scuse me . . . aw, hell, get outta my way!"

Within seconds he popped into the midst of a lopsided fight between a fatigued-looking Rafe Barr and three bluecoats. They were close by a fancy train car with gilt filigree around the many windows, and fancy painted eagles and United States flags adorned the flat sides of the long car.

Cookie took his place beside Rafe, bony fists extended in a jaunty pugilistic pose. Rafe looked down. "What took you so long?" He grinned and drove a quick jab at a burly red-faced, red-haired man.

"Oh, you know," said Cookie, sizing up the other two officers, "takin' in the sights." He darted in and landed a hard punch to the already-bleeding nose of one of the men. The crowd cheered.

"By the way, Rafe, what's all this about?"

Rafe danced to one side, feinted, and delivered a crushing shot to the red-faced man's breadbasket. "This is the thanks I get for trying to warn Grant and his boys that something bad's in the air."

"Oh, I see," said Cookie, not quite avoiding a blow that glanced off his shiny temple. "Might want to work on your diplomacy skills, you big lunk."

"I told you," sneered the red-faced man in a thick Irish accent. "We don't need to be told how to do our jobs. Now off with you."

"Confident, ain't he?" said Cookie.

"Yeah, well," said Rafe. "He talked with his fist, then his mouth."

Rafe lunged forward, and his ham-size fist smeared the Irishman's already-mangled nose, and blood sprayed upward. The man staggered back and Rafe turned to see if he could lend a hand to Cookie, who faced two attackers to his one.

There's only so far you can push any man. *But a man like Cookie,* thought Rafe as he watched his friend windmill and crowhop and carom off the heads of his foes, *takes a lot less pushing than most folks.*

As he had been through his many long years of friendship with Cookie McGee, Rafe was amazed at the pistol-crack dynamo of a man, and pleased he wasn't on the receiving end of Cookie's ire.

Then a gouged leather boot sole slammed Rafe's cheekbone, tolling bells and popping his vision with bursts of light as though he were listening to the chiming tower of an old Mexican church. He felt himself slump to his knees, and heard thuds and groans behind him. The Irishman had struck faster than he thought possible.

"Boy! You got to jump back into the fracas, elsewise we'll be sunk before we float!"

Cookie's voice cut through the clamoring bells. He was right. Rafe shook his head as if to rid himself of a foul thought and growled. Any more knocks like that and he might as well hang up his spurs and settle into a rocker on the front porch. Might happen one of these days, but not yet.

Rafe's vision cleared and he pushed to his feet, his sightlines watery and jumpy, as if he were watching the horizon shimmer at midday in the desert. He saw the leering red face of the Irishman grinning at him as that man, too, gathered his wits and made to meet Rafe head on.

Must be the man had fallen over after he kicked Rafe. Good, that meant Rafe had landed a solid, dizzying blow that affected more than the man's mashed nose.

"Sure, now you're the biggest man I seen since we arrived in this nasty little blister of a town, aren't you?"

It wasn't so much a question as a statement, the Irishman talking to himself. Rafe pulled his fist back. He wished he had a dollar for each Irishman who yammered when he could have spent the time and effort throwing a punch instead. This one, despite the hardscrabble edge about him, was no different.

"Rogues!" he heard Cookie shout, his teeth set in a tight grim smile. Rafe could tell the old buck was enjoying himself.

"I'm endangering you because I'm addled," shouted Rafe, setting his stance in a classic pugilistic pose. "Not fair to you."

"Pish posh," said Cookie. "You let me do the worrying, you ninny. Now throw a final beating on that Irish bastard before I do the same to you." Cookie grinned and toed the skinny little man at his feet.

Rafe wasn't certain how Cookie did it, but he was able to lay low dozens of contenders over the years with little more than sheer grit, clenched teeth, wiry reflexes, and knuckled hands.

At his own feet, in a sodden pile, the begrimed fat Irishman moaned and one eyelid flickered. Rafe leaned down and looked at one side and then the other, as if selecting a muffin from a platter full, and drove another fist at the man's face. The Irishman would not come around for some time.

"Now," said Rafe, rubbing his knuckles and looking around. "Enough of these interruptions. It's time to find Jack."

The entire fight had taken but a couple of minutes, long enough for the law to be alerted. The last thing he needed was to raise the dander of yet another lawdog in yet another city.

"We best skedaddle, son," said Cookie, nodding toward four bluecoats descending the steps at the end of the fancy train car. They were in no obvious hurry, as if they'd seen all this before.

Rafe threaded his way through the crowd, behind Cookie. "It won't pay to wait around and explain things to them — likely we'd get tossed in a cell for our troubles."

CHAPTER THIRTY-THREE: THE COMPANY WE KEEP

Early in his journey, Talbot Timmons concurred that the trek from Yuma to Santa Fe could not have been more trying. The train was a mild improvement over the slogging of mile after mile on horseback, or worse, wedged into a crowded stagecoach with a handful of unwashed, leering passengers, most of whom should be locked up.

At least the swaying rhythm of the train, though jarring at times when it really set to clacking on a harsh curve or steep grade, provided a modicum of relief from the concerns clogging his brain, as events of late had bloomed into a garden of outright headaches.

To make it a thousand times worse, Timmons was accompanied by Turk Mincher, a more frightening man he'd never known. And that was no small consideration, given that he was warden of the most notorious prison in the western United States. Timmons sniffed back the preposterous thought that there existed elsewhere a facility more daunting to fresh-faced felons or more soul-grinding to seasoned residents. No sir, Timmons prided himself on his harsh, though effective, tactics.

The man seated across from him in the otherwise private compartment of the swaying, pounding clack-clack-clacking train seemed to know whenever Timmons sneaked a look at him. Or maybe Mincher had spent the entire trip so far staring at him, hence the lack of surprise.

"Look like you had yourself a thought, Warden. A thought that almost caused you to smile. Could that be right? 'Cause you don't strike me as the sort of man who smiles willy-nilly."

"Mr. Mincher, I don't know what you speak of, but I assure you, if you are intimating I lack a sense of humor, you don't know me in the least."

"Don't get your knickers in a bunch, Warden. I was only funning you. What say you tell me what it is you expect of me yonder in Santa Fe. I like to be prepared for whatever may befall me. You understand, it being business and all."

"I do understand, especially as it is, as you so rightfully put it, a business proposition. However, as I mentioned before, I will not divulge my plan to you or anyone before it is time to do so."

"When do you reckon it will be time?"

Timmons beamed a full smile and shook his head. "Not soon, Mincher."

Mincher matched the smile with one of his own, leaned back in his seat, and tipped his low-crown black hat down over his eyes. "Right then. I expect I have a minute to spare for a pinch of shuteye. When I come around, remind me to tell you about the fella that one time, one time, mind you, was so stubborn about cutting loose with information I required, why . . ." Mincher shifted the matchstick he had been chewing to the corner of his mouth, and said no more.

Timmons couldn't help himself. He had to know. "What happened to him, Mincher?"

Turk poked a long finger up, raising the brim of his hat enough for Timmons to see the man's eyes. "Why, Warden, let's say he raised my ire." Down went the hat.

Timmons's smile drooped away and he felt a distinct tightening between his temples, behind his eyes. From experience, he knew the feeling was not about to go away any time soon. Why had he ever suggested Mincher come along, why had he said he needed his help in Santa Fe? If that blasted Rufus Turlington had any sense about him, Timmons wouldn't have had to make the trip himself.

Hell, if Feeney hadn't allowed himself to get killed by Mincher, the man seated across from him, why, Timmons might still be in Yuma sipping bourbon. But no, Turlington was as incompetent as his dear old dead daddy, Rufus Sr., was reliable and trust-worthy. At least in that case, unfortunately, the son turned out nothing like the father.

CHAPTER THIRTY-FOUR:
WE MEET AGAIN

Following the fracas at the train station, the men made their way back to the stable where Cookie exchanged his fancy suit for his daily garb. They saddled up and spent two fruitless hours searching for their gambling compadre, Jack.

"I got to wet my whistle, Rafe, or I won't be worth a hill of beans. How about a glass of cold beer?"

Rafe shrugged, too tired and sore to disagree. He'd spent a good many hours in the saddle over the past week with precious little to show for it save for a tall stack of bruises, a ringing head, and an aching back. He imagined the buckskin felt much the same.

Rafe caught himself mentally licking his wounds and shook it off. He looked over at Cookie and, despite the dark cloud that seemed to stick with them lately, could not help but smile at his irrepressible friend.

The older of the two jerked his chin. "Let's try over near that Mexican market we passed on our way in. You know, up on the north edge where you gave away all that cash to the waif."

Rafe ignored the good-natured dig. "Fine with me." Five minutes more found them riding up on it.

Cookie reined up. "Well would you look at that odd pair of fellas yonder." He punctuated his statement by letting loose with a sloppy rope of tobacco spittle. He'd been streaking his chin all morning, blaming southern tobacco for being too "loose in its ways."

Rafe was unsure what that meant, but Cookie had been reluctant to give it anything but his best effort, and had chewed with vigor. Each man dismounted and lashed reins around a hitch rail.

The big man looked over the saddle of his horse in the direction Cookie had jerked his chin, and there stood Knifer and Plug. His head still twinged, a dull reminder of the Denver episode. Not only did his zeal for tracking his wife and son's killer cloud his sight, but he'd allowed himself to be caught, clubbed, and thrown in jail. He was now burdened with yet another crime. *And I could do worse,* he thought, *than to pin the blame on those two.*

He eyed the odd pair again, noting their appropriate names, given the bandolier of blades the tall man wore across his thin chest, and the crude knob of a man beside him, the sawed-off shredder held casually in the crook of one tiny arm, snout angled at the chewed porch floor.

A low groan of recognition and menace, like that of an angry bull, curled up out of Rafe's broad chest. His big hands gripped the saddle horn and cantle tight enough that the knuckles whitened.

Cookie lost all interest in his vociferous chewing as he watched the transformation slide down Rafe's face. His own eyes widened. "You know them fellas, I take it?"

Rafe nodded, not taking his eyes from the pair. "Denver."

"Oh, them." Cookie narrowed his eyes. "So, we about to mix it up with them, then?"

A nod and a low-voiced grunt in reply from the big man.

Cookie pushed the loose wad of chaw from his mouth, drooled out the last of the brown chaw juice, and said, "Then let's get to it."

Rafe finally looked at him. "Me, not you. I owe them."

"Two of them, one of you? Them odds

won't do, leastwise not while Cookie Mc-Gee's kicking. You never really told me all of what they did."

"It's what they didn't do . . . yet."

"Huh?"

Rafe's hand trailed out of instinct down to the Colt hanging low on his right side. "They told me they knew something about someone who knew something I need to know."

"Oh," said Cookie nodding, then scrunching his eyes and shrugging. He watched the two men, who didn't seem to be in any hurry. They leaned against the old log length that served as an upright holding up the ramada roof. Even from their distance of fifty feet away, Cookie saw that the post was polished smooth as a baby's backside — as were most of the posts holding up porch roofs fronting saloons all over the West — by the leaning shoulders of countless loafers.

"What's the plan, then?" Cookie looked over at Rafe.

"I'm going to come up on them from behind." He tugged the brim of his fawn hat low.

"What'll I do?" said Cookie.

"Distract them."

"How am I supposed to do that? Maybe

with a conjuring trick?" Cookie's craggy face took on a grim look, as if he were biting down on a pebble. "Sure, ol' Cookie will fire up a stage program right there in the street, that's what he'll do."

Rafe's voice offered the thinnest trace of humor. "You'll think of something, Cook. Always do."

Despite his flare of fluster, Cookie smiled at the offhanded compliment. He could have taken it any of several ways, but to him it was a mark of friendship that Rafe didn't fawn over a man such as Cookie, a man whose many skills were such that he could be trusted in most any situation. He turned once more to Rafe, but the big man had already begun moving off to his right, his long legs carrying him at a steady clip, singular intent driving them.

"Hey now," said Cookie, patting his own provisions. His modified dynamite holster was loaded with sticks, and his skinning knife swung at his left side. Neither would do much good. The boom-boom sticks would take out a pile of architecture, not to mention it would likely kill the two men Rafe wanted to chat with.

And if he unsheathed his big pigsticker, those two hard nuts were like as not to peel him open with slugs or knives of their own, depending on which man acted first. Cookie had a feeling a duo like that was well practiced in such undertakings.

He shrugged and, passing between Rafe's buckskin and Stinky, made straight for the two men. "In for a penny," he said, a phrase he'd heard Rafe utter a lot lately. It was a sweet saying Rafe's wife, Maria, had used — though always with a smile — long years before.

"Think of something," muttered Cookie as he crossed the dusty street. "Sheesh. What if I can't? What then?" That thought slowed his pace until he was nearly stopped.

"Get out of the road, you fool!" The words were followed with the sharp crack of a drover's whip snapping the air above the crown of Cookie's battered topper. The rooster of a man immediately spun, hands balled into bony fists, challenge setting his face into a hard sneer.

"You hop down off'n that seat and we'll settle this has once and for all!" Truthfully, Cookie could barely see the man's face around the two hulking oxen staring down at him. The sun's afternoon glare, wreathing the driver's head, didn't help matters.

"Bah! Fool, I say!" the driver snapped the whip once more, cracking it as if he were taking a bug out of flight, once more above

Cookie's head. But this time the oxen plodded forward, cutting around the riled coot.

Cookie was about to hop aboard the slow-moving wagon and trounce the devil out of that driver when laughter from the side of the street stayed him in his tracks. One thing worse than being called a fool was being taken for one. He spun toward the guffaws and saw it was the two men he'd been on his way to confront in the first place. He quick-stepped on over, a long, bony finger, like the prow on a schooner, leading the way.

"You two think that's funny? Man almost gets hisself run down by crazed, savage beasts right there in the street, and you two . . . whatever you two are, stand there loafing and laughing, as if you ain't got a care in the world!"

"We don't, old-timer!"

Cookie regarded the speaker, the tall man with the knives hanging off him like ornaments on a general's chest.

"Waiting on a señorita to bring us our glasses of beer whilst we take in the scenery. And what do we see? An old man wandering around in the middle of a busy street, looking confused as all get-out. Why, I don't know about you, Plug, but I'd say we was richly rewarded for our efforts." The tall man looked down at the midget by his side.

His short companion showed a mouthful of rank, stubby teeth.

They looked like a set of chaw-stained horse choppers to Cookie, and the sight of the little leering man startled him.

It was at that moment that a familiar face appeared behind the two men, looming down at their slouched forms. Cookie raised his finger high once more and recommenced his cackling, his words further inspiring a swirl of high dudgeon and righteous wrath in himself. He enjoyed cursing out everything from the low morals of the day's horrible parents to the offensive and foul behavior of the two men before him.

It worked — their eyes widened as he proceeded to call them every name he could dredge from his many years roving the trails. He even tossed in a number of words that, to his recollection, weren't words at all. But they sounded good. And offensive. His rant had the desired effect of keeping their attention on him while Rafe did whatever it was Rafe intended.

Turns out it couldn't have been any simpler. The two leaning men pushed upright, intending to make for the wiry old rooster of a man berating them. Before they took a step, Rafe spread his arms wide, one

298

high, one low, and clapped the outer sides of their faces hard inward, his big hands covering the sides of their faces like massive spiders.

The force slammed their heads into the stout post, thudding hard enough to send a tight, dull bell-tone up the post, which Cookie took great satisfaction in hearing.

Their bodies stiffened as they rebounded off the post. Their eyes widened in shock, and their mouths sagged as if they'd sampled too many hot chiles.

"Remember me?" growled Rafe behind them, though they were past hearing anything other than the clanging of church bells in their swelling heads. As they sagged to the porch floor Rafe clapped their heads into the post once more, for good measure. Then he let them slump and crumple.

"Whoo-eee!" Cookie clapped his own hands together and spun in a quick jig, ignoring the stares the proceedings had attracted. Luckily it was midafternoon and the street outside the cantina was sparsely populated. Even at that, those who witnessed the bizarre moment wisely chose to turn their attentions back to the last of the warm beer in their glasses.

"Now what?" said Cookie, once he'd gotten the jigging out of his system and landed a couple of quick toe kicks to the ribs of each of his tormentors.

"Now we drag their sorry hides to the alley in case the law decides to wander on by."

Cookie bent low and laid the shotgun across the short man's gut, then muckled onto the midget's shoulders and followed Rafe as he dragged the tall man, one-handed, along the porch toward the side of the building.

"You really think," Cookie grunted and tugged, "that lawdogs'll be making their rounds in the Mexican quarter during the day? Hell, I can't imagine they put much effort into such matters on a shoot-em-up Saturday night."

"Way my luck has run lately, the cavalry will ride on up, led by General Sherman and Moses himself."

"Can't argue that, boy. Trouble tracks you like stunk on a skunk."

"Thanks, Cookie. I don't know what I'd do without your words of wisdom."

They made it to the angled shade of the alleyway. "You'd be a poorer fella, that much I can tell you, you whelp. Now I got to stop a minute. This little man might not look like much, but he's solid. Wouldn't surprise me if he had bricks in his pockets.

Now, you gonna tell me what it is these boys did to you?"

"You remember Denver?" Rafe grabbed the taller of the two unconscious men once more by the back of his coat collar and recommenced dragging him down the alley.

"Oh, I see now. Those two you told me about. Hmm, no wonder you wanted to get the drop on them from behind. Say, that means you stuck me with coming at them from the front, like a man fool enough to walk up on a nest of newly woke pit vipers and wave his hands in their faces. Why, I'm lucky I still have my wits about me!"

"Who says you do?"

"What? Why you . . .'"

CHAPTER THIRTY-FIVE: EVEN THE BEST OF PLANS

Colonel Rufus Turlington sucked back the last of the mouthful of bourbon he'd been sloshing around his teeth, a habit he'd gotten into years before, after a big meal. He poured himself another couple of fingers of the fiery whiskey — a follow-up drink was yet another habit he'd gotten into of late. Especially since money worries had become money woes.

"What to do, what to do?" he muttered to himself. He knew he had to make this situation into something shiny instead of the dirt mound it had become. But how?

What would Daddy do? He knew how to take care of everything. First thing he would have done, Rufus told himself as he sipped, is to not have spent money that wasn't his. Somehow he had gobbled up all the money Daddy had left him. Most of it ran like water through his damnable fat hands. He held up one pudgy appendage and stared at it through a glassy haze. Yep, right on the green table, hand after hand of cards, chip after chip, until he found himself signing away the deed on his ancestral home.

That there was his low point. He'd had enough of a winning streak after that — plus he'd sobered up for a couple of rounds, that he was able to win back the lion's share of it. He doubted there had ever been a man alive who had sweated bullets like he had.

Then he'd had his brightest shining moment. Talbot Timmons, one of Daddy's oldest acquaintances.

It was nearly a year since he had sat right up in bed, Mala beside him, snoring those soft lady snores like they do — he had marveled that even black women snored like that — when he'd awakened out of a cold-sweat dream, all boozed up in the head, cotton in the mouth, and said, "I got it. I got it."

She'd sat up, said, "What's that?" But he had no time to explain, especially not to her. That day one of Daddy's oldest acquaintances, Talbot Timmons, was in town (nobody could ever say they were friends with that worrisome creature, after all. Who could be a genuine friend to a head jailer of a place like Yuma?) and wanted him to attend a meeting to reform Phoenix Shipping, to act on his daddy's interests. Rufus could not have been prouder. He'd celebrated that night, too. But as he fell asleep, his thoughts grew darker. Ain't no way Timmons truly wanted him there. Man was too smart for that.

That weasel of a warden wanted something from him. Not sure what. But Rufus knew that was the sort of fellow Timmons was. Never something for nothing. Not like Daddy, rest his soul, he was a generous man. Brought Timmons in during the war, he did. Set him up, even got him that job in Yuma. That was the rumor, anyways.

That night, though, Turlington's dark thoughts curled and slicked and slid around each other like a rope of thick snakes until they filled his mind with doubts.

Have to show them Phoenix Shipping boys a thing or three, she'd said. Least he thought it was her. Had to be. Was a woman's voice in his ear. Must have been talking in his sleep about all his worries. She was good for that, anyway. Listening to him, murmuring little words of encouragement. Meant she was good at two things.

Rufus poured himself another drink. It was nearly time, after all that planning. They were plans Timmons actually seemed impressed by, plans Timmons told him he should make happen. They were plans for little poker tournaments leading to the big one. It was Timmons who said they should make the tournament in Santa Fe a big splash, big enough to lure the damnable Yankee president down there so they could make an example of him. It would be a bold-as-all-get-out coming-out party.

It was true that the previous year hadn't gone as he expected. He'd had to make all manner of excuses to Timmons and the others about why he needed money from all of them to set the thing up. But they hadn't balked much — it was a mutual business deal, after all.

While he explained it, he tried his level best to sound like Daddy. And wonder of wonders, they'd all sent him money — the amounts he'd requested, no less! All he had to do was follow through with setting up the biggest poker tournament the world had ever seen — a weeklong event. At least that's the way he had told them all it was going to be.

Timmons said he would take care of luring President Grant there. Said he knew people who knew people. New Orleans had been the top choice of everyone on the council, but Timmons didn't think the President would be as excited to go there.

Likely Grant was too fearful, thought Rufus. So, they'd settled on Santa Fe, a spot the President might find more acceptable as it was more western than southern.

It was Rufus who had insisted, before the entirety of the revived Brotherhood, that he be allowed to hire the men who would remove Grant from office, forever. Rufus saw his insistence had riled Timmons, and he was glad of it. Then Rufus was surprised even more when Timmons reluctantly agreed. Only after the meeting disbanded did Rufus wonder how in the hell he was going to find someone depraved and desperate enough to kill the President. As luck would have it, not two weeks after the meeting he found himself in Denver on business.

He stopped off at the Tivoli Club to hoist a mug with his old pal, Soapy Smith. He expressed his latest woe, without mentioning the potential victim's name, naturally, to Soapy, who smiled and snapped a finger. "Got the two perfect men for the job. A sicker pair you'll not find, but they're reliable as a good pocket watch."

"Who are they? How do I find them?" said Turlington.

"Well now, Colonel. If I was to tell you that, why I'd be out of business in no time at all."

Rufus nodded. "I see. How much, then?"

And that's how Colonel Rufus Turlington the Second, came to hire Knifer and Plug.

His other big task was to locate a Santa Fe venue to host the event. Of course, he had to see to it personally. And while he was there he figured he'd judge the state of play in that town, something he'd not personally done before. While he was there he set up an office and promptly began to make a mess of things.

He hadn't meant to dip into that stack of money he'd been loaned for the purposes of setting up the event. But he had. And the year went on and on and he got poorer and poorer. Good thing Punk was so stupid, he worked for little more than promise and whiskey. It rankled Rufus that he had to pick up Punk's whore tab more often than not, but then again it was cheap enough to have a brute like Punk do his bidding.

This damnable week of poker couldn't have come any sooner. Rufus was strapped, putting every expense he could muster on the cuff, splashing out for all manner of goods and services. He had done his best to show the other members of the council, all of whom had made the trip to town, that he had everything under control.

Still, they had their doubts, and they

weren't afraid to give voice to them. Bastards. Ungrateful bastards. But this newest idea, a lynching, a genuine good, old-fashioned lynching, now that was a stroke of genius. Rufus only wished he had more than one such stroke of genius a year. He figured he'd need one a week at least, if only to climb out of the hole he'd dug for himself.

He tipped his glass up, all the way, and drained it down. His other hand reached for the neck of the bottle he'd been working on — and found it stone empty. "Damn my luck."

"You can say that again, Colonel."

Turlington turned and standing in the doorway was none other than Warden Talbot Timmons himself. And behind him, a man he'd never seen before. A man in a black hat, blood-red shirt, and black vest and trousers, smoking a cigarette, and with that deadeye stare that reminded him of every one of those dark nightmares he'd been having all year long. Reminded him of all those black snakes in all those black dreams, thick as muscled arms, all twisted together and flexing and devilish and so very frightening.

Colonel Rufus Turlington swallowed back a hard knot of something awful and couldn't think of a word to say.

CHAPTER THIRTY-SIX: FIRE IN THE HOLE!

Cookie came to in a cold, dark place. Felt as though his mouth was packed tight with cotton ticking. He ran a thick tongue around his teeth and gums, and parted his lips — they were dry, and his bottom lip split when he parted his mouth and tried to speak. He grimaced and gave it another go. "Rafe?"

His voice was a hoarse wheeze, barely a whisper. What had happened to him? Cookie's burr-covered mind struggled to recall how he had ended up in this bizarre place, feeling as he did. He reached a trembling left hand off his lap. It slipped down past his leg as if lifeless. Dizziness and the quick rise of bile up his throat told him he was about to throw up.

He ached all over his body, and if it was possible, he ached beyond his body. His muscles and bones and teeth and hair and ears and eyes all felt as though some giant creature had grabbed him up in its hands and twisted him, wrung him out like a wet rag. Felt about as dry, too.

Hot needles tickled his left palm. It seemed to take all the effort he could muster to raise the hand again. But he did it and dropped it back to his lap. None of this made any sense. And if he let his hand drop like that again he was going to lose whatever might be in his belly. He sat propped against something, maybe a wall, in the dark. After a moment, the queasy feeling simmered, then something else crept in — a smell, familiar somehow, though faint. But it was comforting. At once he knew the scent — horse. No, more than that. It was horse and hay, maybe a whiff of dung, too. He was in a stable, had to be. But why so blasted dark?

He tested his voice again, but the result was little better than his first effort. Time to get serious, he told himself. I can breathe, that much is plain, or I wouldn't be sitting here in the dark feeling sick and addle-headed.

If I was dead, I'd be feeling . . . well, nothing. Maybe like I was in the midst of a five-day toot, all light and feathery and happy. Might be I'd be hearing harps or pretty singing from ladies with wings and fancy glowing rings above their heads. Halos, that's what they are. No, I doubt I'm dead. Besides, the way I've lived, not so certain there's a place for me up in the clouds.

The thought gripped his innards like a coal-hot hand. What if this was death? What if this was the hellish place? Pictures of flames and walls of shimmering heat worse than the Llano Estacado ever was forced his eyes wide in the dark. *No, no, Cookie,* he thought. *If that was your situation, you'd not be smelling horse nor hay nor dung.*

His wide eyes probed left and right and were rewarded with a thread of something that wasn't black. Had to be light, then! He tried to sit up, to push himself away from whatever it was he lay propped against. Fresh bile bubbled up his throat, pushed through his mouth, and sprayed up and out his mouth and nose. It stung his nostrils and his eyes teared with the stink and the effort and the needle-like pain of it.

He leaned back, his chest heaving, trying to spit whatever it was flecking his lips. Another wave of the funk bubbled up and out, then a third. On and on and Cookie could do nothing save retch, his body not under his control. This was not something he'd ever felt. Sure, he'd been ill of a morning following a night or three of bottle-diving. But not like this, never like this.

After what seemed hours, the convulsive squeezings in his gut and throat slowed, then stopped. He didn't dare move lest a fresh volley of gags and stink kick off again. Long minutes passed and Cookie's breathing leveled. He swallowed, poking his tongue once more out of his mouth slowly, like a desert mouse peeking out of its burrow scanning for snakes. No retching threatened. He did his best to feel his lips with his tongue. They were dry, cracked, tasted awful from the gut troubles. But he noticed something new . . . he felt better than he had before he threw up all over himself.

He wasn't about to shout "whoopee," but he was as pleased as the situation allowed. He also felt his thoughts clearing. And with that sensation, flickering memories of what had happened the day before — could have been the week or month before, he had no way of knowing — trickled, then flooded, in.

Dim at first, but then he recalled . . . Rafe had had to go do something — something he'd learned rummaging in the coat pocket of that tall, ratty-face bastard, Knifer. A telegram? No, a note, a letter, that was it. Rafe had read it, his face got all tight, and Cookie felt sure he was going to powder his teeth, Rafe ground his jaw muscles so tight.

"What is it, boy? What's it say?"

Rafe didn't look up right away. He read the note, then reread it, folded it carefully, and tucked it into his cigar pocket. "I have something to do, something to attend to. I'll be back as soon as I can. You keep an eye on these two. If they come around, keep a double-eye on them. They're slippery and dangerous."

Cookie read the hard look on his pard's face, knew enough not to question him. If Rafe Barr had something to do, and asked you to help him, you did it and you'd get the story later. Once the dust settled. So far in their days riding the trail together, the dust had always settled. Cookie knew there would be a time when it wouldn't. No man ever knows when that day would come, though.

"Git off with ya, you big lummox. I've tended my share of sons-of-bitches before. You do what you need to and get on back here. We'll wake them up then and you can get all the information from them you want."

"I have a good start," said Rafe, patting the pocket with the note and heading for the stable door.

Cookie watched him leave, and muttered under his breath, "Crazy fool, goin' to get

313

himself kilt one of these days. And I'll be right there with him. Ha!"

Cookie's very next thought brought the full horror of his plight gushing back into his mind.

"Those bastards," muttered Cookie. "They poisoned me! Poisoned me and left me to die." That would account for the all-over ache of his body — for he recalled the nightmarish agonies his body had been put through as the poison they'd dosed him with raked through him. Oh, God, never was there a feeling like that. He'd felt deep and bitter hatred for a small number of folks along his life's path, but he'd not wish this poison pain on a single one of them. Even the worst of them.

Except for the two weasels who did this to him, that is. For he was now recalling the full and foul situation: the entire grim scene when those two, the ones he and Rafe had got the drop on, the ones who called themselves Knifer and Plug, had spun the table on him and laid him low.

Knifer nodded at Plug. "Haul out that little bottle. Let's give him a dose."

The little man grunted.

"Grant? Don't you worry about him. Plenty to go 'round."

Cookie wasn't certain what all this meant, but he didn't like the sounds of it, nor the fact that these two not only had the upper hand, but seemed to be taking pleasure in something. And pleasure to these pigs could only be bad for him.

Knifer snatched a small green glass bottle with a cork stopper from Plug's tiny hand. He stepped over to Cookie, straddled him, and laid a long hand across Cookie's forehead, forcing his head back. "Open up!"

Cookie jerked his head left, right, growled and cursed, and kept his mouth closed tight. He didn't know what was in that bottle, but it couldn't be anything healthful.

They struggled like that for half a minute, Plug standing off to the side, giggling and rubbing the side of his head.

Knifer stood, the little bottle clutched in one hand, and with the other pointed a long, dirty finger down at Cookie. "You'll drink it, damn your hide!" The tall man sneered, his tobacco-stained lips set tight in a toothless pucker.

"Breathe on somebody else, you jackass." Cookie considered working up a gob of spit and launching it at the man's homely face.

"No, huh?" Knifer jerked his head at his compadre. Plug, his foul face worse with each passing second, purple lumps swelling one side, grinned and scooted behind Cookie. The cantankerous old rooster felt the little man's clawlike hand grapple onto his jaw and jam his head hard backward.

Cookie struggled, trying to whip his head to either side, but Plug's grip was too powerful and he could only stare upward at the little man's hideous face.

Cookie kept his teeth and lips jammed together tight but the smiling Plug shook his head. "Nah, nah," he said, and with his free hand pinched Cookie's nostrils tight. Cookie struggled, but ropes bound his hands and legs in a tight, knotted cocoon. Knifer bent low over him once more, this time jamming a knee against Cookie's chest, and held up the little bottle.

"Somebody's about to get himself a big surprise."

Cookie gagged and writhed, then cracked open the corner of his mouth and pulled in air.

"Oh come on, dammit, old man! I got things to do, people to kill!" Knifer drove a hard quick fist into Cookie's gut and Cookie gasped. As soon as his mouth opened, Knifer upended the little bottle and dumped its glugging contents into Cookie's mouth.

Cookie spluttered and sprayed it and tried to force whatever it was — tasted like cat piss churned up with scrapings from the bottom of a doctor's leather bag — out of his mouth. But Plug jammed harder on his chin and wrenched his nose. Reflex gained the upper hand and he swallowed. That was all it took.

Almost immediately he felt something like hot branches from a campfire jammed down his throat, only to be met with hundreds of needles of ice racing up from his guts. They collided and whatever had taken over his body was off to the races. The odd sensations lasted but a moment. Then his entire body went numb like a hammerstruck thumb.

Claws of a dozen wildcats raked him left and right, all from the inside. Foam bubbled up out of his mouth, something that felt like tears or sweat or blood ran from his nose, and he was barely aware of the little man and Knifer staring down at him.

Never in all his days had Cookie felt such mounting agony. It was the worst pain he could ever imagine, and it grew worse with each second that passed.

His body thrashed and whipsawed left, right, over and over; even though he was bound, wrapped tight, somehow his thrashing loosened the ropes. Soon one arm was freed and he clawed at himself, at the stable floor, at the air, anything, but nothing helped. Then as soon as it began, his body slammed to a stop as if he'd been dropped from a cliff down onto a massive boulder far below. But that was the only thing that stopped — the pain kept on. Cookie heard a thread of sound, a scream forced through a pinhole. It was him, howling in agony but making thin noise.

His eyes were hot coals, pushing their way out of his head, doing their best to leave the place they'd sat for all these years, his tongue jutted, rigid like a stick, and his fingers and toes stiffened at the ends of plank-stiff limbs.

"Best grab my rope off him," Knifer said to Plug. "A'fore he commences to thrashing again." He wiped his hands on his trousers. "That bastard won't need rope — nor much of anything — where he's headed."

The little man made a strangled, garbled sound.

Knifer laughed and shook his head. "You say you'd piss on him but you don't believe you have it in you yet? Plug, you are a cold sumbitch, you know that?"

Cookie had heard them talking but with each second that passed he made out fewer and fewer words. Instead, odd moaning sounds came at him as if bellowed through long colored tubes. What light there was in the stable flickered and blinked like starlight through wind-tossed trees. And then everything had grown worse. Much worse.

CHAPTER THIRTY-SEVEN: GUESS WHO'S IN TOWN?

As he strode with purpose behind the buildings that lined the long front street, Rafe barely recalled anything he'd said to Cookie. Didn't matter. Cookie was reliable, he'd be able to keep a lid on those two simmering fools if they woke up before he got back, with a better idea of what to do with them. In the meantime, he'd seen something — one name — on the letter he pulled from Knifer's pocket.

Rafe patted his own breast pocket as if to remind himself the letter was still there. The action reminded him of his cigars and almost without thought he plucked a half-smoked cigar from the same pocket and thumbed alight a match. He drew on the squat brown nub, rolling it and coaxing a glowing head to life. The thick blue smoke was satisfying and calmed him. He still felt twitchy from seeing the two bastards who'd lied to him in Denver, then left him for dead

— or at least to take the fall for the bank robbery. And it had worked.

Cookie saved his backside then and he reckoned the old buzzard was doing it now, too. He'd have to repay him somehow, somewhere down the line. He owed Cook much — the very least was his life, but all that would have to wait. He had far more urgent matters, as Cookie would say, to cogitate on. The man latched onto a new word and rode it hard every time, and was not afraid in the least of misusing it.

But seeing those two men, a pair of men he had not expected to see again, was shock enough. And had to be nothing short of co-incidence, hadn't it? Certainly the world was a big place, the West only slightly smaller — or so it seemed, so vast was it. But what drew them down here? He hadn't intended to hammer their heads so hard. It would be some time before they came around enough to be of use to him.

But it was the name, or rather the title, of someone mentioned in the letter that cinched the top of the sack tight for Rafe. Timmons. The one and only warden of Yuma. Of course, he had been referred to only as "warden," but how many others with connections to anything with the name of Phoenix attached could there be? Rafe hoped for the world's sake there was only the one of them.

The letter had been sent by a Colonel Rufus Turlington the Second. In it, he'd said a mutual acquaintance, referred to in the brief letter only as "the warden," had recommended their services to him. The sender's name was familiar to him, though Rafe recalled it had been the man's father, of the same name, he and Cookie had helped expose during the war. The Phoenix Shipping affair . . .

He didn't have any clear idea of where to go, but he knew he needed to scare up some answers. And sitting there in the unused stable with Cookie, waiting for those two fools to come around, didn't hold much appeal. If only Jack had been there. There was too much about this escapade that was unsettled. It left him feeling as if he wasn't thinking hard enough, as if something big was about to happen, but for the life of him he couldn't make heads nor tails of the signs.

Jack's cryptic telegram was baffling — and worrisome — enough.

PHOENIX ABOUT TO RISE IN SANTA FE STOP USG DUE SOON STOP SURPRISE

PLANNED STOP COME QUICK STOP JACK

Rafe could recite it word for word at this point. The only Phoenix he was aware of had been that slaving front thriving even while the war was going on. But he and Cookie — with the help of a couple other operatives — had foiled that mess. Or so he thought.

Now Timmons was, likely, in the letter he'd found on Knifer. And given that Jack was a black man in the very lap of rich white southern men, playing their game — and if he knew Jack he was playing it far better than any of them combined, and riling them up because of it — that didn't bode well for the dandified ex-slave.

CHAPTER THIRTY-EIGHT: THE MORE THINGS CHANGE

Jack awoke to banging sounds. "What the . . . ?" That's when all that befell him the previous day tumbled into his mind like a brick wall collapsing. Hot pains stitched up his bum leg. He gritted his teeth and stifled a groan.

"Ah, I see you're awake, Mr. Gambler Man. Good, good."

The voice came to Jack through the watery waves of pain that crashed in on him as he tried to focus his vision.

"You wasn't so slow and lazy, you'd see you're not alone in your plight."

Jack grunted, working harder to open his eyes. He heard a whimper, a woman's voice, and knew who it was before he could get those blasted eyelids up. Mala. He said her name. Or tried to. Nothing but a croaking sound. He locked his lips, and tried again. Her name came out as a whisper. "Mala?"

Another whimper, then, "Jack . . . is that you?"

"Yeh." Seemed to take all his strength to push out that word. He felt something collide with him, collapse on top of him. The pain was brutal, and threatened to smother his senses once more. It was the cry of pain from someone else, Mala, had to be, that kept him from going under once more.

"There, now you two want to be together, suit yourselves. Me, I got work to do."

With that, Jack heard a wooden clunk, and felt a whoosh as what he guessed was a door slammed shut, heavy steps retreating. Then silence.

"Jack?" Mala's voice was little more than a whisper. "Jack, what's going on? Are you okay?"

He grunted again, tried to speak, and managed to say, "Okay, Mala."

She shifted and that's when he felt her weight on him. There went the pain again, so intense, shooting up and down his entire body as if he were being dragged through blazing coals in a smithy's forge. He groaned, clenched his teeth, breathing sharp, hard, fast. It seemed to help. She shifted again and managed to get off of him.

"Jack, what's wrong? What have they done to you?"

"Leg, my bad leg . . ."

"I get my hands untied I'll help you."

"Mala . . . you okay?"

"Jack, stop talking. Save your strength. Give me a second." She growled in frustration. "I can't get my hands untied."

"Mala, Mala, stop." He breathed heavily, swallowing. "Listen to me, where are we? What's going on?"

"It's Rufus, Jack. He's gone crazy. I . . . I think he's going to kill us. I have to get untied, get you out of here."

"Shh . . . I think he's coming back."

Mala stopped struggling and they both listened. It wasn't the heavy footsteps they'd heard before, but it was a loud, cracking sound. They both held their breath, wondering what the sound was. Then, without warning, the lid of the feed bin was yanked upward and bright light sliced in on them. They both squinted, looking up at the leering face of Punk Clements, then Colonel Turlington appeared beside him. They both stared down at Jack and Mala. The colonel chuckled and Punk followed with a giggle, as if given permission.

"See, what we got in store for you two is more than a quick stop at the end of a short rope." The fat man rubbed his hands together. "You two animals are —"

Mala sniffed, then spat up at him.

A drip of spittle clung to Turlington's left jowl, slowly dripping. All four of the participants, Jack, Mala, Turlington, and Punk, were quiet for a moment, then the fat man sucked a sharp breath through his rubbery lips and tight-set teeth and dragged a yellowed handkerchief over his cheek.

"You little hussy. After all I've done for you? And here I am about to bestow on you the greatest honor a little tramp like you could ever hope to gain in life?" He turned to Punk. "Bah, why do I bother?"

The underling shrugged and giggled.

"Get back to work, damn you. I want the rest of those planks stripped clean off the upper half of this barn so nothing's left but the carcass. We want everyone to see what the Brotherhood of the Phoenix can grow on its twisty vines. And it's a fruit like no other, I'm here to tell you. One that will send a mighty message to anyone who cares to think about it."

"You like to hear yourself talk, Colonel?" Jack forced the words out, trying not to let the pain he was feeling crawl up onto his face. It didn't work.

Over the banging and cracking of planking being stripped off the beams of the stable, Turlington laughed. "Something like that, fella. By the way, you look terrible. Sort of like you been all beat to hell and put away mad." He chuckled again.

"Rufus, what is it you want? What are you going to do with us? I don't know what you think is going on between me and Jack, but you're wrong."

Turlington held up a fat hand. "Don't want to hear any more of your lies, woman. You think I'm stupid?"

She snorted.

Turlington's eyes narrowed, but he continued. "I knowed from the second you caught sight of each other at the tournament that you'd met before. Hell, I don't know much about your breed, could be you took a likin' to each other right then and there. I don't know, but I tell you what, I ain't one to put up with such shenanigans.

"Then you start a-pumping me for information about the Brotherhood. I thought at first it was because you was interested in my business, then this one gets caught snooping in my affairs and I put the pieces together all right."

"You figured all that out by yourself?" Jack forced a smile and a sad headshake.

"Shut up. Ol' Colonel Turlington's gonna have the last laugh, and . . ." He tugged on his watch chain, popping the face of the timepiece open. "Oh, it won't be long now." He clicked it shut and shouted, "Punk, hurry up with them last boards. I got things to do and I need you down here to make certain this here grain bin with our special guests stays good and locked 'til I come back. You got me, boy?"

"Yes, sir. Nearly through, though why you want me to peel perfectly good planking off'n this here barn is a mystery."

"That's why you're an idiot and I'm head of the Brotherhood." Turlington looked back to his captives. "Let you in on a little secret, you two. This here?" He jerked his head backward as if he'd taken a pop to the chin. "This here's all for you. Oh, and one other person you'll be sharing the stage with. He ain't black, but he's a lover of such as yourselves."

"Thought you were, too, Rufus." Mala tried to keep her voice firm, but it shook with rage.

"Oh, we had some fun, girl. But that's all it ever was going to be. Something warm and nice now and again. But as my pap always said, 'Dung seeks its own level.' You think on that some, you hussy, while you gaze on this!" Turlington flung a fat arm wide, sweeping at the great bone rack of high beams behind and above him. "What will surely be remembered as the most impressive and unusual scaffolding for multiple hangings you ever will see!"

"What?" Mala bucked and thrashed, slamming into Jack in the confines of the wooden feed bin. "You . . . Rufus, you can't be serious! After all this time . . . Rufus?" Her breath stuttered in and out.

"Now, now, my dear," said the fat man as a wide smile crawled across his fleshy face. "I know what you're thinking — why here? Why not build a proper scaffold in the plaza? I'll let you in on a secret. Just now, the Brotherhood is trying to keep its doings under lock and key, so to speak. But this old barn? Right beside the plaza? Oh yes, I saw the possibilities. So ideal in so many ways. The unveiling will be grand, though. I assure you. Trust me!"

He yanked on the lid of the bin and swung it downward once more. "And you'll have the best seats in the house! Think of it as the greatest honor of your damned life. Don't think of it as an end, but as a new beginning, a rebirth, if you will, of the Brotherhood of the Phoenix!"

His giggle turned into a chuckle that bloomed into an all-out gut laugh as the lid slammed shut on Mala's screams and Jack's wide eyes and pain-gray face.

CHAPTER THIRTY-NINE: A NEST OF VIPERS

It had been a long time since Rafe had seen so many fat white men garbed in their best frock-coat finery. Six or seven years since, when he and Cookie had infiltrated the dockside offices of Phoenix Shipping in Savannah. That had been a quick fight, and had gone far smoother than he would have liked. In his long experience in such matters, that sometimes was the case. People weren't always on their guard. And that night, even the guards weren't on their guard.

The first, as he recalled, had been asleep, likely from too much wine, which Rafe had smelled with nose-wrinkling displeasure. With each breath out, the guard fortified the sour stink-cloud that surrounded him.

Rafe had had to convince Cookie that dynamite would attract attention and kill innocent dock workers whose only crime may well have been that they were hungry and needed a job. Even if it was working for a hive of murderers and thieves who made a brisk business of buying and selling people, dragging them in chains from all over the world, even as the nation fought to end the trade.

And now, all these years later, the slavers were still around, still squirming toward the light. Rafe bit back the urge to burst in on them, this latest incarnation of Phoenix. He held back. It wouldn't do to get himself punctured like a pin cushion at this early stage of play. He'd feel better if he could find Jack first. Dread like a caged rat gnawed at him. What if he was too late and Jack was . . . ? No, no sense in thinking like that. But where in the hell was Jack?

"Gentlemen." The voice was loud, working to rise above the din of voices. It was also beginning to thicken from drink.

Rafe squinted through the gap in the planking that made up the wall of a back room in what appeared to be an office. On a hunch, he'd followed three portly cigar-smoking men in white suits to this spot and it looked to be paying off.

The vertical boards had been there a long time, and smelled good, a mix of the dry, tobacco-warmth of old piñon leached through with the musty pungence of hay and horse. The room had once been — might still be — used to stable a horse. Now it was outfitted with a crude plank table around which sat cigar-smoking southern men in suits.

Through the gap Rafe saw part of another fat man, no surprise there. This one seemed to think highly of himself, perhaps held a position of high standing in the organization. So far Rafe didn't recognize anyone, but then again, the years can change a person, as he well knew.

"Gentlemen, please, if I may have your attention." The man shifted the too-large cigar to rest between curled, pudgy fingers. He snugged the same fingers on the other hand in his vest watch-pocket, jostling a gold chain that rested against the light gray vest sheathing a pendulous belly.

"I know you are all curious to know when the boss will arrive."

"Don't you mean the President?" This voice came from somewhere to Rafe's left, hidden by boards. Rafe didn't dare to shift, for fear that men might be standing nearby and hear him through the plank wall.

"No," said the fat man with a conjured patience that looked barely controlled. He forced a smile. "Grant? No, he would be the puppet."

"Puppet, eh? Thought that was you," said a rough voice, thick with a southern accent and slow as tired mud. A ripple of chuckles circled the room.

That struck a nerve with the fat man, whose nostrils flared as if he were desperately trying to take in more air. "The boss, as I was saying, will be here tomorrow. He is coming all the way from Yuma for this event."

Rafe's jaw set tight. Timmons, had to be. He willed it to be Timmons. Here in Santa Fe. Tomorrow. Rafe could hardly wait.

"Good," said the slow-voiced speaker, to the far right in Rafe's range of view. "We've all spent enough cash on this elaborate setup. If I for one don't see results, and more to the point feel gold in my hands, this one and this one," the man speaking held up two meaty paws before his own ample gut, palms up, "there's gonna be a heap of trouble and it's all gonna drop on your head, Young Rufus."

"But, but I assured you, all of you —"

The man with the hands shook his head, eyes closed. "Save it for someone who cares, junior. I knowed your daddy a long time and when he passed on and left his seat on the council to you, why I about ate my hat. But I went along with the rest of them, seeing as how a good many of them were whelps of my peers, same as yourself. Figured some of them might know something new about the world, something us old codgers ain't yet learnt. But all I have gained is a hole in my pocket where my money used to set, nice and warm against my baby maker."

Another ripple of laughter trailed around the room.

He held up his hands and continued. "That said, I believe we all have to admit this poker tournament idea, while not all yours, I might add, is shaping up to be a good thing. Especially considering we needed some way to get that slave-loving so-called president down here. But you got us all worried. I expect we'll hold out for another day, until this all is set to come to a head. But after that, though, we best have a big payoff, in both money and in power."

The speaker scanned the quiet assemblage. "The Brotherhood, or whatever you youngsters are calling the council these days, damn well better make good on all the promises you been blowing up my backside like fragrant hickory smoke. If the South don't rise again, you and the other whelps would do best to stay down in the mud with it. And don't even think of taking me with you."

Rufus Turlington bared his teeth, a solid set of choppers nested in the furry pouch of a mouth ringed with poorly tended whiskers and whiskey-wet lips. "While I respect your age and . . . oh, what to call it? Wisdom, shall we say? You have no call to talk to me like that. I have done nothing but my level best for you all, and this is the thanks I get?" He hung his head, turning his empty glass in his pudgy hands. He looked as if he were about to weep at the sad plight foisted on him.

"Yeah, well, we heard you was having trouble controlling that slave girl you been keeping on a short leash. Or have those roles reversed? She got you by the giblets, Young Rufus?"

Giggles all around. Rafe almost sighed. If this is what the council or "Brotherhood" or whatever these fools called themselves got up to in their meetings, it's no wonder the South hadn't struggled up from its deathbed.

Nonetheless, to Rafe the intent was all too clear. This little fat man — whom Rafe surmised was the son of one of the early Phoenix ringleaders, since the name 'Rufus Turlington,' which he read in Knifer's letter, was familiar to him — was on thin ice in his fellows' eyes. But what was this chatter about him having a black woman on a short leash? Rafe assumed that meant she was his mistress. The irony was bitter — Rafe didn't doubt such a thing would be tolerated by this bunch, perhaps even envied as an odd sign of power. But from the tone of the yammering, it seemed the least in a long list of offenses this young fat man had committed.

Rafe got the sense the next day would spell the fat man's success or failure in his fellows' eyes. And to what degree they would celebrate or denigrate him depended on the outcome of the proceedings, likely the poker tournament. That and this business with the President would dictate the fat man's continued position of power or, perhaps, his death.

If these men were anything like the Phoenix Shipping crew, and apparently, a number of them were the offspring of that gaggle, there was little they would not dare do to protect their money. *And that's why I have to punch them low,* thought Rafe. *Right in the wallets.* Suddenly he knew his way in to the problem. Now he had to figure out a way to get out of there without being heard.

Before Rafe could pull back away from the wall, the fat young man, Turlington, unleashed a broad, jowly smile. "I tell you now as I have told you in the past. All is in hand. Do not worry yourselves over nothing. All is under my control and what's more, I have a particular surprise for the boss, and for you all, too."

"What is it this time, Rufus? Slave girls for us all?"

The fellow who said that couldn't have been more than twenty-five, thought Rafe. But already he had the telltale beginnings of a paunch himself. *Born into it,* thought Rafe. The young man leaned back in his chair, smoothing the lapels on his fawn-colored suit, half-smiling at the chuckles his comment drew forth. He continued. "Hell, that ain't nothing. We was all weaned on such things. Impress me, dammit!" He smacked a hand on the table top with such speed even Rafe flinched at the sound.

"Impress you, eh?" The fat man puffed on his cigar, but it had gone out. He regarded the tip a moment with a sneer, then tugged on his smile once more. "All right, then." He took his time looking around the table. "How would you all like to attend a lynching?"

For the first time since Rafe had begun listening in on the odd proceedings, no one said a word, no one coughed, scratched a nose, no one moved.

"What are you on about, boy?" It was the old gent, eyes narrowed and a curious look on his face.

Exactly what I was about to ask, thought Rafe.

"You ain't about to string up your dark piece, are you?"

"Might be I am, might be I ain't," said Turlington, rocking back on his heels, enjoying the moment too much. "Might be she's one half of the proceedings. Might be," his fat lips nursed on his cigar once more, then he remembered and pulled it out with a slight sucking sound. "Might be she got herself caught dallying with a buck of her own kind."

Bells of warning tolled far back in Rafe's mind.

"You ain't man enough for her, eh?" It was the young man. He looked around himself, but none of his fellows paid him any mind. Neither did Turlington.

"Might be he's a stranger, the very one been a burr under our saddles all this livelong week at the tables. Ain't nobody that talented at poker and still be honest. And too damned uppity for his own good! Free man, my ass." The fat man's face widened into a bitter sneer that made him look nastier than he had since Rafe began watching.

And then, as if the fat man read his mind, he seemed to look straight at the crack through which Rafe was watching. Rafe didn't move. Movement is what gives away the prey to the predator. *Keep still, Rafe,* he told himself. Though his thoughts were aswim. Had to be Jack this bastard was talking about.

The fat man's gaze flicked away and he kept talking.

"Tell us more then, Young Rufus."

"All due respect, Montclair, I aim to hold off on announcing anything more until the boss arrives. Don't want to steal his thunder, eh?" He brayed like an overweight donkey, then clapped his hands and said, "Thank you, gents. We'll draw this here meeting to a close. We all have lots to do — some of us more than others!"

Rafe had heard enough. He made his way to the safety of concealment behind a rick of musty hay, a spot from which he could defend himself to either side should he be discovered. He was barely a dozen yards from the back room, but could hear the chortling men as they scraped their chairs and made to vacate their illicit meeting. They had chosen the spot well. Rafe

340

crouched in the shadows, the smell of the dried, brittle hay threatening to incite a sneezing fit in him.

Thinking back on all he had seen and heard, it seemed incredible to Rafe that the collective of buffoons he'd witnessed could choose much of anything useful, let alone cobble together a plan clever and bold enough to lure the President of the United States down to Santa Fe for, of all things, a poker tournament. And yet somehow they had.

Since the President had guards of his own, Rafe's immediate concern was finding the two people who were going to be lynched, one of whom he was fairly certain was Jack. And the thought chilled him deep.

CHAPTER FORTY:
BAD LUCK AND GOOD FRIENDS

Rafe made his way back to the stable at which he'd left Cookie, and paused outside the tight-shut door, listening. No sounds from within. He was hoping he'd hear Cookie verbally abusing their two captives. As eager as Rafe was to get in there and grill the two brutes, something stayed his hand. He waited another five, ten seconds. A dog yipped some streets eastward, someone laughed, closer he heard a basin of water — or worse — dumped out, the splash a quick sound on an otherwise quiet part of the day. Siesta for many folks. Somehow he didn't think Cookie would be indulging in a nap with Knifer and Plug in his charge.

Rafe tugged open the door, keeping to one side and low. He removed his hat and peered in around the door's edge. He saw no one, smelled horse sweat and musty, dry hay, and . . . something else. A bitter tang on the air. Like the drunken leavings that were behind barrooms everywhere. Vomit.

As his eyes adjusted to the darkened interior, Rafe saw no sign of the odd pair of criminals, no sign of Cookie, either.

He scooted low, stuck to the wall and low-walked toward where he'd left them a couple of hours before. His Colt felt reassuring and heavy in his hand, but in uncertain situations, no gun would be enough to make a man feel safe. Only a fool would trust completely in his gun. He squinted away drops of sweat slipping along the creases on his face, sliding into his eyes and stinging.

Then he saw a shape stretched out ten feet away. He walked closer, sensing nothing else in the dim space that shouldn't be there, no quick movements in the shadows of killers about to pounce. Then he saw it was Cookie.

The old codger looked dead. Rafe dove forward, and plowed a furrow with his knee in the dirt floor.

"Cookie!" Rafe shook him. No response. He backhanded his old compadre roughly on the face. "Wake up! Cook — you with me?"

The effect was far more dramatic than Rafe had expected. Finding his chum sprawled out on the hay, stinking of vomit and with the limp look of a freshly killed man, he had expected the worst. But once again Cookie McGee surprised him.

"Why . . ." he coughed and gagged, eyelids fluttered, then his eyes opened and he swung his old meat-hooks, one gnarled hand finding purchase on Rafe's chin. "Who's hitting me? What's going on here?"

Rafe grabbed Cookie's arms and used the man's own thrashing momentum to help raise him to a sitting position. "Easy, Cookie, easy. It's me, Rafe. You okay?"

"Course I ain't okay. Been through it, all right. Through it . . ." His voice trailed off. Rafe smacked him again across the cheek.

"Dammitalltohellanyway!" Cookie growled, trying to edge away from whatever it was that was hitting him.

"Cookie, from the looks of it, you've been poisoned."

"Yes, yes I have, let me at 'em . . ."

Rafe put a hand on Cookie's chest, the stink of bile wafting off his friend. "Cook, can you sit up? Let me help you."

It took a long minute before Cookie was able to lean against the plank stall on his own. Rafe was surprised to find their two horses and gear still there. He would have sworn the two men would have stolen them.

Must be they wanted out of there in such haste. But where was the old Mexican who ran the place?

Rafe almost hated to go exploring. He felt guilty that they'd brought the two men back there. And then he felt worse moments later when he found the old man slumped, his life's juices leaked out. He'd been stabbed too many times to count.

Rafe's first thought was that this would be one more crime he'd need to prove he had no hand in. Except he had, in an odd way.

He sighed and patted the old gent's shoulder. "My apologies, amigo."

Back out in the dark barn, he saddled Horse and Stinky and tied a lead line from Stinky to his saddle. Then he helped Cookie up into his own saddle and climbed up behind him, a tricky feat given that Cookie was nearly useless and ready to slide off the saddle without Rafe's hand steadying him. "You ready to ride?" he said, Horse's reins in one hand, his other wrapped around Cookie's bony midsection.

"Ride, hell, been riding before you were a squallerin' bairn . . . don't you forget it." Cookie's slurred words were reassuring, though they lacked the verve they were most often delivered with.

"Good to hear," said Rafe. "Let's get out

of here and get you some place where you can heal up."

"Don't need healing. Need to get my hands on those two . . ."

Progress was slow as they made their way out of town northward, snailing along back alleys and dusty streets with few people about. Stinky followed without his usual fuss, for which Rafe was grateful.

He kept watch on their surroundings, on every shadowed gap between buildings, but no one jumped them, not much moved, in fact. He led them toward a well-used campsite they'd passed on their way in.

It seemed with each step the horses took, Cookie gained in strength and coherence. His gaze sharpened and focused, and he even groused about the hot sun.

"Could be worse," said Rafe, wondering how he was going to get help for Cookie. Already his mind ticked through his limited options. Being an outlaw had its downsides. Nothing for it, he'd have to get a medical man out there. First, he'd set up Cookie in a campsite, make sure he was comfortable, then he'd ride the short distance back into town and visit an apothecary.

"Hey," said Cookie, startling Rafe, who'd been intent on scouting their backtrail. "That . . . Doc . . . ?"

346

Rafe squinted. "Yep. No other wagon like it."

"Why . . . he here?"

Rafe plucked the stub from his mouth. "Assuaging his guilt, I expect."

"Ass— what?" Cookie shook his head weakly as they rode closer. "That fella. I wish he'd get himself a . . ."

"Get himself a what?" Rafe suppressed a smile. He knew Cookie was about to tip his hand to the fact that he had taken a shine to Arlene and he viewed Doc as an interloper.

"Oh, nothin'," said Cookie. "Nothin' at all."

For the sake of his ears, Rafe chose to keep his mouth shut.

The familiar team of horses was picketed nearby, cropping coarse green growth. It took them mere moments more to locate Doc. The legs of the grizzled inventor poked from beneath the modified wagon. He looked either to be tinkering on his contraption or dead drunk and passed out beneath it. They both hoped it was the former. An inebriated Doc was something they did not need at present.

"Doc?" said Rafe, bending low and peeking beneath the rig.

Cookie wasn't so polite. Still wobbly on

347

his legs, he sagged against the wagon and managed to kick one of Doc's scuffed brogans.

"Huh?"

The legs flailed and caught Cookie in the shin, nearly upending him. Cookie flailed and grabbed the top of the wheel before he fell over.

Doc grunted his paunchy little body out from beneath Ethel's chassis. "Oh, gents. Good to see you. Yes, yes, been hoping to find you. So much to tell you, so much to show you, where do I begin?"

"Doc, what are you doing here?" said Rafe. "It's good to see you and all, but this is no place for you."

"Truth of the matter, gents," said the medical man, thumbing grime in a circle on the lenses of his spectacles and not looking either one in the face, "is I am wracked with guilt. As soon as you left the ranch I stewed in my own juices. It was Arlene, dear woman, who convinced me to bring Ethel to you. So here I am. Brilliant notion from a brilliant woman." He smiled at them both. His smile slipped and he leaned forward, sliding his spectacles down his nose. "Cookie, you look rather rough."

A low, threatening growl rose up from Cookie's throat. "Been poisoned."

"What's done is done, Doc," said Rafe, hoping to head off any unpleasantries sure to bubble up out of his friend's mouth. He eyed the wagon and wondered if maybe his luck was shifting to the good after all. "I'm glad to see you, Doc. As he said, Cookie's ill. I suspect he'll live, but I'm no medical man."

Rafe moved to the rear of the wagon, and rummaged in the chuck box, which thankfully still contained cooking supplies.

"I'll see to Mr. McGee. And be sure to partake of those scones from Arlene," said Doc. Rafe held up a small canvas sack, and Doc nodded, then resumed lifting Cookie's eyelids, swatting away the cantankerous man's feeble hand gestures. "I can tell you something I overheard amongst fellow travelers."

"What did you hear?" said Rafe, chewing away on a scone. He was mighty peckish, though he felt guilty about eating while Cookie looked so awful.

"Hmm . . ." Doc stroked his cheek with a finger, oblivious to the fact he was trailing grease all over his face as he drummed his cheek and chin, and fiddled with his lips. "Anyone . . . Oh," he snapped his fingers. "Yes," he smiled up at them, though how he could see through his grease-smeared spectacles was a mystery.

"Well," said Cookie, one bleary eye fixed on Doc. "You gonna cut loose with your news?"

"Easy now, Cook," said Rafe. Cookie amazed him. He looked like homemade hell but kept at the fight, bobbing his head and forcing his eyes to stay open, like a battered rooster who doesn't know the meaning of defeat.

Doc was still smiling, oblivious to the fact that he'd elevated Cookie's dander to new heights.

"Doc . . ."

"Yes, yes," said Doc. "Well now, let's see." Doc squinted and looked up at the sky as if the answer was written in the dark-streaked clouds.

Cookie growled and Rafe put a hand on his chest, feeling the tension building. "Doc, if you don't speak up soon, winter's liable to be on us."

"Something about a party. No, no, not that. Now let me see . . ." Doc snapped a finger. "Yes, now I recall them saying something about a revival, or a rebirth of some sort. They said riders from town were spreading the word to everyone hereabouts that it's to be a big celebration. It all sounds quite jolly, actually."

Rafe set down the scone he was about to bite into, "Doc, did you say 'rebirth'?"

The begrimed man nodded. "Yes, I'm quite certain that's what they called it. Odd choice of word for a party, come to think of it."

Cookie gazed from Rafe to Doc. "They say what day this party was happening?"

"I believe they meant today. Yes, yes, I'm quite certain of it."

Rafe was already in motion. *Today,* he thought as he stomped up the steps into Ethel, rummaging in the tight quarters, flinging open the gun cabinet. He could have sworn that damned Phoenix fool said tomorrow. Thought he still had time to find Jack.

Rafe snatched up a Winchester carbine, grabbed a box of shells from the neat stack inside, and headed back out the door.

"Did they say where?"

"On a square . . . by a church," said Doc, eyes wide with concern. "Yep — a square by a church, that's it. Why, Rafe? Is something the matter?"

"Rebirth . . . phoenix . . ." said Rafe, unbuckling a saddlebag and stuffing in shells.

"Oh, phoenix!" said Doc, raising a finger as if testing the wind. "Jack mentioned a phoenix in his telegram."

"Yep," said Rafe. "Not a coincidence. And if what I heard comes true, Jack may well be the guest of honor at this party. Now Doc, is this thing in running order?"

The medical man flicked his bottom lip with a finger, lost in thought staring at the wagon.

"Doc! You have to listen now. This is no time for flights of mental fancy, you got me?" Rafe rarely spoke to others in such a hard, clipped manner. Doc, whom he'd known but a short time, had grown accustomed to the big man's even demeanor. So when Rafe barked, he listened.

"Yes, why, yes, Rafe. It got me here and while it's not fully operational in regards to what I have envisioned for —"

"That's fine, Doc. I need you to do two things — doctor some more on Cookie, bring him around. Try that hangover cure you're so fond of. I'm guessing you have the recipe memorized."

The doctor grinned, tapping his temple. "I can do you one better than that, Rafe. I have a bottle of it close at hand — in the chuck box, to be precise. Doesn't do to leave home without it."

"Then dose him up in good shape. I . . . we have to do all we can for him . . ."

Doc patted Rafe's arm. "I know what he means to you, Rafe. To us all. He's a good egg — if cantankerous."

"Cantank . . ." Cookie's right eyelid rose drowsily. "Why I oughtta . . ."

"Cook," Rafe smiled. "Glad to hear you're back among the living."

"Take a damn sight more than those two buzzards . . ." Cookie's voice drifted off even as his eyelids fluttered in protest.

"Let Doc do what he does best. And make it snappy, you two. I need you both with the wagon to get to that plaza."

As he spoke Rafe swung up on the buckskin, hat tugged low, his rifle cradled in the crook of his right arm, twin Colts strapped down on his thighs.

"Wait, Rafe!" Doc waved a hand from the back end of the wagon, rummaging in the chuck box. "How will I find the plaza?"

"Head for the crowd," shouted Rafe, then he sunk his heels and the buckskin thundered townward in a cloud of dust.

"Cookie, my friend," said Doc, plucking a green bottle from a shelf and eyeing the tincture within. He thumbed down the cork stopper and shook it violently, then smiled. "This bottle is nearly as green as you are about to become." He giggled and knelt beside the prostrate form.

Cookie groaned again and forced his eyes open. "Doc? What . . . what're you fixing to do to me?"

"Cure you — though you may not feel that way for some time to come. Keep in mind I am doing this for your own good."

"Then why are you smilin'?"

"I'm not — it's a grimace of sympathy."

"A what?"

Doc propped Cookie's head higher, wadding the folded wool army blanket tight beneath him. He tilted the sick man's head back, pinched his nose, and said, "Open wide!"

The effects of Doc's miracle hangover cure were expeditious. At least to Doc's practiced eye. Barely two minutes after he'd double-dosed the limp little rooster of a man with his tincture, and made darned certain he was out of the way of Cookie's sudden windmilling limbs, Cookie's eyes bulged and his teeth popped open and shut as if he were trying to get a purchase on a particularly tough bite of steak.

"You son of a greenhorn landlubber! You trying to kill me?" Cookie rattled off long, unintelligible strings of words joined by gasps of breath. "Ain't no way that there goop can be good for me!"

"Would you rather have the poison stay inside you?"

"What do you mean? Still in there, ain't it?"

"Not for long," said Doc, counting the moving hand on the face of his pocket watch.

"What's that suppose to . . . oh, God, Doc, something's happening . . ." From a dozen feet away Doc heard the pulsing rumble, rising in pitch and fervency, emanating from Cookie's gut.

"Perhaps a double dose was imprudent." He backed away.

"Doc?" whimpered Cookie, holding a callused hand to his middle.

"To the bushes with you, Cookie McGee!" Doc pointed. "Make haste!"

Cookie ran toward a clot of brambles, crowding close by the base of a cluster of aspen.

"And don't hold back," shouted Doc. "The sooner that poison is out of you, the better. Rafe needs us!"

"Don't worry!" whimpered Cookie from deep within the thicket. "Couldn't hold back if'n I wanted to — neither end. Oh, lordy me . . ."

Doc tried to ignore the commotion and busied himself on the far side of the wagon, tidying and readying Ethel for movement. But, he soon found he had to soothe the horses, so agitated had they become at the sounds — and smells — boiling out of the undergrowth.

"Well, Stinky," said Doc, patting Cookie's little mustang on the shoulder. "I'd say you and your master share the same name," he said with a grimace.

"See here, Doc," said Cookie, emerging from the bushes on wobbly legs. "Untie my horse. I have to ride."

"Not in your condition. You'd best ride in the wagon with me." Even as he said it Doc knew he would have cause to regret the decision. Poor Cookie carried with him a significant whiff of taint. "Do you feel well enough to travel? I sensed urgency on Rafe's part."

Cookie nodded, dragging a shirt sleeve across his trembling mouth. "Ain't come the day yet when Cookie McGee failed to show up for his pards. Let's go . . ." The last word pinched out into a worried "Ohhh," as Cookie spun and bolted once more for the trees.

"Hmm," said Doc. "I always wondered what a double dose would do."

By the time Cookie ambled back, still the color of pea soup but now with a tinge of redness coloring his cheeks and forehead, Doc had Ethel the War Wagon buttoned up, the horses rigged and hitched, and he was crouched in the short side-doorway, one hand holding a cord tied to a ring at the bottom of the three steps. "Hurry, man. No time to waste!"

"I'm a-comin' . . . No thanks to you! Double dose, my foot! Wait till this mess is behind us."

"I'd say in your case at least that's a foregone conclusion." Doc smirked.

"This ain't no time for smartin' off, Doc. All the same to you, I'll ride up front, drive the team out in the open air."

"Nothing doing," said Doc, wagging his hand at Cookie. "You'll note the lines are rigged to run through that narrow horizontal slit, below where the seat resides."

"What? Why?"

"That's what makes it a war wagon, my good man. All will be revealed. As to driving it, I believe I'll start us out and then once you get a feel for things you can take over. Perhaps I can navigate. I fancy myself somewhat of an amateur explorer. Back at university I was known as Intrepid Jones because of my way with a map. I spent hours in the archives, poring over ancient —"

"Doc!"

"Hmm? Yes, Cookie?" He nudged his sliding spectacles back up to the top of his nose.

"Shut yer yapper and close that door afore my gut decides to cut loose again! We got to find Rafe!"

From inside Ethel's belly, Cookie shouted, "I'll be back for you, Stinky!"

CHAPTER FORTY-ONE:
HIGHER, EVER HIGHER

"Where are you taking us?" Mala jerked her body out of Turlington's flaccid grip, but he snatched at her again and held tight as he thrust her into Punk's waiting hands.

"I should think that would be obvious, my dear," he said, jerking his jowls upward. At the top of the steps, skylined against the blue beyond, three fresh nooses swung gently in a breeze.

"Two of us," said Jack, sneering, doing his best to tamp down the hot white pains lancing up his injured leg. "But three neckties," he said.

Turlington plucked the cigar from his pooched lips. "My, but you are an astute one, aren't you? Yes, yes, the third, and dare I say, most important — no offense, mind you — guest of honor should arrive any time now."

As if on cue, a ruckus at the rear doors of the barn swung their heads around. "Ah, there they are now."

In walked three figures, the two most odd flanking a stumbling, portly man. He wore a wool suit of dark gray, with a white shirt beneath a gray vest on which swung a gold watch chain. But the man's head was covered with a grimy feed sack.

Turlington giggled, "Oh, but I am glad to see you two decided to follow through with our plans and brought that criminal into our midst. But really, even though the man deserves exactly what he's soon to receive, a filthy sack such as what you've covered his head with is . . . well, it's a little uncouth, don't you think?"

The shorter of the two newcomers looked up at his partner. The tall man returned the look and shrugged. "I know, I know, Plug. The man thinks he can fill the air with words and everything will take care of itself." He turned his gaze on Turlington. "Now, Colonel, 'afore we turn this one over to you . . ." He kicked the stumbling man in the ankle.

A groan filtered through the dirty bag covering the man's face and the sacking pulled in, pushed out, with each hard breath the prisoner took.

"We need to see the cash, in hard coins. None of that Confederate funny money.

Ain't worth a tinker's fart."

Turlington's eyes narrowed and once more he pulled the cigar from his wet lips. "I told you, when the deed is done, then you will be paid."

"And I told you that me and Plug get paid when we fulfill our end of the deal. And here it is." Knifer jerked on the nearest of his prisoner's bound arms. "Where's my money?"

The midget growled.

"Right, sorry, Plug. Where's *our* money?"

Silence draped over the small scene like a damp washcloth.

A single door opened at the front of the building and a man passed through shadow and walked toward them. The newcomer cleared his voice and stepped into the light. "As amusing as this is, it is a waste of time." Talbot Timmons faced Turlington. "Colonel Rufus, I suggest you pay the man. As exciting as I'm certain you are finding all this foofaraw, it is little more than that. The crowd outside is amassing, your cohorts are waiting impatiently, and I, for one, have many important things to attend to. I suggest you get on with the proceedings with all haste and let the Brotherhood rise . . . before we all die of old age."

"Now see here, Boss, I . . ."

Turlington's brief flame of anger pinched out like a doused sulfur match as Timmons said, "Yes? Do go on, Rufus."

Turlington stuck out his jaw, nodding at Knifer, Plug, and their prisoner once more. "Fine, but I will need to see the goods before I pay you a red damn cent. Take that rag off'n his head."

The two outlaws nudged their limping charge forward. Knifer, still clutching a sizable Bowie knife, reached up with his right hand and grabbed hold of the top of the bag covering the man's head. The hilt of the heavy knife clunked the man hard on the temple. He groaned once more, his head twitching to the side.

"Oops," giggled Knifer.

Plug snorted.

Knifer tugged the sack all the way off the man's head and several of the folks in attendance gasped. That the man was United States President Ulysses S. Grant was in little doubt. But it was the red lumps knotting his face that shocked them.

The man groaned once more, his eyelids fluttering as he lightly shook his head as if to clear his thoughts.

"I won't pay for damaged goods!" Turlington barked.

Quick as a fingersnap, Knifer strode

forward, covering the five yards between him and the colonel. "You will pay, or I will gut-and-nut you right now. Not necessarily in that order, neither."

"Now, now, gentlemen." Timmons smiled.

As sudden as smoke, a thin cowboy in a low-crown black hat, black vest, black pants, and a tied-down gun rig stepped out of the shadows behind the warden. He smoked a quirley and the dim light in the barn flashed briefly off white teeth and a red shirt as he raised his arm to puff his cigarette.

"I am certain, Rufus," said Timmons. "That our guest of honor put up a fight — we know he likes to fight — leaving Knifer and Plug here to do what they felt they had to in order to secure their quarry. Am I right, gentlemen?"

Plug growled low in his throat and nodded, eyes gleaming, lips parted slightly. He shifted his grip on the sawed-off shredder cradled in his right arm.

"You damn straight you're right. Why," Knifer smiled wide, nodding toward Grant, "this son-of-a-bitch needed a good ol' whompin' on account of some of the things he said about us. I ain't never heard such words out of a man's mouth before. And some of them aimed at my sainted mammy, too!" He winked and loosed a gob of phlegm that caromed off the boot of his prisoner. Plug found this amusing and wheezed like a tiny donkey.

"I suggest that my employer here," the stranger in black nodded at Timmons, who puffed up a bit despite himself, "was merely trying to smooth your feathers, eh boys?"

"I knowed I knowed you! You're . . . ."

"Never mind who I am," said the man in black. "You turn over your charge and you'll get paid, right, Warden?"

The warden nodded and turned to Turlington. "Right, Rufus?"

The fat man in turn nodded and rummaged in his pocket. "Never said I wouldn't pay, only want my show to go on as planned."

"*Your* show, Rufus?" said Timmons, one eye cocked and a half-smile threatening.

"Oh, hell, the Brotherhood. All of it."

"Yes, all of it. Now, someone gag our three guests of honor, hood them, and escort them upstairs."

Rufus scowled at Timmons. "I was about to say that." He turned to Punk and said, "Get on it, then! I have to tell you how to do everything?"

CHAPTER FORTY-TWO: NAH, CAN'T BE . . .

Much as he wanted to avoid trouble, Rafe found himself riding straight for it. He'd hoped to find Jack and get the heck out of town before he tempted fate any more than he had. Every lawman and bounty hunter west of St. Louis had to be on the scout for him, especially after not turning Sue Pendleton over to the blackmailing Warden Timmons per their arrangement.

And it was a sure bet there were more hired guns than ever on his trail now that he was an escapee from the marshal's cells in Denver — a man the public viewed as a bank robber who aided thieving killers. He thought back on the mess in the bank and couldn't wait to track down Knifer and Plug. Not only for what they did to him but for trying to kill Cookie. The thought made Rafe bite through the stub of cigar clamped in his teeth.

He was still spitting flecks of soggy tobacco as he slowed up and circled a swelling throng of spectators. They were all gathered around a fountain in a normally busy market section of town, everyone chattering, all with expectant, curious looks on their faces.

It looked to Rafe as if nobody in attendance, himself included, knew quite why they were there. And yet something had drawn them all there — likely Grant's presence in town. Maybe he was going to speechify. Rafe hoped it was as simple as that, but the talk of lynching he'd overheard was worrisome.

He guided Horse to his left, in part to avoid walking into folks at the edges of the milling crowd.

Off to the east side of the plaza stood a two-story barn, the upper reaches of which appeared to have been stripped of planking. A half-dozen new tarpaulins the color of threshed wheat had been draped high, overlapping and secured with hemp ropes. It looked as though the barn was in the final stages of construction and the carpenters had expected rain. But something about it seemed off, odd.

He continued to rove the edges of the crowd, scanning for a sign, any indication that the scant information Doc had given him was true. Snatches of conversation, none useful, filled the air.

". . . said any time now . . ."

"Man told us something big was planned . . ."

". . . you sure it was here?"

"Heard Grant was coming down to the plaza . . ."

"Rebirth? Like a prayer meeting?"

There was that word again, thought Rafe. *These folks all sound as confused as I am, though the mention of Grant made sense.* He would draw a big crowd.

From Rafe's vantage point atop the big, champing buckskin, he did his best to eye every face in the crowd, see if he could pick out someone up to no good, or at least someone who seemed as if they didn't belong. He saw fat dandies, gamblers, he suspected, called out for the same reason everyone else was here — the promise of spectacle.

Then off to his right, at the western edge of the plaza, arranged in a loose three rows, stood a dozen southern gents; he'd know the look anywhere. They wore white suits, gray suits, black suits, all of the finest cloth, string ties, and low-crown hats. Cigars abounded and gold watch chains dangled from the thick curves of not a few round bellies. The men were attended by women balancing parasols on their shoulders.

He recognized many of them from earlier, when he'd been a silent, hidden party to their secret meeting. To a man, Rafe judged them as the leftover holdouts of Phoenix Shipping or Brotherhood or whatever they wanted to call themselves. It wouldn't matter what name they went by, their stock in trade had been the buying and selling of human beings. Their attendance at this mysterious gathering was a telltale sign of bad things about to happen. If he didn't know their secret intentions, he could almost find them laughable.

But nothing about lynchings was joke-worthy. And as the offspring and leftovers of the old guard, the original "council" as they'd called themselves, they were certain to be doubly dangerous. They would be desperate to reclaim vast fortunes lost in the war, they would nurture a hatred of northerners and blacks. And they would pine for what they were certain to feel were the glory days of their lives before the war. They would want the Confederacy to thrive — at any cost.

He'd all but given up hope on anything of note happening with this crowd. Rafe turned the buckskin and began threading his way through the increasingly tight-packed crowd. He reached the far periphery and leaned down, his saddle creaking. Wouldn't hurt to verify what Doc had heard. "Excuse me, ma'am?"

An old Mexican woman, smiling and with wide eyes, turned them reluctantly on him, as if she were afraid she'd miss something.

"What's happening here?"

She reacted as if he'd slapped her. She shook her head. "El Presidente Grant! He comes, sí?"

"Ah, yes, of course, thank you, ma'am. Gracias." Rafe touched his hat bill.

She shook her head at the fool she'd wasted her time on and Rafe felt sufficiently chastened. Maybe this was going to be nothing more than a presidential speech. But then the words "rebirth" and "phoenix" clanged in his head like the peals of a tolling bell. He looked up in time to see movement ripple through the crowd, accompanied a second later by a shout, every person turning and pointing beyond Rafe. Pointing toward the barn shrouded with tarpaulins, or rather the barn that had been shrouded.

As Rafe turned in his saddle, he heard a whooshing sound and saw the mass of tarpaulins and ropes covering the shrouded structure drop away to reveal the hand-hewn, raw-beamed framework of the upper reaches of the two-story barn.

Three nooses of brand-new hempen rope dangled, knotted and spaced, from the topmost crosspiece. Long ropes tethered them, tied below, out of sight.

But it was what filled the nooses that chilled his blood and stoppered the breath of everyone in the crowd. Three people, hands tied behind their backs, heads covered with soiled grain sacks.

At one end stood a woman, judging from her shape and the torn, begrimed dress she wore. At the other end stood a man in a dark suit and bloodied dress shirt that would never be white again. It was obvious the man had a bum leg, given the angle at which it bent and the way he favored it. Rafe knew without doubt it was Jack.

The noose in the middle was occupied by a corpulent man with a similarly grimy suit, dark gray, from the look of it. He leaned, then jerked himself upright once more, as if dazed. President Grant. Had to be.

"No," whispered Rafe, taking it all in within seconds.

His reaction was much the same as the rest of the crowd. This was not what anyone expected to see. Judging from the hands covering mouths, from the drawn-back faces, from the gasps, they all felt as did Rafe. They had been expecting to see a famous man address them — Ulysses S. Grant, the President of the United States. Not this.

The initial shocked sounds dwindled, replaced with louder cries of confusion, then of nervous laughter, as if it were all a strange, elaborate hoax.

As people in the crowd turned to their neighbors with quizzical looks, a grunting, red-faced figure climbed into view.

"No, no, don't move, folks! Stay right where you are — you will be treated to all you expected to see — and a little bit more!" He smiled wide, clapping his hands in glee.

Rafe recognized him from the odd secret meeting as Colonel Rufus Turlington the Second. And Rafe's gut told him the surprise he was about to unveil was something he sorely didn't want to see.

CHAPTER FORTY-THREE: CLIMBING THE MOUNTAIN

There looked to Rafe to be no way he could make it past the double row of armed fools the Brotherhood had assembled downstairs at the front of the barn. He had to find another way up there. A last resort would be to find a suitable spot to snipe Turlington — and any other Phoenix members who dared creep into view. But that would not save Jack or the president or the woman from a hard, quick death by rope. Had to be people, out of sight, manning the ropes.

He had to get closer. His best chance was to make his way to the top, free the three lynching victims, shoot any of the fools from below as they made their way up the stairs to the staging area. Simple as that. Rafe growled and heeled the buckskin into action.

He hoped Turlington tried to kill him. Better yet, Timmons. That weasel had to be around somewhere. Rafe prayed the man drew on him — it would give him a chance to kill him first. No way was he going to expire in this lifetime before Talbot Timmons. He could not let that happen. But let him draw first and Rafe could live with that little slice of conscience.

He swiveled his head, roved with his eyes, and spotted a suitable set-up at the side of the building. That alley to the left looked promising. Halfway down it he spied a wagon laden high with goods, parked and waiting for the proceedings to be over with, he guessed.

No eyes were on him as he slid down from the buckskin's back and, leading the horse by the reins, angled around the crowd and into the alley. The lower his height the less attention he might attract as he moved. With little more thought than that, Rafe bit back the urge to leap once more atop the horse, rather than try his luck on foot — but he knew he'd never make it in time. And trusting Turlington to stay his hand was a fool's errand.

Rafe snaked his way through the crowd, roughly shoving people out of the way, and angled straight for the demure work wagon piled high with crates and barrels and sacks of feed. He hoped his estimation of its distance from the jutting end of a carrying beam was enough for him to leap and gain purchase, swing himself up, and clamber in time from there to save Jack and the others.

As with so many plans, no matter the amount of time put into them, this one wobbled from the start.

The big horse shied more than he expected — perhaps it was the crowd. He managed to make it to the wagon, keeping one eye on the proceedings far above. He raised himself up, stood on the saddle, and grabbed as high as he could to the roped stack of goods topping the worn wagon.

The slick soles of his boots slipped and he went down hard, driving his chin into a burlap-covered crate. Good thing he hadn't been talking with Cookie, the tip of his tongue would be laying in the dirt somewhere below.

Prickles of light pulsed and danced, threatening to pinch out his vision. He shook his head, which made it worse, and, unbidden, a swift image of a smiling Jack Smith flitted into his mind.

Rafe gritted his teeth, and hauled his aching jaw and the rest of his battered body upward. He wasn't certain if anyone from the Brotherhood had seen him angle down the alley, but it was too late to worry about that now.

One last jump and he reached upward, muckled onto the beam with one arm, and felt the uneven dents left by the adze in squaring off the top, the fingers of his left arm the only thing keeping him from swinging inward and dropping back. He was too high up to fall without some sort of bone-snapping injury.

Below and to his right, he saw the buckskin, dipping his big head in what Rafe interpreted as anger and annoyance at Rafe's foolhardy moves. If he made it through the next ten minutes without getting killed, he vowed he'd reward the buckskin with an extra feed, if only for being smarter than Rafe himself felt.

The big man blinked hard and shook his still-throbbing head — sharp and dull pains fought for supremacy as they radiated upward from his smacked chin — swinging as he was from one hand. Every time he tried to swing his right arm up and onto the beam, he pendulumed too far inward toward the structure.

He'd give anything for something solid, like the boards that should have been there, against which he could jam his boots. But wishing never did anyone any good, as far as he could tell. And so he did what he always did — Rafe Barr gritted his teeth and forced the situation to bend to his sizable will.

That damnable right hand slapped once, twice more at the beam. He felt like bellowing in rage, but still hoped he was unseen from above. And from somewhere above he heard snatches of shouts. It was Turlington's voice, excited and droning all at once, carrying on, filling the air with shouts of greatness and promises of a future in which the South reigned supreme. The sound was like a hundred mosquitoes swarming his head and he with no way to swat at them.

Even in his darkest moments, wrongfully buried alive in the living hell of Yuma Prison for the murder of his wife and son, Rafe Barr had always been able to scrabble around in the deepest pit of his mind and come up with a last fistful of grit to muscle through any situation his hard life had served him. Always he'd been able to do so.

Now, when he called on himself to find it once more, that relied-upon reserve of determination that had always spanned the gulf between success and failure, between trying and doing, this time Rafe felt something foreign, the feeling of unavoidable failure.

This time there was nothing there, no reserve, no help. Even the fleeting image of his friend, mangled and noosed somewhere up above, failed to muster the strength he was desperate for. And then he heard the bitter snarl of laughter he'd come to despise; the sound had tormented him, echoed in his head, drove him up off his hard cell bed each morning in Yuma — the rank sound of Warden Talbot Timmons's laughter. Was that bastard up there, too? Down below? Hard to tell.

It was a confident, tight, clipped laugh, and no matter where it was, Rafe wanted to smear it out. Almost as much as he wanted to gut with a dull wooden spoon the killer of his family. Almost. But that was enough; all he needed to drive his right arm upward once more.

His cold, clawing fingers snatched at the half-barked beam, snagging there, straining, his short fingernails snapping at the tips, splitting. He felt as if his very finger bones would shred . . . .

And then he was up, had the left arm up and over the beam, one floor from the top. He rested there but seconds before continuing on toward the staircase that would lead him to the scaffolding. A grim smile spread wide on Rafe's lean face.

CHAPTER FORTY-FOUR:
A CONVERGENCE OF EVENTS

"Give me those lines and poke your head up outta this contraption, can't hardly see where I'm headed tucked inside the belly of this beast!"

Doc sniffed and regarded Cookie coolly. "I'm beginning to wonder if ministering to your medical ailments was such a good idea."

"Whine at me later, Doc. Right now, Rafe needs our help. The man don't ask for such unless he's serious. Now make like a prairie dog and tell me where we're headed! You wanted to navigate, get on with it!"

Cookie sawed the lines, squinting through the narrow gap that gave him little more of a view than of the rumps of the two thundering horses. "By God, Doc. You could have figured on a little more of a gap for the eyeballs. I can't see anything but the part of a horse no body wants to stare at."

The words were lost on Doc — busy as

he was scanning the increasingly busy street before them through a side door he begrudgingly admitted to himself was too small. He'd managed to wedge his head through the horizontal gap, but hadn't accounted for the fact that his ears didn't want to return in the same direction from whence they came.

"Oh, hell," he mumbled, then shouted, "Left, turn left here!"

"What?"

"Left! Left!"

"Why didn't you say so? Ain't no call to shout at me, Doc." Cookie shook his head and took the corner hard, with Ethel threatening to roll as two of the four reinforced wheels rose from the ground with the sharp curve. They slammed down hard and the wagon raced onward.

Cookie still wasn't feeling in fine fettle but he was a damn sight better than he'd been earlier. Of course, it wouldn't do to admit that to Doc. But he would most certainly borrow a bottle of that hangover cure from the man. Just this once Cookie figured he'd give the man his due — Doc was on to something there.

"The road splits ahead — I suspect we want the far right avenue, as that's where the people are most numerous."

"English, Doc. I need plain speechifying!"

"Right, right then!"

"You agreeing with me or telling me a direction?"

Doc's groan of disgust was audible even to Cookie. The medical man tried once more to pull his unprotected head back in through the door's gap, and nearly decapitated himself. He managed one ear as he shouted, "When I agree with you I'll say 'correct' and when you get a direction, it will be right or left! Do you understand that, you broken-down old cowpoke?"

"Gee, Doc. Ain't no need to get personal about it. Make certain we are both reading from the same book, if you get my meaning." Cookie shook his head and did his best to navigate the wagon through the swelling crowd. They received a good many stares, shouts of surprise, and raised fists as people felt the grinding wagon wheels slice by too close for comfort.

"Oh, dear!" shouted Doc.

"What? What's happening?"

Doc pulled his head all the way in, ignoring the swelling red lump his ear had become at the wrenching it had received. He put a hand on Cookie's shoulder and jerked his chin forward. "Ahead, the barn — it's a scaffolding."

"Scaffolding? Like for a lynching?" Cookie peered out and as the dust he'd raised blew away, his eyes widened as much as Doc's. "There's three folks up there —" He glanced at Doc, then back out the gap. "And one of them's Jack! Oh, Rafe, what's the plan, what's the plan? A distraction, that's what he'd say."

Cookie snapped his fingers. "Here, Doc. You take the lines. Keep heading around the crowd. We got to get closer to the action. All anybody knows, we're a driverless carriage, eh? Now where'd you squirrel away the boom-boom sticks?"

"The what?"

"My best friend, next to Rafe!"

Doc squinted at Cookie as if he'd begun barking like a dog.

"Dynamite, man, where's it at?" Cookie yanked open small drawers and cupboards, one latched compartment after another.

"Under your feet," said Doc, gritting his teeth at a near miss with a spectator, "in a steel-lined container. I thought it would be safer there."

"Good thinking, Doc. 'Specially when I'm around." He rummaged in the floor's compartment. "Ah ha! You got my mini sticks!" He grinned. "Perfect for a distraction."

It took him seconds to render a quarter

stick of dynamite into an even smaller load, then he whipped open another side door, this one scarcely larger than the door on the other side that nearly claimed Doc's ears.

"Doc? Next time you go into the wagon-modifyin' business, you might want to consult with folks who will be using your contraption. Now, see the barn?"

"No, I fail to see a barn, I —"

"Lookin' half-built, with the scaffolding atop! I need you to drive straight at it."

"Why?"

"Why? Good God, man, so's I can blow it up! Why do you think?"

"Blow it up? Whatever for?"

Cookie sighed and stamped a boot. "A distraction, Doc. That's what Rafe would want me to do. Besides, I ain't going to blow it up, only toss a charge on up there is all."

"But we don't even know where Mr. Barr is, we —"

"Trust me, Doc. If he's drawing breath, he'll be up there at the scaffolding any time now, and he'll need a distraction. Welcome it, I'd say."

"What if he's not?"

"Cross that river when we get to it, Doc! And don't be such a worrier, man. This here's what you built Ethel for, ain't it?"

"Yes, I . . . I guess so."

"Then get me over to that barn. Or else."

"Or else, what?" said Doc, dragging the lines hard and steering two horses to the left.

"You don't want to know, Doc." Cookie giggled and patted his pockets for a match.

High above the crowd stood the fat man, whom many in town had come to recognize, if not entirely like, over the busy weeks leading up to the poker tournament. He cupped his pudgy hands to his face. "Can you all hear me?"

Murmurs but no bold shouts of response from the crowd prompted him to try again. "I said, 'Can you all hear me?' "

This time headshakes and shouts of "Yes!" greeted him. Curiosity, Rufus knew, was on his side. This could be tricky, but fortunately he had enough men with guns called in to keep the crowd genial should it come to that.

So far the confused looks of the locals told him all he needed to know — they were curious, to be sure, but they were also like people the world over — bloodthirsty and eager for a death scene given the opportunity to view one. Well, he was about to offer them a trio of them.

"Now, now," he patted the air before him.

"Before we get to the main event, the very thing you all are waiting for, I would like to tell you the reason behind it. That is to say I am sure you all are wondering what it is I am doing up here with these three criminals waiting in the wings behind me."

A muffled scream burst from one of the people about to be hanged. That it was a woman was obvious by the sound and by her once-pretty blue and white satin dress. Now it was a soiled, ripped thing, sagged and streaked with blood. Her own? The crowd wondered but did not look away.

"Shut her up, will you, Punk? Why in the hell do I pay you, anyway?"

Emboldened perhaps by the bizarre scene in which he found himself, Punk snarled, "Ain't paid me in a month of Sundays, Colonel." Even as he said it he backhanded the cloth sack covering the woman's face. The crowd's reaction was immediate. Gasps told Rufus the action had been too much too soon.

"Okay, Punk." Rufus sneered at his hired man. "Ah, why don't you . . . take the rest of the afternoon for yourself. Away from here. Your presence is disturbing the situation."

Punk snorted. "You got to be kidding me." Then he realized the boss was giving him the day off, so he bolted for the stairs.

"I think it's time to get this show on the road, don't you?" Rufus shouted to the crowd, but the response was another round of confused looks and mumbles. "I am Colonel Rufus Turlington the Second, and I am here for one reason and one reason only." He thumbed his lapels and rocked back on his heels. "And that is to reveal that you are witness to a miracle, a rebirth of sorts, yes that's it." He nodded in agreement with himself. It was sounding good so far. Keep using fancy words and they will eat out of your hand, Rufus. "Ahem, yes, a rebirth, a rising from the ashes! Hence the name . . . Brotherhood of the Phoenix!"

The crowd was quieter than ever, brows drawn tight in confusion.

Rufus plowed ahead. "But you, my dear people, will one day tell your children's children that you were there, or rather here, on that fateful day when the South rose from the ashes that the Northern Aggressors had so haughtily assumed had covered the Confederacy once and for all!"

Rufus paused, scanning the crowd, a smug grin tight on his mouth. He directed his gaze toward the back, and saw his cohorts in the Brotherhood. But they were not smiling in support. He saw only a small band of confused, scowling faces.

Behind him, Grant tried to shout, but managed little more than a garbled growl. It sounded to Rufus as if the man were saying his own name. But between the beating those two repugnant characters had given him and the gag Punk had cinched tight around Grant's bearded face, there was little more the President could do than writhe and snarl. Rufus felt a tiny thrill at seeing the grimy sack puff in and out in time with Grant's frenzied breathing.

Fresh shouts drew his attention back to the crowd. This was not going as well as he had hoped. Had he been incorrect in assuming these people would be supportive of such a grandiose scheme? Where was the boss? Timmons would know what to do, he was one fiery orator, had stirred the Brotherhood at gatherings in recent years. But Turlington saw no sign of the boss nor of the strange, menacing gunhand who'd arrived with him.

"Boss! Hey, Timmons!" growled Turlington while keeping a forced smile on his face. "Where are you at? You should be here, dammit!"

Rufus realized he was alone on the roof with the three folks he had long dreamed of lynching. Well, one of them anyway. The other two, Mala, sweet Mala, and the bastard who'd taken a shine to her, well they were going along for the ride. A short, quick one, but still.

He'd joked earlier that they were there to add a bit of color to the proceedings. Punk had not caught on. A fine, wasted joke.

Everyone down there stared up at him. They were getting all fidgety. This was not the way he had planned it. In his mind's eye he had orchestrated this magnificent symbolic event and that alone was going to be enough to convince the crowd and the other members of the Brotherhood that he and only he was the worthiest to run the show. That the boss, Timmons, was next to useless, had been for some time, sitting on his little throne way down there near Mexico at Yuma. *To hell with him,* Turlington had long thought. *This was going to be a mighty overthrow and a mighty resurgence. All at once.*

But it wasn't happening like that. Not like that at all.

"What are you doing up there?" one voice hurled up at him.

Another shouted, "This a stage play? Where's President Grant?"

At mention of his name, Grant emitted another loud bellow, shook his head, and stomped in place, the noose preventing him from further movement.

A woman shouted, "We were told he was going to be here, that Grant himself was going to deliver an oration!"

Rufus held his hands up again, and managed to quiet the crowd once more. "Now, now," he said, "This is what I'm talking about, see? The President, he's . . . he's . . ." all of a sudden it occurred to him that it might not be the wisest move to reveal that the President was the one in the middle with the bag over his head. About to be lynched.

This crowd seemed angrier than he ever anticipated. Might be they'd turn on him. Turlington looked down and around at the surrounding street. People were still congregating far below, spreading outward from the plaza. A wagon threaded its way through, slowly drawing closer to the barn and this makeshift scaffold. Looked as though it was trying to figure out a way around the crowd.

To hell with it — time to show the world Colonel Rufus Turlington the Second was his own man. "President Grant," shouted Rufus. "His time has come and gone, you see? He's, hell . . ."

The shouts grew louder, threatening to drown him out.

"Well, he ain't here. Not for long, he's . . ."

"What are you saying?" said a man in a bowler hat looking upward from the near edge of the crowd. "You aren't really going to hang those folks, are you?"

"Madre dios!" shouted a woman, crossing herself, her white shawl ruffling with the movement. Others shouted; women screamed and pointed. Children laughed and chased each other through the crowd.

They truly thought it was a stage play of some sort. Rufus was good and confused now. Should he cut bait and run or plow on ahead?

Then something whipped upward from the crowd, from the wagon threading its way toward the barn. It arced high, spinning, trailing smoke . . . *like an incendiary from the war,* thought Rufus. Not that he had actually fought in the war, but he had seen enough things exploding, including the old home place, to know when something was about to erupt in flame and debris. But those thoughts came too slow, for the thing — what looked to be a tiny stick of dynamite — clunked right at his feet, hissing and spraying smoke and sparks.

"Oh, God!" shouted Rufus, diving for cover. He misstepped, and with a shriek, plowed ass-over-bandbox down the stairs that led back down to the stable. His arms whipped left and right, clawing at the wood railing, finding no purchase as he caromed off the steps. He came to a flaccid heap halfway down, moaning and trembling, crying weakly for someone, anyone to help. Where were they all?

He looked up in time to see a large man, wide at the shoulder, staring down at him. The man said, "Remember me? No, of course you don't, but your pathetic father would have."

"Waah? Who . . . you?" Rufus snotted himself and thought maybe, given the warm sensation down below his watch chain, he'd fouled his own trousers.

The big man shook his head, lips curled as if he'd stepped in a dog turd, and drove a mighty fist straight into the rubbery center of Turlington's fat face. Blood pitched outward in a berrylike spray and the fat man lay still, unconscious.

"Good," said Rafe, stepping over the man. "Your whining and stench was getting tiresome."

One thing that bothered Rafe was the fact that Timmons was in town, likely in on this lynching charge, and yet when Rafe got up to the partially stripped upper story of the barn, the man was nowhere to be found. He could have sworn he'd find him there.

"Wishful thinking," growled Rafe.

Timmons might be unsavory, but he was no rash-acting fool. Rafe bet himself a cold beer that the man had some ulterior motive in all this. Had to, otherwise why ally himself with an idiot such as Turlington? Out of duty to the dumb man's dead father? Not likely. He would certainly not put himself on a stage like this.

Then it came to him — what's the one thing men the world over lusted for, killed for, risked their own necks for? Money. As simple as that. And where was the money this week in Santa Fe? At the poker tournament. He bet himself a second beer — and a fine cigar — that he'd find the money when he found Timmons, or the other way 'round.

He'd worry about that later, if later came. Right now, he had to save Jack, the President, and whoever else was up there.

The crack of a rifle shot was followed by a sizzling, buzzing sound right beside Rafe's head as he emerged from the open-topped stairwell. He ducked down, biting back a curse. "Looks like the easy part's over," he said.

He heard a muffled scream followed by

391

the word "help" — the word was clear enough. It was a woman's voice, one of the three folks about to be lynched. He had to get up there, no telling when a bullet would cut through a rope and cause one of these folks to drop. Rafe peered up again, eyes level with the rough plank floor. There were the three folks, and all seemed to still be alive.

Jack was sagged, his game leg looked busted up worse than ever, and he was struggling mightily to hold himself up on his good leg, but he was losing the battle. The good leg trembled with the strain and the noose rope grew tighter by the second as Jack's leg slowly gave out on him. Jack's hands clenched and unclenched in futility, bound as they were at the wrist by iron manacles.

The man in the middle, a heavy-set fellow, was likely Grant — had to be, no one but desperate ex-Confederates would have balls enough to kidnap the President. Where in hell were the President's guards, anyway?

If they hadn't been killed, they should be tossed in prison for doing such a lousy job.

"Jack!"

Nothing. The man still slumped slowly downward, leg quivering more than ever.

"Jack! It's Rafe — hang in there — tighten

up, I'm coming!"

That did it. He saw renewed strength there, the hands paused for a moment, then gripped together tighter, balled into fists. Then another rifle shot whipped in, followed by another. Rafe looked to the three tied ropes preventing the three necks from dropping and snapping. As he suspected, the shooter was aiming for the ropes. Specifically, the middle rope. President Grant's rope.

The woman writhed, and screamed again.

"Easy now, I'm a friend," growled Rafe. "Hold on . . ."

The figure in the middle spun, jerking too hard against the rope. "Gaaah! Help!" The voice came out thick, likely gagged.

"Hang tight, I'm working on keeping your neck short."

Rafe had no plan. Whoever was sniping out there wasn't about to wait for him to attempt a rescue. The shooter — or shooters — was enjoying this game. Otherwise, why not kill the President? One less link of blame in the chain? Easier to lay guilt on a rope than a bullet.

Rafe crouched low on the steps, and shot a glance downward where he'd left the fat man — and Turlington was gone. Should have trussed him up, dammit. *My punching hand must be weakening,* he thought.

He checked his revolvers, pulled in a deep breath, and was about to race up onto the lynching floor when he heard something clunk to the wood above. He peered out once more and saw another smoking stick of what looked like small dynamite. It expelled clouds of smoke, hissed like a riled snake, and showered sparks like a celebratory fireworks show, but didn't explode.

"Cookie," said Rafe, smiling. "Perfect timing, perfect distraction." He wasted none of the smoke — sure to whisk away in the mild breeze that had kicked up in recent minutes.

Rafe crept low, hauling out a Colt, cocked and ready, in his big left hand, as he waded through the smoke. He shucked his skinning knife with the other, and made quick work of Jack's noose, slicing through the rope a foot above the man's head. Jack sagged backward, his strength all but gone. Rafe guided him to the floor, laid him on his back, and tugged off the hood. He cut free the tight gag tied around Jack's bruised and bloodied face.

Rafe played no favorites but went down the line, slicing through Grant's rope. A volley of rifle and pistol shots whanged in from two directions. Matter of time before a guessed shot got lucky.

He tugged off the dirty sack covering the President's face. He, too, was a much-beaten and gagged mess. But there was no mistaking the man's visage — that beard and piercing eyes. Rafe pulled on the gag enough to slip his knife tip beneath, then cut it free. "Keep low, sir. I'll be back."

The bullets rained in harder and the smoke was all but gone. He cranked off four shots as fast as his thumb and forefinger could work the hammer and trigger, and sawed at the rope holding the trembling woman. She stayed upright, turning left, then right, as if she might get a glimpse of her attackers.

"Keep down," he growled, tugging off the hood covering her head. He cut her gag free and dragged her down to her knees. Even through the bruising and eyes puffed with rage and tears, he could tell she was a pretty woman.

He flicked his big knife and cut the ropes binding her hands behind her — she could help him with Jack better if her hands were free. "Down, keep down!"

There was something familiar about her, though what he could not say. *Later,* he thought. *Time enough later. If there was to be a later.* He had to get the three off the roof. The smoke was all but gone and

Cookie, despite Rafe's silent urgings, had not tossed another of his distractions.

"To the stairs — hurry!" shouted Rafe, half-dragging the woman.

She made it down the first step, then spun and bolted past Rafe. "Jack!" she made it to his side and held his face so tenderly between her hands. "Jack? Are you, are you all right?"

He said something, moved, groaned, and she hugged him.

Rafe shook his head but continued pushing and pulling the President toward the stairs. "Now see here, I've had enough —"

"You will have when they pump your old war-torn hide full of lead pills . . . sir! Now get down those stairs before we both get shot!" The last thing Rafe was worried about was bowing and scraping to a government official, even if he was President of the nation.

Rafe gave scant thought to the fact that he'd been scrabbling all over that roof, out in plain sight for all the snipers to see. None of the four of them had yet to feel so much as a nibble from one of the dozens of bullets that pelted at them.

Jack proved the easiest of the three to deal with. Rafe slung him over his shoulder and low-walked to the steps. "Get down here now," he shouted at the President, who seemed bent on making himself as big a target as his sizable girth would allow. Rafe all but accidentally kicked the woman on down the steep steps. She was ahead of him but kept stopping and reaching for Jack.

"Ma'am, get down there now!"

Near the bottom she turned on him and pointed a finger nearly up his nose. "You see here, I have had about enough of taking orders from bossy white men, you hear me, mister?"

From his ignoble spot, draped as he was over Rafe's right shoulder, Jack chuckled. Of all the sounds Rafe did not expect to hear, it was the sound of Jack laughing that he least expected. "That's my Mala," said Jack.

"Damn right," said the woman, not taking her flinty eyes from Rafe. "Who are you, anyway?"

"Later," said Rafe, wondering what Jack meant. "I'll explain later. Right now, we have to get you all out of here. And if my luck's holding, we might have a chariot waiting."

"Let me guess," said Jack, wincing with each step Rafe took. "Cookie?"

"Yep," said Rafe. "And Doc . . . and Ethel."

"Ethel?"

"Long story for later. Come on, Mr. President, no time for laggards!"

They made it to the bottom of the stairs. The much-abused Grant rubbed his rope-chafed wrists and nodded, his scrutiny of each person around him revealing suspicion.

Rafe glanced back at him once more, about to give him another shout, when gunfire opened up outside, too close for Rafe's liking. His own barked orders were drowned out by a tumble of shouts and screams of many dozens of people, fleeing? He hoped it was the crowd running away from this blossoming melee.

Sudden, hard, whistling thuds of bullets hit the barn door before them, the walls to either side, and the back wall, as well.

Surrounded, great. Rafe bit back the urge to swear — there was a lady present, after all — and thumbed back the hammer on a Colt. "Get down, everyone to the center of the room, behind that feed bin!"

"Here, sir!" He thrust the other uncocked Colt at Grant. "I trust you're familiar with the working end of one of these."

The firearm in the man's burly hand seemed to give him instant vigor. He stood taller and hiked up his shoulders. "You bet I am, young man. Let me at the bastards!"

"Easy now, sir. We're pinned down. I'm expecting reinforcements, but until then we only have so many bullets between us and them." Rafe jerked a chin at the door.

All four folks huddled together, Rafe doing his best to scan all sides of the dim interior of the barn.

"I don't like doing nothing," said Grant.

"Same here, sir," hissed Jack. "Got a plan, Rafe?"

"Nah, you know me, Jack. Playing it by ear."

Something that was not a bullet clunked against the double doors at the front of the barn. For a moment, the rain of bullets slowed, nearly stopped, the voices without quieted. Rafe's eyes opened wide. "Get down! Get down!"

The last of his words were lacerated by flame and smoke and shredded planks blasting inward as the front of the building disappeared in a convulsive explosion.

It took the four trapped people a lifetime to regain their senses. Rafe had covered the others as much as he could with his body. Dust filled his mouth and the stink of smoky gunpowder clouded his nostrils. Sounds pulsed and wavered as he blinked his eyes and shook his head to dispel the clamor of ringing bells in his ears.

He rose, pushing broken planks and smoking straw and burlap off the others. "You okay? Okay?"

The woman, crouched over Jack as if to shield the wounded man, even as his hands were wrapped around her head to do the same, looked up at Rafe and nodded. Jack and Grant, heads bent close together, looked up and also nodded.

A shout behind him pulled Rafe back to the deadly moment.

"Hoo doggie! That was a hot one! Over here, boy! And make it snappy — ain't much time!" Emerging from the smoke-filled, ragged hole where the south wall of the barn once stood, Cookie McGee waved his arms like an enraged scarecrow. "Hurry it up! There's a passel of folks out here think we've done something wrong!" He shouted over his shoulder. "Hold 'er steady, Doc! Won't be a minute!"

Rafe saw people already closing in, pulling aside boards and shouting. He had no idea who they were — the President's men? Hired guns of the Brotherhood? The law? None of them held appeal.

"Now, dammit!" Cookie hopped from one boot to the other, windmilling an arm and ushering the stumbling four toward a narrow door in the side of Ethel the War

400

Wagon. Rafe escorted Jack and the woman in, then shoved President Grant as gracefully as he could up the two steps and inside the cramped interior of the wagon. As Grant stepped in Rafe pulled the Colt from the man's hand. "I'll need that, sir."

Cookie poked his head back out the door. "Rafe, get your ass in here!" But the big man was already swinging the narrow door closed.

"I'll meet up with you! I have a bird to kill!"

"What? A bird? Boy that don't make no sense!"

But Rafe had already turned and disappeared into the shadows of the barn, bent low, guns drawn, scanning for sign of Turlington, Timmons, and the others.

Cookie barked one last shout, squinting into the gloom, then slammed the wagon door as angry fists and a rifle barrel poked into the gap. Cookie slashed downward with his big belt knife and felt the satisfying soft give as the keen steel edge bit deep into a man's hand. A vicious scream slipped through the gap, echoing in the cramped wagon.

The rifle barrel slid out of the nearly closed door and Cookie mashed other fingers hard with the heel of his boot. The door smacked shut. "God, Doc! Go! Don't spare the horses!"

"But I fear they've taken fire!"

"Drive 'em, I said! They'll falter soon enough if bullets found them. We need to get out of here!"

Ethel lurched back toward the plaza, everyone inside slamming side to side as drawers and cupboards flew open and random bits of gear and supplies rained down on them.

"Must devise proper latches for those compartments," mumbled Doc.

"Give me those lines, Doc. You tend to Jack. He's hurt. We can ride faster than they can run and most of those brutes was on foot!"

The wagon rumbled and clattered across the cobbled plaza, the rooster of a man shouting oaths and curses through gritted teeth at the thinning crowd before him. "Why are they angry with us? We saved the President, didn't we?"

"Indeed you did, sir. And I thank you!"

Cookie looked over his shoulder to see the purpled, bruised face of none other than U.S. President Ulysses S. Grant close by his left shoulder. He'd jockeyed forward in the wagon to give Doc room to minister to the ailing man.

"You call me sir, sir?"

"I guess I did. Now who in the hell are you?"

Cookie was about to extend a hand for a shake when a shotgun blast slammed into the side of the wagon. Ethel absorbed it, her plate-steel sides deflecting the worst of. She rocked side to side, and stayed upright, but the shot threw the lunging horses off their rhythm.

"Damn it all to hell . . . sir!" Cookie growled. "It's a wonder nobody's killed the horses yet. But we best lay off the palaverin' until we're safe and away from here."

"Uh, Cookie," said Doc. "I hate to be the bearer of ill tidings, however . . ."

"Blast it man, can't you say a thing without talkin' it to death first? What is it?"

"Fire!" shouted the woman. "The wagon's on fire!"

"Thank you, ma'am. See? Ain't so hard, is it, Doc?"

Blue-black smoke rolled forward from the rear chuck compartment, the most vulnerable spot on the wagon.

"The bastards have torched us!" shouted Grant, teeth grim and gritted.

"Mr. President, sir, take these lines and drive like your ass is on fire! 'Cause it is!" Cookie jammed the leather straps into

403

Grant's big mitts and squirreled up the side of the wagon, stepping on shelves and mashing his boot into a stack of neatly rolled maps.

Doc whimpered. "Ethel, what have they done to you?"

"Hush now, Doc."

"Oh no, Cookie, what are you gonna do?" Jack shook his head as he watched his friend snatch up two half-sticks of dynamite.

He grinned. "They want fire? I'll give it to 'em!"

Despite the protesting voices chasing him, Cookie tugged free a deadbolt on a hatch in the ceiling. "Need your shoulder, sir."

Grant stiffened his broad back and nodded. "Go ahead."

Cookie stepped on the President's shoulder and with a single motion flung open the hinged hatch above him. Quicker than his age would indicate, he slipped upward through the opening, revolver already drawn.

"Here, Cookie!" shouted Doc, thrusting a thick folded square of canvas up at him. "Beat the flames down with this!"

"You got it, Doc. Ethel won't die on my watch!" He poked his head back down, smiling at the four people below him. "Hey, we pretty near outrun 'em! Keep 'em going, Grant. Sir."

"They still have bullets, Cookie," shouted Jack. "Look out!"

"Pish posh!" shouted the old rooster. Then he slammed shut the hatch and they heard him clunking along the roof, crawling aft. Presently they heard the muffled sounds of him swearing and whacking away with the canvas. "She's good!" he shouted.

New hoofbeats drummed hard and fast from both sides, as if someone had been lying in wait along their lane.

"Hey!" Cookie shouted. "Where'd you come from? Give you a taste of boom —"

The riders in the wagon heard a clunk, then nothing else.

"Cookie?" Doc shouted. He hoisted himself up, poking his head through the hatch. "He's gone!" He looked back down below. "Mr. President, sir, we have to go back! Cookie's gone! He may be hurt."

"I'm sorry, but the needs of the many . . ."

"What? I . . . . I voted for you, mister!" Doc stood in the middle of the wagon, shaking his clenched, work-grimed fists at the President.

"And I appreciate that. But I have to think of the safety of you three as well as myself. At the risk of sounding too puffed up, if something happens to me there will be

405

much confusion — and not only in Washington!" He thrust a meaty finger skyward.

The throaty click of a revolver's hammer being drawn back overrode even the slamming, crashing sounds of the wagon careening forward.

"Begging your pardon, sir," said Jack, a six-gun aimed at the ceiling. "But you're as safe as you're gonna get, at least for the time being. You best be turning this buggy around. Our friend is in need of our help."

Without looking behind him, Grant sighed and snapped even harder on the lines. "To be clear, I am not turning around. I'll hear no more of it. I am quite certain I misheard, but if there's a gun drawn in this wagon, it best be aimed anywhere but at me."

Mala shook her head at Jack, who released the hammer and sank back against the wall of the thundering wagon. Doc glared at the back of the President's head and said nothing more.

Scant seconds later, Grant shouted, "Jackson? Melville?" He squinted through the viewing slit. His bruised face broke into a grin and he yarned back hard on the lines, slowing the lathered, crazed horses.

"My men! They've come through. Excellent! Excellent!" Grant slowed the team and turned to face his fellows in the wagon.

"We're saved, folks! My men have overtaken us. Must be the ones who had been firing on us, thinking I was being kidnapped yet again. What a day."

The inherent doom of his last phrase did not match the smile cracking his blood-crusted beard or the bruised, puffy eyes that regarded them. "Cheer up — your friend may yet be well. Now we can go back for him."

Outside, moments later, the President's two men, each bearing signs of a beating, slowly lowered their weapons as Grant convinced them the people with whom he'd shared a wagon were his rescuers and not his abductors.

Jack spoke up. "Sir, you should know that the man who did all the saving is none other than Rafe Barr. And I know you know who he is."

The change that came over Grant's face was sudden and stone-like. "But that man . . . he's supposed to be in prison for the unthinkable act he committed. And a traitor to his country before that."

"Wrong on both counts, Grant," said Doc, raising his fists once more. They were met with Jackson and Melville's drawn and cocked weapons.

"Now, now," said Grant, touching his

bruised temple. "I don't know what to think right now. But I know there's time for this all to sort out. Time for explanations now that the . . ." he cut his eyes involuntarily to Mala and Jack, "lynching was avoided."

"This time," said Jack, shaking his head.

"Jack, we're alive," said Mala. "That's enough for this minute."

"Yeah, but what about Cookie?"

Grant turned to his men. "You didn't pass anybody on the road out here? An old bald man with a . . ."

"Big mouth," said Doc affectionately.

"Yes," said Grant. "And dynamite."

"No, sir," said the man known as Melville. "That is to say, I think I saw someone on top of the wagon as we gave chase, but then they weren't there. Too much smoke to see, sir."

"Then he has to be somewhere along the road, between here and town," said Jack, leaning forward. "We have to find him." He winced and groaned, the pain in his leg turning his face the color of cold stove ash.

"Relax young man. Jackson," said Grant. Turning once more to his men. "You search the roadside. We'll be along under escort by Melville."

They found the spot where it looked as if Cookie may have landed in the roadside ditch. But of the man they sought, no sign was in evidence, save for a couple of scuff marks. Further on toward town, they found the burned-away remnant of the canvas tarpaulin he'd used to put out the fire. His tracks headed back toward Santa Fe.

"Thank God for that," said Grant when he was told, sensing relief on the faces of the others. "I'd like to get back to town, get on the train, and get the hell out of here. I hope the reinforcements you sent for are on their way, Melville?"

"Yes, sir, there should be fifty troops here within a day. Until then, we have full compliance with the law in town and the local sheriff as well. No one goes in or out of Santa Fe without us knowing about it."

"Good," said Grant. "And the other six men of my guard? All dead?"

Melville nodded. "Yes, sir. We were ambushed." He looked down. "Unprepared, if I am honest."

"Damn and blast." Grant sighed low and scratched his fingertips through his beard. "Well, there will be time enough for sorting through the events once we're back in Washington."

CHAPTER FORTY-FIVE:
COMING AROUND . . . AGAIN

When he came to, Cookie determined that the tumble from atop the wagon did nothing to help the discomfort in his gut. Nor did it help the overall ache he'd felt since being dosed first with poison from those two oddballs and then from Doc's vile tincture. He wasn't sure which was designed to kill him, but he'd lay odds down the middle they were both able to do the job.

Right now, he thought, sitting up and looking around himself. *I need to figure out where in the heck I am.* He looked to his right, and there sat town. To his left the road on which they'd been rambling bent and curved out of sight, eastward. He stood, forcing himself upright despite protest from his knees and back and head. Come to think on it, even his elbows ached. The toe of his boot nudged something. He looked down and saw one of his half-sticks of dynamite.

It brought a smile to his face as he retrieved it.

That's right, he was about to lob a stick at whoever had set fire to the wagon. When he'd prairie-dogged up out of the wagon, he hoped to see their pursuers falling far behind. By the time he'd doused the fire with that canvas Doc handed to him, two riders had pounded onto the road right alongside, as if they'd been in wait for them. They started throwing lead and it was all Cookie could do to keep from being punctured, let alone scratch a match and light a stick.

"Spineless hounds," sneered Cookie. "Else they would have stuck like hide glue."

Then that blasted Grant had hit every rut and stone in the road, and before he knew it Cookie had been bounced right off that wagon top. "And now here I am," he said. "Afoot and annoyed. About right for one of Rafe's hare-brained adventures. Leastwise we got Jack and his lady friend on out of there. President, too, though time will tell if that was a good idea or no."

Cookie squared off toward town and let out a deep breath. "All right then, let's go track Rafe, see if he needs me to save his mangy hide again." Angling across an uneven stretch of ground, Cookie veered wide

411

of the road and found himself down a gulley, out of earshot when Ethel and the riders rumbled on back to town, scouting for him.

CHAPTER FORTY-SIX:
TIME FOR A TRIP

From the sounds of the odd scene of battle back at the plaza, the crowd had broken up and gunshots had become less frequent. Rafe had faith that, even under the weather, Cookie would see to it that Jack, the woman Jack seemed to know, and President Grant would make it to some safe spot.

He nudged piled junk and shadowy stacks of old sacking with his toe, gun aimed before him, hoping to find a cowering fat man with a busted nose. With luck, he'd find others.

Rafe had no idea how many members of the Brotherhood, or more to the point their hired guns, were lurking about, bent on killing Grant and anyone else in their way. He knew Knifer and Plug were in town, had heard rumor that Timmons was there, but beyond that, all bets were off.

Right now he had to find Turlington. He'd popped him a solid blow on the face, but the son of a gun had disappeared. Couldn't have gotten far.

Rafe jammed his boot into the last two piles of old hay still in the stable, but the only sign of life was the white-toothed flash and screech of a brown rat making for new cover.

"Wrong rat," said Rafe. He thought about pulling out a cigar, but put it out of his mind. In truth, the only thing he really wanted was a glass of whiskey and a spot by the cookstove. *Must be getting old,* he thought.

If he were Knifer and Plug, he'd have made tracks on out of town. He still didn't know why they were in town in the first place. Unless they were involved with the Brotherhood somehow?

Once Rafe got out of the half-dismembered barn, it wasn't difficult to track the fat man. He'd left a trail of toe scuffs, dragged heels, and blood droplets — and one soiled white hanky — straight to the side door of a low building not far from the stable. Rafe thought he recognized it — it was side entrance of the same building where he'd spied on the Brotherhood's meeting, though he'd come on it from the other end.

"Should have had Cookie blow them all

up in their nest," he murmured as he slid in close beside the door where Turlington's trail led.

He ducked low, tried the door latch, and found it unlocked. A quick nudge and the heavy wood door swung inward. The room inside was darker than outdoors. He heard nothing from within.

"Turlington?" his voice was loud enough for the man to hear. No reply.

"Turlington, I know you're in there." Still nothing. "Look, I'll make a deal with you . . ." Rafe let that linger, easy to do considering he had no notion of offering the would-be murderer a thing.

"What sort of deal?"

The voice was hesitant, but bold at the same time, as if he were trying to remember he was a man of some importance, if only to himself. That's all the verification Rafe needed. He kept low, but nudged the door wider, and in one quick motion snatched off his hat and tossed it in the room. No gunshots, nothing but a sharp intake of breath. He'd surprised the fat man, and the man was apparently unarmed.

Rafe followed the hat, barreling into the room himself. He almost bowled over the fat man. Both men were surprised. Turlington's shock was more evident by his scream.

He dropped to his knees on the wood floor, cowering, and held his arms up in front of his blood-streaked face, slopping whiskey all over himself from the glass clutched in his right hand.

"You! You're the one who hit me in the face! Oh Lord, don't hurt me more! Have mercy on me, I am being set upon from all quarters. If you only knew the tribulations I have undergone . . ."

Rafe said nothing. He slipped his Colt back into the holster and stood over the cringing man, arms folded across his wide chest. From the looks of the fat man he'd taken in as much whiskey as he'd spilled on himself.

Disgust thinned Rafe's lips into a rare sneer as he waited for the man to stop groveling. After a half-minute more of Rufus's howling and mewling with no response from Rafe, Turlington grew quiet, turned red eyes on the big man, and in a small voice, between stifled sobs, said, "You going to rob me, ain't you? I knew it, I'm being robbed."

"The only thing you'll experience less of because of me is freedom."

"Wha . . . what's that mean?"

Rafe moved with snake-strike speed and snatched up the whining man's shirtfront and string tie in a big fist. The wad of cloth made a serviceable handle to haul the bloated fool to his feet.

"It means," said Rafe, gritting his teeth with the effort. "That you will be looking at the world from now on through bars."

The fat man puckered his lips to respond, but Rafe shook his head. He looked the fat man up and down. "Take off those braces."

Turlington's eyes widened. "Why? What are you going to do to me?"

Rafe sighed, lifting a Colt from its holster. Before he cleared leather the drunk backed up, clunked into a big wooden desk, and said, "Okay, all right, I'll do it, I'll do it!"

His pudgy pink hands trembled as he fumbled with the buttons holding his leather braces to his trousers. He freed them and they dropped to the floor.

"Pick them up," said Rafe.

The man did as he asked.

"Now hand them to me . . . easy-like."

Again, Turlington complied.

"Turn around, hands behind your back."

"But . . . my trousers will fall down."

"Not my concern. Turn around."

Turlington whimpered as his pants dropped right down to a formidable pool of smelly gray cloth around his ankles. His spindly legs sported voluminous soiled undershorts and socks with garters.

If the man was not so foul to him in every way, Rafe would like to have laughed. But disgust won out and he repeated his directive. "Hands behind your back."

He tied the man's fat hands tight — too tight, for they began to swell and purple — and Turlington whimpered and weaved in place over his mighty misfortune.

"Now," Rafe pinched up his battered hat, plopping it on his head. "Get going." He kicked the simpering Turlington in the backside and sent him sprawling into the dirt out the door he'd come through.

He found he didn't much care if he was seen by anyone who might be of the lawdog persuasion. He had plans for Turlington and he wanted to get them over with as soon as possible. He had other people to track down in this town.

"Get up. Now."

Turlington lay on his face, trousers bunched around his feet, hands tied behind his back, nose a pulped mess, underpants soiled, and cried like a whipped child.

Rafe shucked a Colt once more, held it beside the fat man's bulbous head, and cocked it slowly, the clicks ominous in the otherwise silent street. "Get up."

Turlington struggled to his knees, swayed,

gasping and sobbing, then managed to get his feet under him.

"What kind of a lawman are you?"

Rafe blew out a cloud of blue smoke. "I'm as far from a lawman as you're liable to find, Turlington."

"What do you want with me, then?"

Rafe leaned closer to his captive's ear. His voice was low and cold. "You and your kind hurt my friends and many others for far too long. You're lucky I don't kill you and leave you in an alley for stray dogs to feed on. Likely you'd make them sick. You have that effect on people."

The fat man whimpered and a string of snot trailed out of his greasy, broken nose.

"Now march," said Rafe.

The fat man shuffled slowly forward in front of him, trousers bunching and impeding his progress.

Rafe lit a stogie, enjoying himself for the first time in hours.

"Where . . . where are you taking me?"

"To catch a train."

CHAPTER FORTY-SEVEN:
A PRIZE HOG

The mahogany door of the private rail car swung open and President Grant made his way, stiffly, into the plush interior. Melville lit an oil lamp, then another. They kept the curtains drawn and would do so until the President's train was well away from the trouble spot Santa Fe had become.

"Sir!"

It was Melville. He jerked his head downward, and the other two men looked upon the thing that caught his gaze. There on the carpet, in the middle of the train car's floor, lay a befouled fat man.

Melville already had his sidearm drawn, a match burning down to his thumbnail in his other hand. "Ow!" He shook it, but kept his eyes on the sight before him in the middle of the floor on the carpet.

"Who is it? Is he dead?" said Jackson.

Melville reached a tentative hand toward the confusing bundle of a man. He felt the

420

man's neck. "No, unconscious either from a beating or, from the stink rising off him, from booze."

President Grant bent low and looked at the unconscious man's face. He straightened, still regarding the trussed-up, soiled mass of a man who'd all but lynched him. "Now that goes a long way toward making up for the nightmare of these last hours."

Melville and Jackson flanked the President and stared at the fat man with the wide eyes and bloodied face.

"Who is he?" said Melville.

"That," said Grant, patting his soiled coat for a cigar. "Is none other than Rufus Turlington the Second. I was, unfortunately, acquainted with his father a number of years ago. Foul man. And I see no change in the pedigree."

He found no cigar, and limped over to the desk in his private rail car. As he selected and prepared a cigar he continued. "If the young woman, Mala, is correct, and I have no reason to doubt her, that pile of waste, gentlemen, is the mastermind behind this Brotherhood of the Phoenix plot."

Melville whistled. "How on earth did he get here?"

Grant puffed his cigar thoughtfully. "I have a feeling I know exactly who delivered

421

him, all wrapped up, missing nothing but a bow on his damnable head."

"Who was it, sir?"

"Good question, Jackson. A hero, a legend, an outlaw? I believe the answer depends on who knows the truth about such things in this life." He sighed and poured three stiff drinks. "Melville, Jackson, join me in a drink. Then take that worm to the horse car, chain him there securely, and one of you keep a watch on him at all times. I have a feeling we'll learn much from him. Before we send him to Yuma for the rest of his days."

Once the two guards disappeared, a quick, soft knock came on the closed door of the train car. Grant slid open a top drawer of the desk and pulled out a nickel-plate derringer. He cocked it and, standing to one side of the door, said, "Who is it?"

"It's the man your lousy hostler skills nearly killed!"

Grant's eyebrows drew together. He stepped back, pistol trained on the door. "Come in."

In stepped Cookie McGee.

"Ah, so you are alive. We all but gave up on you, figured you were somehow turned into vapor or smoke."

The skinny man shook his head. "I can't

make heads nor tails of your palaver, Mr. President, but I wanted to be certain you got my friends back here safe. Figured you'd beeline here, after all." He looked around the wagon. "Anyone with such fancy digs wouldn't be likely to leave 'em behind."

"You're right there, sir. I thank you for your part in my rescue. As to your friend, I believe he has already visited and gave me yet another reason to be beholden to him."

"Rafe was here? I mean . . . ah, hell, sir. It's a name, lots of folks have that name."

"Relax, Mr. McGee. I know who he is. I am no prosecutor and this is no court of law. And besides, he is not here."

"Gone, eh? Didn't happen to leave a note telling where he'd got to, did he?"

"Alas, no. But when you next run into him, please give him my regards."

"What he needs a heap more than regards, if you'll pardon me saying so, Grant, is a good word from someone in a position such as yours. He's about sick of being railroaded. And that rascal Timmons down in Yuma, he's mixed up in all this, too. Ringleader of the entire damned Brotherhood, if you ask me. You mark my words." Cookie's bony finger pointed at the President's bearded face. "Sorry, some folks tell me I get carried away."

Grant scratched his hair above his right ear, winced at the bruising there, and said, "Funny you bring up Talbot Timmons's name, as I met with him not ten minutes ago on my way to the train station. He's an old acquaintance of mine." Grant regarded Cookie through his cigar smoke, then shrugged. "The man said he has no idea what this 'Brotherhood' business is all about, can't understand how his name came up in connection with it."

"I'll bet." Cookie folded his arms on his chest. "What's he doing in town, then?"

"What is anyone doing in town? Gambling, hoping to win the big pot." He winked.

"How about all those southern fat cats? Dandies, the lot of 'em." Cookie snorted and shook his head. "Can't be a coincidence half of 'em had daddies who ran that Phoenix Shipping crew me and Rafe busted apart down Savannah way during the war. Wasn't nothing but a front for selling folks as slaves!"

Grant nodded. "I remember it well. But there's little if any evidence tying this so-called Brotherhood to the poker tournament. I strongly suspect it's a scam perpetrated by Turlington, a mad scheme to avenge the loss of his family's plantation in the war. Like so many others, he never got over it. Timmons assured me he has no associations with this fool, Turlington, no matter his blatherings to the contrary. However, Talbot did say he'd be more than happy to host the man at his fine establishment in Yuma."

Cookie thrust a finger once more in Grant's direction. "That's another thing! That rascal Timmons was in on the Phoenix deal from way back. I seen him, I was there! How he ever ended up running Yuma Prison is beyond me. Should be an inmate there, not the damned warden!"

Grant sighed and rubbed his temples. "I do understand your concern, Mr. McGee, but even if your friend, Rafe Barr, were to speak against Timmons, or any other of the so-called southern gentlemen, who would take his word? He's on the run from the law, he's a convicted murderer, he's still regarded by many as a traitor to his country, and he's an escapee from a penitentiary."

"Now you listen here —"

"No, sir! I have had enough!" barked President Grant. "It is you who had better listen to me. I am telling you the facts. I'm also being far more lenient than I need to be toward you and your friends. Consider it a brief kindness. After this, my hands will be tied and the law will have to sort your fates. Do we understand each other, Mr. McGee?"

The two men eyed each other for some silent seconds, then Cookie dragged his cuff under his nose and sniffed. "I reckon."

"Well, we won't get to the bottom of it all in the next five minutes, that much I know." Grant gestured toward the sideboard. "Have a drink with me. It will no doubt calm our nerves." He splashed whiskey into two crystal glasses, handing one to Cookie. "Care for a cigar?"

"Nope, never took to them," said Cookie in a quiet voice. Then he brightened. "Now Rafe, he appreciates a fine cigar more'n anybody I know."

Grant opened a polished box and pulled out two large brown cigars. "Excellent. Then give these to him when next you see him. From my private reserve." He tilted the lid back but the box was empty. "Hmm, I would have given you more but I'm running low. I could have sworn . . . Never mind," he shook his head. "My compliments and my thanks go with them. Too little, I know, but it is a gesture."

Cookie smiled as if he knew a fine little secret, and tucked the offered cigars into his dynamite holster. "Will do, Grant." He finished his whiskey, and inched for the door.

"You and your friends are welcome to accompany me to Washington, of course."

"Thanks, all the same," said Cookie, keeping close to the exit of the fancy train car, "but I expect we'll be moseying on home."

"Oh, where's that?" Grant said, lips pooched around his stogie, squinting against the smoke and acting as if the question and its answer meant nothing to him.

"Oh, here and there, Grant," said Cookie, resting his hand on the doorknob. "Here and there. Travel safe, sir. Maybe our paths will cross again one day. One more thing, Grant. Leave the wagon wrangling to others, eh?" Cookie McGee offered the President a quick salute, then closed the door behind himself.

CHAPTER FORTY-EIGHT: TAKE THAT!

It was a solid hit, one that stretched the knuckles 'til they felt as if they would burst. But man, did it feel good.

Rufus Turlington's soft head snapped back, looking as if it were on a spring.

"That's for Mala . . . my little sister." Jack drew back for another hit — he ached to deliver another fist to the man's fat face, but he'd knocked him out, a sagged bag of fat, lips drooped and pooched, a string of bloody drool spooling from his mouth, drizzling down his baby-hair beard and onto his soiled vest front. He hoped to hell the man would rot in prison. But in his long experience, no rich man like this ever got his deserts.

Jack was beholden to Grant's two guards who left him in there while they tended to matters. Now that they were short-staffed they were grateful for his offer of watching over Turlington for five minutes. Said they'd be right back. Plenty enough time for Jack.

He winced as he shifted in his seat — the leg, the busted-to-hell leg — was on fire, would likely never heal right. He was laid up at the ranch for months the last time it knitted. This time, how on earth would he ever heal? Not likely.

He'd heard horrible stories of men whose bones were broken in the war by bullets and horse stompings and bludgeonings from the enemy, slowly withering away, dying like un-picked grapes on the vine, skinnying to nothing as they rotted out from the inside. All from busted bones that went bad, and began to fester.

"Had a chance before you and your man stomped me!" Jack lashed out, his throb-bing knuckles smacked into the soft flesh of the man's face one more, this time as a backhanded slap. The unconscious man's head bobbled again, settled, and slopped backward.

He'd been wanting to do that to a fat white southern man for a long, long time. Long before the tournament began. But alas, that would have curtailed his play. Not that it mattered much in the end, he'd lost all his savings, and Cookie's too. "Too big for your britches, Jack," that's what he said to himself, rubbing his aching hands, his teeth set tight against the jolts of pain in his leg, his ribs.

So much could have been, but now would never be. Jack's mind fluttered, landing gently on the memory of that pretty young Mexican woman he'd helped in the bar that first night in Santa Fe. Made up as an old beggar. Why? Who was she? He'd never know now. He felt certain there would be little such opportunities in his future days.

He was done for. Humbled by half. And now what? Time to go home with his tail betwixt his legs and wait for the end. Home? What home? The ranch? That was Cookie and Rafe's place. He was a stray they took in, time and again, nothing more.

"You licking your wounds, son?"

Jack looked up. As if on cue, there stood Cookie.

"You look almost as bad as I feel, Cookie. We were worried about you, thought maybe you fell asleep and tumbled off the roof of that crazy wagon Doc built."

Cookie managed a weak smile. "Day I fall asleep on the job is the day you'll be lowerin' ol' Cookie McGee into his final resting plot. And that day's a long ways off, you whelp."

Jack nodded and looked back down at the unconscious man on the floor at his feet.

430

Cookie's voice broke in again. "We got to leave that worthless man to his captors now. I expect you and that pretty sister of yours, Mala, need some tending. Doc's going to take you all home in Ethel. He's got her righted around again, though I can't speak as to how comfortable the ride will be."

"You're coming, too, aren't you?"

Cookie looked out the open door of the rail car and scanned the busy depot. "No, not yet. Have to find Stinky, then that big lummox, Rafe. Then I'll be along."

Jack nodded. "He delivered this fat bastard to the President. Rafe is all right, Cookie. I expect he's off doing the same thing he was doing when you found him up Denver way. Searching for answers."

Cookie rasped a hand across his unshaven chin. "You may be right. But I'll spend a day or so kicking around town. You never know."

"Don't wait too long, you heard what Grant's man said — half a hundred troops are riding hard from Fort Marcy to get here, and then it'll be martial law all over town. You won't be able to get in or out."

The old trail dog snapped out of his reverie and regarded Jack coolly. "Who says I won't?" Then he winked and made for the door. "All I need is a distraction." He patted the worn brown leather of his peculiar holster.

Jack saw the wicks of a couple sticks of dynamite curling over the top. He shook his head. "Cookie?" Jack cleared his throat, looked down at the floor. "About your money . . ."

Cookie waved a hand as if shooing a fly. "Don't you fret. What would I do with it, anyhow? Buy fancy clothes? Ha! Long as you and the rest of our little family are safe — even Doc, though don't you allow as how I said so, or I'll give you what-for — why, that's all that matters."

With that, he stomped down the wooden ramp of the rail car and made for the center of Santa Fe, determination guiding each step.

CHAPTER FORTY-NINE:
A TIME TO RIDE

Thirty minutes later found President Ulysses S. Grant ensconced in his rail car, listening to the clanking and rumbling of the train as it readied to leave the station. He leaned back in his chair, his aching head on an embroidered pillow, eyes closed.

"It's a shame we weren't able to apprehend the two vicious bastards who cold-cocked me. They were an odd pair, much as I can remember. Though what I do recall leads me to question my own mind."

"What was odd about them, sir?" Melville gazed out the window at the westbound train, also readying for departure.

"I caught but a brief glimpse of them before they dragged that smelly sack over my head. They were an odd pair, as I said, one tall and one short. If I didn't know better, I'd swear one was a midget with bad teeth and a sawed-off shotgun. The other his opposite in height, no teeth to speak of,

433

and a strange way of talking. He also bore knives, many, many blades about his person." A shudder rippled through his tired frame.

"A close call, sir," said Melville.

Grant nodded. "Say, Melville, you're from the South. How come you're not as bitter as all these so-called southern gentlemen seem to be?"

Still gazing out the window, Melville stretched casually and nodded to a well-dressed man walking by the train.

"Who says I'm not, sir?"

Grant's eyes snapped open and he regarded the back of his chief guard's head.

Melville nodded once more to the stranger and watched as the man mounted the steps of the westbound train, lugging a bulging satchel and smiling.

"Talbot Timmons is the warden of Yuma Territorial Prison, isn't he?" said Melville.

"What about him?" said Grant, eyes narrowing.

"Oh, nothing. Thinking out loud, sir." Melville turned to face his employer. "Too bad all that tournament money went missing in the hubbub, sir."

"Yes." Grant grinned, rubbing his hands together. "I would have liked to have played a hand or two. I doubt all that money will ever be recovered."

"Oh, it will pop up, good as new, one of these days, sir." Melville smiled. "I bet on it."

CHAPTER FIFTY:
LOST AND FOUND

For two hours after he dumped the blubbering Colonel Rufus Turlington the Second in President Grant's rail car — and helped himself to a handful of fine cigars from a wonderful, earthy-smelling carved humidor on the desk — Rafe Barr made his quiet way in broadening circles in the environs of the little barn-turned-gallows.

People milled about, including a half-dozen lawmen of all sizes and standings, but the afternoon's bizarre proceedings, guessed Rafe, were so fresh no one knew quite how to set order to the confusion. That suited Rafe — he needed to find Knifer, Plug, and Timmons. Any order would do. And he suspected he had little time to do it in, if any of them were still around.

Grant would no doubt have called in troops from Fort Marcy. By Rafe's reckoning that would give him but an hour before they arrived. The local law had already begun detaining folks.

Loath as he was to turn his back on the task, Rafe had to retrieve his horse — if he was lucky enough to find it — from the side street where he'd tied him before Cookie blew the front of the barn off. Horse wasn't one to suffer sudden sounds with tolerance. Likely the beast had run off, though Rafe hoped the buckskin's preference for sweet hay might have led him to any stable nearby the scene. Now he had to find out which one. Night had come almost before he realized it and with it, bone-deep exhaustion.

Rafe turned down a dark passageway he hoped connected with a cross street closer to the plaza. The closer he walked toward the far end, the less promising it seemed. A crude plank wall faced him and the day's events seemed to pin him there, one shoulder leaning against the wall. He rubbed his eyes with a thumb and forefinger and couldn't quite suppress a yawn. When had he last slept? What was it he was searching for, anyway?

"Timmons," he whispered. "He has to know. So close . . ."

From behind him came a soft, quick rustling sound, like a bird taking flight. It happened in the time it takes to pull in a breath. He turned to see it, to face it, but whatever it was hit him on the side of his head, above the ear. His aching, aching head.

Rafe Barr collapsed against the wall, rattling the boards, then dropped to the dirt like a sack of wet sand.

He looked up as his eyesight came back to him, dim and revealing little but a fuzzy shape, hazy, the outline of a figure looking down at him. Rafe smelled smoke from a quirley, but had no time to consider it, for a voice cracked the silence.

"Yes, so close, eh, Barr?" The voice was low, a dry sound, cold as if steel could talk. The voice blew smoke in his face and sighed. "Oh, by the way, I know what it is you're so dogged in searching out. I been watching you for quite some time. You might say I have taken a special interest in you."

Rafe struggled to clear his head, blinking away the bursting stars, the clanging of bells in his tormented head. Snatches of memory flitted in and out of his mind, on the trail, camped alone, smelled cigarette smoke at night — this man. Rafe tried to speak, but managed only a malformed word.

The man above, the smoker, blew more smoke and said, "What's that? 'Who,' you say? Well, friend, I will tell you."

438

Rafe struggled to get an elbow under himself but the man said, "Uh uh uh, not so fast, Mr. Barr."

Rafe felt something hard press against his chest, slide up to his throat, and press there, holding him, pinning him down. Why couldn't he move his arms, dammit? No strength, he had no strength for this anymore. So tired his head . . . so sore.

"Now, where was I?"

The sound of breath drawing in, the fire-eye glow of the cigarette, the plume of smoke.

"Oh yes. Now, the boy, see, he whimpered, I don't mind sayin'. But the woman, now she was, what's the word? Stoic, yes, that's it. Stoic to the end. Through it all, I might add. Long after she tried to claw her way free. Stoic, yes, sir, that is the word."

The man leaned down. Rafe shook, tried to rise, and felt the boot push harder into his throat.

"Oh, what did I do then? Oh, well I will tell you. After the fun, well . . . then I killed them."

The man sighed as Rafe struggled beneath his boot. "You have disappointed me, Rafe Barr, I don't mind sayin'. I expected more from you. You are not nearly as fun as they were, 'specially the woman. Oh, well. I guess it's like the fella said, 'It ain't the destination so much as it is the journey gettin' there,' eh, Rafe Barr?"

A solid rock of raw anger filled the throat of the big man as he lay on his back, pinned and truly helpless for the first time in his life.

"Well, as you said, Barr — so close, so very close. Pity."

The last thing Rafe heard was the sound of alley grit grinding beneath boots as the man walked away.

The last thing he felt was a chill, like a midwinter breath, slowly replacing the warmth of his blood as it leaked into the dirt.

The last thing he thought was how he had failed his wife, his son.

EPILOGUE:
CAREFUL WHAT YOU WISH FOR . . .

"Miss Pendergrast?" The solid man behind the desk, Allan Pinkerton himself, didn't look up when Sue walked into the office. He didn't do much of anything but nibble his bottom lip, squint through his half-moon spectacles, and frown at the papers he held in his pudgy hands.

She closed the door and stood before the massive oak desk, her hands clasped behind her. And she waited. For two, then three minutes. She fidgeted, then she cleared her throat.

Pinkerton looked up. "Oh, yes, Miss Pendergrast." He glanced at a heavy bronze-cased clock anchoring the corner of his cluttered desk. "You're late."

She opened her mouth, but their eyes met and she saw a challenge there. He was testing her, had to be. She closed her mouth. "Yes, sir. My apologies. You wanted to see me, sir?"

The big man leaned back in his chair. It squeaked and popped. He folded his hands together over his belly, hiding the gold watch chain that always hung there. "Miss Pendergrast, you have been here for oh, let's see," he closed his eyes and his lips moved slightly, tallying days in his head. "A couple of weeks now? Close enough at any rate."

"Sir, I —"

"Calm yourself, young lady. When you arrived, you were of little consequence to me. The fact that you sought out employment here is of slightly more consequence to me, though only so far as I am able to find your abilities of use to us here. I will admit you have made a difference. You make decent coffee; the file room, such as it was, is shipshape. It's less a cluttered repository of accumulated detritus from all manner of previous excursions my operatives have undertaken than it had been. All this and other things, too, lead me to regard you in a different light. Now."

Sue wasn't certain what all this was leading to, but a tremor of foreboding crawled up her spine. "Sir, I can do better work, I assure you. I would like only to be given the opportunity."

"Confound it, girl," he smacked a hand on the arm of his chair and heaved himself forward. "That's what I'm getting at. You talk before I'm finished again and you will be the one who's finished. Now let me get to my point. Windy or no, it's my business and you will have to listen to me. Now, where was I?"

Sue bit back the urge to tell him he hadn't been getting much of anywhere. She kept her mouth closed; her cheeks had heated up considerably in the past seconds. She watched as Pinkerton rummaged on his desk, flicking papers to and fro as if sorting coins. "Ah yes, here they are." He went through the infuriating ritual of adjusting the spectacles on his nose, leaning back in the chair, and perusing the papers in his hand.

"As you no doubt are unaware of, precisely because the incident has been kept as much as possible out of the public's scrutinizing gaze, there have been events of late, troubling events of national and international import. Certain . . . people with whom I maintain ties, both personally, fiscally, and professionally, believe without doubt there is one person behind these unfortunate incidents. One man alone, a name from this nation's recent past who we had all thought was sequestered beyond reach for good and for all and forever."

Pinkerton nibbled his bottom lip and let out a long breath, still not looking up from the paper in his hand. He spoke once more. "As it happens, I concur with these . . . people." Here he paused, looking at her with drawn brows as if was awaiting a response.

Sue was about to speak when she recalled his recent admonition to keep her mouth shut until he was finished speaking. How was she to know when that was? She wished he would get to the point he was so painfully trying to make.

"I find I am short of staff at present, given the oddly volatile days in which we live. All the reprobates insist on breaking laws and going underground at the same time. Alas, my trusted operatives all have their hands full. I am particularly appalled at the dearth of female operatives in my employ. Not that there is much of a call for gender-specific services, but occasionally such a need arises. That time has once again arisen."

Pinkerton squinted at her over the rims of his spectacles, again seeming to await a response. She held her tongue.

"The man I mentioned who has enacted a string of horrible crimes too foul to tell at this moment is, alas, also a man who enjoys the company of women. Our intelligence is unimpeachable in this regard. He has been witnessed firsthand on a number of occasions in the company of at least two women, one of them as luck would have it, is not unlike yourself in regards to stature, perhaps even hair color.

"In short, Miss Pendergrast, I need an operative who will be able to infiltrate the hideout of this notorious man. Alas, he does not operate alone, though he has the reputation of being a lone wolf. He is a killer, a bank robber, and a cold-blooded banditi."

"What has this man done so recently, sir?"

Pinkerton narrowed his eyes, and for a moment Sue thought she might have overstepped that line he had warned her of, but he merely nodded.

"I am glad you asked that most obvious of questions first. Mere weeks ago in Denver he robbed the Precious Metals Exchange. We have it on unimpeachable authority he operated in concert with two other criminals of his acquaintance, likely in his employ. They are known to us, as they also have pulled jobs on their own. They call themselves Knifer and Plug, a mismatched duo, according to eyewitness accounts. The taller of the two, Knifer, carries all manner of bladed weapons on his person, and his ruthlessness is evident in the callous disregard with which he treats all around him, save for his partner, the one called Plug. He is equally as foul, though in a diminutive size."

"Sir?"

"He's a midget. But deadly. He cradles a sawed-off shotgun always and shows no compunction for keeping it quiet. Oddly enough, they turned on their boss whilst in the midst of the caper, and made off with the bank's money."

"So the authorities in Denver were able to capture this elusive criminal?"

"Yes, in a manner of speaking. They found him at the scene, unconscious, the victim of his underlings' shenanigans. The marshal there was able to lug him to jail. Our story takes an unfortunate turn at this point. Another of his operatives, an older man proficient in the use of disguises, posing as the man's high-powered attorney, was able to free the criminal."

A twinge of recognition curled like wispy smoke into Sue's mind. Could it be? "Sir, do you have the name of this bad man?"

"All in good time, Miss Pendergrast. All in good time. Now, where was I? Oh, yes, the false lawyer managed to break the man free of his confinement in the cells below Denver City Hall. While he was in Denver, incidentally, he was witnessed rubbing

446

elbows with the worst of the worst of that city's Dukes of Debauchery, Soapy Smith and Doc Baggs. If that does not seal his guilt, nothing does. Alas, would that our story ends there, but it most assuredly does not.

"No, this desperado made his way to Santa Fe to what I am certain seemed to him to be a situation ripe for easy picking. A nationwide poker tournament that summoned the best of the best gamblers with a purse rumored to be $10,000. But this man was not satisfied with merely robbing the winners and leaving town. No, while there he carried out a plot most foul, most fiendish in its elaborateness, and in its admirable simplicity, it must be said." He licked his lips and continued, color climbing high up his plump cheeks.

"We should have expected no less from a man who at one time was a notorious war-hero-turned-turncoat-traitor, a double agent whose twin urges of greed and lust knew no bounds. In Santa Fe he and his cohorts robbed, pillaged, and tried to lynch two unfortunate former slaves — one of them a woman, for heaven's sake — and then kidnapped none other than the President of the United States, Ulysses S. Grant."

"Oh that's terrible, sir."

"Yes, yes, it is," said Pinkerton. "Luckily his plot was foiled before he made off with the man, no doubt to ransom him, then kill him. World economies quivered on their very foundations. And yet, despite it all, he managed to get away scot-free with the money." Pinkerton leaned back again in his creaking and popping chair and regarded Sue through half-lidded eyes.

"Something tells me, Miss Pendergrast, that you of all my operatives have the ability to infiltrate this hardened gang and send word as to its location and weaknesses, its hideout, and of the notorious killer himself." He leaned forward, his eyes boring into hers. "A man known as Rafe Barr. Yes, he most assuredly would be known to you, Miss Pendergrast."

"Me?" said Sue, not half as shocked as she might have been had she heard his name recited coldly at the beginning of this one-sided conversation. For she knew that Rafe was not capable of such mayhem. Oh, he might well have caused plenty of ruckus, but it had to have been for a good cause. And she did not doubt that he was on the correct end of each situation that arose.

Unfortunately, the rest of the nation, perhaps the world, did not see it that way. She had to figure out a way to help him clear his name, to help exhume the truth, come hell or high, fast water.

"Miss Pendergrast? Have I bothered you with all my chatter?"

"What? Oh, no sir. Not at all." Sue felt her face redden.

"Well, what do you say?"

"Say? To what, sir?"

"Confound it, girl, will you take on the case or should I wander out onto the sidewalk and pull in a stranger with more qualifications than you are plainly exhibiting?"

"Sir, I . . ."

Pinkerton leaned forward, eyes wide, waiting. "Yes? Yes?"

"I am just the man for the job, sir. Rest assured."

He leaned back. "Yes, well, we'll see. Time tells all, Miss Pendergrast. For the present I want you to retreat to the outer office, familiarize yourself with the case file on this notorious Barr, and report back here early tomorrow morning. You will be fully briefed, then sent on your way to toddle among the giants."

It was Sue's chance to stare wide-eyed. Could this be happening? She really was getting called into active duty as an . . . operative? And on her own case, too.

"That will be all." Pinkerton resumed the same pose of deep concentration he'd been engrossed in when she was summoned, some long minutes before.

Sue nodded. "Thank you, sir. For everything. I won't let you down."

He grunted and she took that as her cue to leave.

Sue had almost closed the door when he spoke. "Good luck . . . Miss Pendleton."

Sue froze in the doorway for long moments, her hand on the knob. How long had he known her real name? If he knew that, then he must know . . . everything? Sue swallowed back a knot of fear and confusion and quietly closed the door.

Inside the office, Allan Pinkerton looked at the closed door over the top of his half-moon spectacles, and smiled.

The end.

The Outfit will return . . .

ABOUT THE AUTHOR

Matthew P. Mayo is an award-winning
author of thirty books and dozens of short
stories. His novel, *Tucker's Reckoning*, won
the Western Writers of America's Spur
Award for Best Western Novel, and his short
stories have been Spur Award and Peace-
maker Award finalists. His many novels
include *Winters' War; Wrong Town; Hot Lead,
Cold Heart; The Outfit: To Hell and Back;
North of Forsaken; The Hunted; Shotgun
Charlie;* and others.

Matthew's numerous nonfiction books
include the bestselling *Cowboys, Mountain
Men & Grizzly Bears; Haunted Old West;
Jerks in New England History;* and *Hornswog-
glers, Fourflushers & Snake-Oil Salesmen.*
He has been an on-screen expert for a
popular BBC-TV series about lost treasure
in the American West and has had three
books optioned for film.

Matthew and his wife, photographer Jennifer Smith-Mayo, rove the byways of North America in search of hot coffee, tasty whiskey, and high adventure. For more information, drop by Matthew's website at www.MatthewMayo.com.

The employees of Thorndike Press hope you have enjoyed this Large Print book. All our Thorndike, Wheeler, and Kennebec Large Print titles are designed for easy reading, and all our books are made to last. Other Thorndike Press Large Print books are available at your library, through selected bookstores, or directly from us.

For information about titles, please call:
(800) 223-1244

or visit our Web site at:
http://gale.com/thorndike

To share your comments, please write:

Publisher
Thorndike Press
10 Water St., Suite 310
Waterville, ME 04901